The *Valley* Without Her

Amie M. Johnson

Ps 23:4

5 Fold Media
Visit us at www.5foldmedia.com

The Valley Without Her
Copyright © 2013 by Amie M. Johnson
Published by 5 Fold Media, LLC
www.5foldmedia.com

All rights reserved. No part of this book may be reproduced, stored in a retrieval system, or transmitted in any form or by any means-electronic, mechanical, photocopy, recording, or otherwise-without prior written permission of the copyright owner, except by a reviewer who wishes to quote brief passages in connection with a review for inclusion in a magazine, website, newspaper, podcast, or broadcast. Cover imagery © deviantART-Fotolia.com The views and opinions expressed from the writer are not necessarily those of 5 Fold Media, LLC.

This is a work of fiction. Aside from reference to known public figures, places, or resources, all names, characters, places, and incidents have been constructed by the author, and any resemblance to actual persons, places, or events is coincidental.

Scripture quotations are taken from the Holy Bible, New Living Translation, copyright 1996, 2004. Used by permission of Tyndale House Publishers, Inc., Wheaton, Illinois 60189. All rights reserved.

ISBN: 978-1-936578-71-9
Library of Congress Control Number: 2013942659

Endorsements

"The Valley Without Her will draw you in from the very first page. The author describes each character so completely that it won't be long until you will feel you know this community intimately. You will smile and cry with them as their story unfolds concerning the disappearance of their well-loved Emma. As you walk with them on their journey, you will experience their shattered dreams and fading hope that life will ever be 'normal' again. Their faith is tested to its limit, but God's Word rings true in the valley, 'Weeping may last through the night, but joy comes with the morning' (Psalm 30:5b)."

~LuAnn Gerig Fulton, author of *Image Seeker*

"This story demonstrates the importance of having close friends as we go through life's trials. Amie also encourages her readers to have a relationship with God and to tap into His strength and wisdom so that we may face the challenges we encounter. It is a good read with reminders of God's faithfulness."

~Lisa Frye, Family First Ministries

For Keith, who found me;

for Jesse and for Sam, who teach me to be the best version of myself;

and for the friends and family who walked beside me on this journey

and used the word *love*.

Prologue

It was her. This wasn't like the other times; the times she had been mistaken. Granted, there was the initial quick-glance-double-take-heart-skip, like times before. But this time there was no sinking in the stomach, a stabbing reminder of cruel reality and, again, the deep sadness. No. There was no mistake this time. It was her.

The morning had been a little hectic, but still the overall mood of the family was happy and calm. Kate Thomas's family was taking their five-hour drive back home to Gardenville when they pulled off the road at a gas station. The early morning sun was slanting pleasantly through the windows of their SUV. A playful breeze ruffled her light brown hair. Alan had gone inside to pay for gas. Claire and James were back from their trips to the restroom and the candy aisle and were already enjoying their quest for cavities when it happened.

Kate was slumped in her seat, half-dozing and reflecting on their lovely vacation to her aunt's lake house, and thinking, in spite of everything, what a blessed life she led. She glanced back at her two children. Claire, sixteen, shy and smart, a little bookish with her glasses, but with a beauty that one day, Kate knew, would blossom into something everyone would notice the first moment they saw her. James was seventeen, nearly eighteen, and outgoing. He had dark hair like his sister (and their father), but with her own gray-green eyes. Once again she thanked God for her children, that they were healthy and safe. At that moment as she was turning back in her seat, her eyes fell on the girl sitting in a pick-up truck four parking spaces away.

This had happened before. A cruel jolt of recognition after a glimpse at some young girl, Claire's age, with just the right shade of hair. Or just the right bouncy walk. Kate was expecting that same routine: *It only* looks *like her. It isn't really her. It will never be her.* She looked more closely at the young girl. Her eyes were downcast, a weary expression out of place on a face so young. Kate's eyes widened as she stared at the girl. She felt the blood drain from her face. Her body went numb, her mouth dry, and for a moment she was incapable of speech. A strangled noise escaped her throat and her heart felt like a frightened bird trapped in her chest. She began to shake.

"Emma?" she breathed. Then louder, she could hear the trembling in her own voice, a voice that sounded strange even to her, "Emma!"

"Mom?" Claire had noticed her mother's behavior, and she sounded afraid. "Mom, what's wrong?"

Kate stared at the girl in the truck—copper-colored wavy hair, brown eyes—a girl the same age as Claire. It was her.

Kate felt herself beginning to hyperventilate, but knew she had to pull herself together. Now James was concerned as well, "Mom, what's wrong with you? Your face is all white."

Finally Kate sprang into action. She dug her cell phone out of her purse and threw it at James, wishing she had more than one phone in the car. One tiny part of her mind snorted at the irony of their flat refusal to buy the kids their own phones no matter how they begged.

"Ow! Mom, what 're you—"

She was trying to unbuckle her seat belt, but her hands didn't seem to work.

"Call 911!"

"Wha-at?"

"Do it!" she ordered.

Claire's voice sounded more frightened than before, "Mom, please tell us what's wrong."

Just then Alan returned. He opened the door, his body obscuring Kate's view of the girl. She tossed her body back and forth in irritation, not wanting to lose sight of her; as if losing sight meant really losing. Again.

"Sorry it took me so long, the guy…"

"We can't let her get away," she gasped. "We've got to keep her, keep her here! Dear God, stop them, stop them!" she babbled.

She knew she wasn't making sense, but she also knew there was no time. Alan looked at her as if she had sprouted antlers.

"What are you talking about?"

All three of them were now looking at her with fear and concern, James still holding her phone, forgotten, in his hand. She ignored their expressions and flailed her hand in the girl's direction. Kate was reaching true panic.

"It's Emma! There! It's Emma Leonard."

* * *

Each of them had a different reaction to Kate's words. James leaned around his sister to see the girl his mother said was Emma, and after a moment of open-mouthed shock, began to dial 911 with trembling fingers. His breathing was fast, his eyes wet.

Claire had burst into hysterical tears and was trying to escape the car, presumably to fly to the girl in the truck, but was being restrained by both her parents.

Alan, bewildered now by all three of his family members looked at his wife. He struggled to keep a hold on his squirming, sobbing daughter. He, obviously preoccupied by the emotional bedlam, wasn't listening.

"Who?"

Claire's sobs became a wail. Kate thought she might scream in frustration. She let go of Claire's knee.

"Emma!" Kate shouted at him. Suddenly, memories of the past two years were a snowball fight bouncing around inside her skull. She wanted to shake him. "Emma Leonard. Look at her!"

Somewhere in the world, James' voice was stammering. He was getting help. Help should be coming. *Dear Father in heaven, let help be coming.*

Alan turned to see the girl for himself. He turned back and looked at Kate with a mask on his face that she associated with physical pain.

"Claire's friend, Emma? The one who…"

"Yes!"

By now Claire was beside herself. "Daddy, *please* we have to get her!" She turned toward the girl, her breath ragged, "Emma!" She choked out.

"Now hold on a second, we can't just…we have to think, we don't know what kind of people…"

"They're on their way!" James shouted, clutching the phone as if he were trying to crush it.

"The people she's with will be back any second," Kate whispered.

Alan met Kate's eyes.

"Let's go," he said, reaching in his pocket for his pocketknife. "You two stay here," he commanded in his most serious dad voice. Claire reached over and clung to her brother, they watched as their parents got out of the car and made their way toward the girl they knew was Emma—Mom wobbling slowly toward the girl, Dad heading to the rear of the pickup.

Kate felt as if her legs were made of jelly. She thought her heart may burst. As they got closer to her, she looked up and saw them. Her face passed from its dispirited aspect to slow recognition to something very like fear and disbelief. She began to shake her head slowly. Her look of bewilderment intensified when Alan stabbed the rear tire of the truck with his knife.

Kate held out her hand. She moved gently as if approaching a frightened animal that might scamper away and disappear. She didn't bother to wipe her own tears as the girl framed in the window began to cry.

"Emma? Sweetheart?"

Emma Leonard looked from Kate to Alan and then behind them toward the SUV. Seeing Claire and James seemed too much for her and she curled in on herself, wrapping her arms around her head as if trying to ward off an attack. Her shoulders shook. Kate reached through the open window and brushed back the girl's soft hair with her fingertips.

The Valley Without Her

"It's okay, it's all right. It's okay now," Kate heard herself repeating over and over, not sure who she was trying to convince.

Chapter 1

Two Years Earlier

"Let's pray." Pastor Josh bowed his head and led the youth group in prayer, closing their Wednesday night meeting. Claire listened as he asked God to grant them wisdom, which had been the topic of the lesson that evening.

"Now remember," he began after ending the prayer, "you need to be there a little early so we can get everything set up." His voice increased in volume as he spoke. He was now competing with multiple teenage conversations. The second he had said amen, they had popped out of nowhere like nighttime mushrooms.

"Don't forget to wear your t-shirts, and bring money for lunch. Be there no later than 9:00!" He was nearly shouting now, but it didn't really matter. He had been drilling the details of the rummage sale into their heads for weeks. Claire knew all the information. Mom had it written on the calendar at home, but, not wanting to be disrespectful to Pastor Josh, Claire listened dutifully to his spiel yet again. She waited for him to finish before tuning in to what her friend was saying to her.

"...or does she need to call her?"

Claire stared at her. "Huh?"

Emma rolled her eyes, "My mom wants to know if your mom wants me to bring anything Friday night."

13

"Oh." Claire smiled. Emma's mom, Joni, was always thinking about things like that. "I don't think so. Have you picked a movie?"

On the other side of Emma, Melody Holloway huffed, "I wish I could come, but we have to go to my aunt's."

Her two friends nodded sympathetically. "I know. I wish you could, too," Claire told her.

They continued discussing their weekend plans as they followed the stream of kids leaving the youth room. They waved good-bye to their friends as they went. All of them were talking, laughing, and bouncing around like a cross between puppies and pinballs. Claire loved sleepovers. Her family got pizza or made tacos, Claire's favorite, and the girls each picked out a movie. Sometimes other friends besides Emma would come—Melody, or sometimes Brayle if she didn't have to take care of her sister and brothers. They would spend most of the evening giggling and talking about teachers and boys and the camp they attended in the summer. Claire's brother, James, usually made himself scarce during these chick flick charged adventures. This was a shame, really, because, though Emma never said so, Claire suspected her friend had a little crush on him. Unfortunately, or in this case perhaps fortunately, James was oblivious as usual. As if summoned by her musings, James showed up at his sister's elbow right at that moment they stepped outside.

"Mom and Dad decided to stay for the meeting. They said to go ahead and walk home."

To Emma and Melody he said nothing. He didn't intend to be rude he was just...oblivious. To Emma's credit, she took it in stride. Claire was pretty sure she was the only one who knew her secret.

"Sorry, Em. Do you want to walk part of the way with us since we were your ride home?" Claire asked, pushing her glasses up on her nose.

Emma shrugged, "Might as well. Mom's working tonight and Dad won't be home for another hour at least, so they won't be worrying that I'm late anyway." Joni was a nurse and Emma's dad, Greg, was a mechanic. Melody's parents were calling for her, so she said her quick good-byes and ran off after them.

"Well, let's go, I still have to finish my English paper," James said. They turned to leave.

"Hey, you guys ready for Saturday?" It was Pastor Josh. He was walking past them on the way to his car. Pastor Josh McMillan was always enthusiastic about whatever he had planned for his teens. Even during his lessons, he would pace around and talk with his hands, really getting into it. Sometimes when they played games, he got even more worked up than the kids. Pastor Ward said that was one of the reasons he was so good with young people.

Claire and Emma watched as James' face fell into an expression of bemusement that would have made a troll look scholarly.

"Saturday?" he grunted. "What's happening on Saturday?"

Pastor Josh's enthusiasm immediately turned to disappointment. With his longish sandy-colored curly hair and blue eyes, he looked like a little boy denied a visit to grandma and grandpa's. After two beats Emma and Claire dissolved into giggles. James grinned.

"Just messing with you, dude," he said, "How could we forget? It's not like you haven't mentioned it every five seconds." He, at least, had the courtesy to look mildly ashamed.

Pastor Josh snorted, shaking his head, "I should've known." He turned his attention to the girls. "You excited about the fundraiser?" he asked them.

"Of course, we are," said Emma confidently, "Claire and I could make fun out of anything." She grinned.

"That's true," Claire agreed, nodding.

Pastor Josh noticed where they were headed, "Hey, do you guys need a ride home?"

"Nah, we'll just walk. Thanks, though," Emma answered.

"Sure, see you later," he said, bumping his fist against Emma's shoulder in his typical Pastor Josh salute.

Claire and Emma strolled toward their respective homes while James strode ahead, other things on his mind than girl talk. They gabbed happily about nothing in particular until they reached Emma's street when she would go in one direction and James and Claire in another.

"Well, see you tomorrow!" she said brightly.

"Yep, see ya!" Claire smiled.

"Later, Emma," James called over his shoulder.

Emma showed the tiniest smile of pleasure before waving one last time at her friend and heading toward home, her bouncy gait concealing her barely discernible limp and her coppery hair shining prettily behind her.

* * *

"Why do I need this stuff anyway?" Claire complained, slamming her textbook closed on her finished assignment. "Like I'm really gonna need to find the value of 'x' in my real life, ever."

She adopted a snooty-strict librarian tone, "Oh no, Miss Thomas, I'm afraid we only consider for employment candidates who have found the value of 'x'."

She rubbed her eyes beneath her glasses.

Alan tried not to smile. He and Claire sat at the table in their dining room where Kate had lovingly decorated the slate blue walls with photos of the four of them. The difference between the sweet smile in Claire's pictures and the pout she now wore was comical.

He set his newspaper aside. "You'll get through it," he told her, "just keep at it."

She gave him a mock glare. "Easy for you to say," she grumbled, "nobody's making *you* find 'x'. What if Mom told you that you couldn't have dinner unless you found 'x'? That'd be another story, wouldn't it?"

Alan laughed. She had a seemingly effortless way of cracking him up. People were always saying how shy she was and asking him if she was "doing all right." He told them they should see her at home with her family. She was witty and charming. He guiltily was a little grateful for her backwardness around others. Not only was Claire funny and quick, she was the cutest girl in the world and Alan didn't want to think about all the unworthy boys who could be chasing after her.

"Your mom and I have a deal," he said seriously, "I kill the spiders and she doesn't make me find 'x'."

Claire raised her eyebrows. "So that's the secret to a happy marriage? Spider killing?"

"Yep." He nodded. "Everything else is smooth sailing after that."

Now Claire laughed, too, and the lines of homework-induced tension finally left her face. This had been his goal. She was about to make a snappy remark when the phone rang. She was momentarily distracted, but soon the ringing stopped. Kate had picked up. Claire turned her attention back to him.

"But really, Dad, sometimes I think they're just giving us stuff to do to keep us busy because they don't know what else to do with us."

Alan nodded sympathetically. "Sorry, kid, I'd like to tell you it gets better." He pinched her nose in a gesture of affection he had used since she was an infant.

Kate appeared in the doorway behind him.

"Who was that on the phone, Mom?"

"Joni."

Claire winced slightly. "She wanted to know if Emma needed to bring anything, right? Sorry, I forgot to tell you she asked. Was she mad at me?"

Typical Claire. Alan and Kate had discussed how she was overcautious about offending others. They didn't think it was about people pleasing, though. It had more to do with being self-conscious—in the same way that she listened to every word Pastor Josh said even though she already knew what he was going to say. She was afraid of calling attention to herself and being singled out, and the idea of all eyes on her was more than terrifying for Claire. They were hoping to help her overcome this insecurity. However, in this case, Claire's concern may have had more to do with Joni herself. Joni Leonard was sunshine personified, and Claire adored her.

Kate gave her a look and sighed. "Yes, she wanted to know if Emma needed to bring anything with her. No, Joni wasn't mad at you. Have you ever even seen Joni get angry?"

"No."

"Me neither. Now you need to clear up your things and call James down here so you two can set the table for dinner."

Kate melted into a chair as Claire gathered her homework things and headed upstairs to get James.

"Rough day?" Alan asked her. He had noticed the telltale signs of stress in his wife when she came into the room, looking tense.

"Just busy," she answered, rubbing her neck. "There's so much to do to get ready for the weekend. I want to be ready for the apple festival on Saturday, and we seemed to have a steady stream of customers today."

Kate ran a little shop called "Line Dried Laundry." The "y" in "laundry" was made to resemble an old-fashioned clothespin. It was a cute little two-story place that sold antiques, quilts, and quaint little treasures that made houses "homey." Just the other day, Kate had been all excited about finding an old birdcage to display in the front window. On the first floor of the shop, there was a little tearoom that people rented out for parties sometimes. It was a popular spot for a light lunch, or for someone just in the mood for a yummy dessert. People came from all over the area for the apple festival and lots of people stopped in at Kate's charming little store. The festival was always good for business. Kate's employee, Marty, had taken a few days off, and Kate was swamped.

When the kids came back into the room, the four of them got the table ready and sat down to eat dinner. The conversation centered mostly around the upcoming Gardenville Apple Festival. It was a huge event. There were games, raffles, and vendors selling everything from rings made out of old spoons to antique tools. There would be toys, pony rides, face painting, and in the evening, concerts by local bands, vocalists, and musicians. There was even an Apple Blossom Queen. But the main event was, of course, the *apples*. They were baked, fried, à la mode, in dumplings, and every other way you could imagine. There was even one popular stand that sold apples wrapped in bacon. The apple festival was the biggest event of the year and people came from miles around to enjoy it. The local newspaper, *The Gardenville Grapevine* (affectionately known as *The Vine*) always made a huge fuss about the apple festival as it was always the most exciting thing that happened in Gardenville all year.

The youth group would be taking care of the church's rummage sale this year. It was a big job and lots of work. A few adults would be there to help supervise, while the kids set up, carried the items to be sold and helped the customers. Even though it wasn't an apple-related event, they still did pretty well and always had fun.

"Last year we made over eight hundred dollars!" Claire said. "It helped a lot with kids going to camp."

The church was really good about making sure that everyone who wanted to go to camp had a way to get there. Kids like Emma and Claire's friend, Brayle, probably wouldn't be able to go otherwise and events like the rummage sale at the apple festival made it possible.

From there the conversation turned to summer teen camp. James and Claire both looked forward to it all year and could talk for hours about the good times they had while they were there with all their camp friends. Alan had to put a stop to the endless "do-you-remembers" and declared it was time to clean up the dinner mess and finish any homework before bed.

* * *

"So can you come over to Claire's for a while tonight?" Emma asked, bouncing excitedly on her toes. She slung her backpack over her shoulder.

"Yeah," came Brayle's voice from the depths of her locker as she selected the books she would need to take home with her. She reappeared, "Mom doesn't care."

Claire hid her dismay at the double meaning. "Mel wanted to come, too, but her family already had plans." She was about to ask Brayle what she wanted on her pizza and to get her movie preference when she was interrupted by an unwelcome voice. All three girls inwardly groaned.

"Why would anyone want to hang out with *Braille*? I think you've got some bumps on your face, *Braille*," sneered Lindsay Glass, her voice like sandpaper. This was Lindsay's attempt at making fun of Brayle's freckles. Lindsay was the bane of the ninth grade, she and her ever-present henchman, Dena Roberts. She always made a big deal out of mispronouncing Brayle's name, which, pronounced correctly, rhymed with Haley. Dena snickered loudly at the old joke.

"Oh, I suppose if I were a loser who didn't have anything better to do." She directed this last gem at Claire and Emma. Claire always wondered how she managed to summon so much disdain in one facial expression. Lindsay would be remarkably pretty if she weren't always snarling and glowering. Dena was categorically boring. Claire supposed this was because she took her every cue from Lindsay and never thought for, or made any decision, herself. It was what made her the spectacular lackey she was. Lindsay, tall and thin with shimmery golden hair, was notoriously competitive and suspicious. On the other hand, while she could be mean as a snake, she could turn positively angelic if it worked to her advantage. Around most adults, for example, she was respectful and demure, which meant she rarely got caught in her cruelties. For these reasons she had few friends. Dena, slightly overweight with dirty-blonde hair and eyes that seemed too small for her face, was the only one who would put up with her.

Brayle was a strawberry blonde with a dusting of Anne-of-Green-Gables freckles across her nose and cheeks. Claire and Emma both thought Brayle was adorable and suspected that Lindsay did too, and tortured her out of jealousy of her cuteness, punishing her lest someone think Brayle more attractive than Lindsay herself. They weren't the only ones Lindsay enjoyed bullying, either. Their good friend, Melody, had suffered endlessly during the semester she had taken gym class with Lindsay. Melody was a perky blonde and not very tall. Lindsay found a multitiude of ways to taunt Melody due to her height, often reducing sensitive Melody to tears.

"I mean, haven't you ever heard of contact lenses?" she continued her address, referring to Claire's glasses. "I think I'd kill myself if I had to come to school every day looking like an *owl*."

Dena continued to laugh unkindly until Lindsay nudged her sharply in the ribs with her elbow. She looked around in surprise while Lindsay arranged her face into smooth lines.

"Hi, James," she batted her eyes. Since Dena did whatever Lindsay did, she batted her eyes, too, only when Dena did it, it looked more like she was squinting into the sun.

James spared them a glance. "Hey," he grunted. He looked at his sister. "You got an extra pen? I lost mine."

Claire was mildly annoyed by his request, but mostly she was glad he had shown up. He was just about the only person Lindsay was always nice to, due to her enormous crush on him, and therefore Claire was spared a moment of Lindsay's horribleness. Claire often wondered why Lindsay would risk being so intentionally unkind to her crush's sister. She could only guess what absurdity Lindsay told herself to justify her own duplicity. Claire sighed and handed him one of her pens.

"Just try not to lose that one too, 'kay?"

"You bet," he said, and turned and walked away.

Before anyone had a chance to recover from the interruption, Claire steered her friends away from the two mean girls. "Well, we'd better get going," she muttered at them as she hurried them down the hall and around a corner in hope of losing the bullies. She'd pull her friends into an empty classroom and shut the door if she had to. Claire knew Lindsay was just getting warmed up. She hadn't gotten to Emma yet and with Emma she was especially brutal. Usually Emma could laugh it off and sometimes even have Lindsay stammering for a comeback. Sometimes though, her words struck Emma to her core. Claire realized she had been wrong in thinking she was the only one who suspected her friend's feelings for her brother. Lindsay had a jealous nature and because of this she suspected the truth, too. Lindsay absolutely hated Emma.

Chapter 2

"What're they doing up there anyway?" James grumbled. He stared up at the ceiling as if it held the answers to this one of many female mysteries. "How can three dinky little girls sound like a herd of elephants?"

Kate sat curled in her favorite coffee-colored armchair in the family room. It sat adjacent to the matching oversized couch that pulled out into a bed. Her chair was the closest piece of furniture to the fireplace and she was looking forward to enjoying a fire now that the weather was getting cooler. Kate put down the book she was reading and raised an eyebrow, looking over her shoulder at him, sitting in the little alcove where the family computer was kept. "Oh, and when you have Ben or Nate over, you're just a studious little pod of church mice? Or even better, Ben *and* Nate."

"That's different."

She tilted her head and squinted at him. "How?"

He was saved from having to defend himself when the noise became louder as the girls came downstairs into the living room. Brayle detached herself from the merriment and began to gather her things from the little bench in the hallway.

"Thanks again for dinner, Mrs. Thomas," she said through the doorway that led from the hall into the living room.

"You're leaving?"

She was pulling on her jacket. "Yeah, I'd better go help Brayce and the twins get their dinner and get ready for bed."

"Well, all right. I'm sorry you can't stay." Kate kept her tone light, but she was angry. *Why should Brayle be the one to take care of everyone? She's just a child herself. And Brayce is only twelve!*

"Yeah," Claire pouted. "We were looking forward to hanging out with you tonight."

Emma nodded, looking mournful.

"It's okay," Brayle told them, although her eyes betrayed her own disappointment. She took a deep breath. "Well, see you all tomorrow at the festival!"

The girls went to see her to the door. James turned back toward the computer and the guitars he was perusing online. He was hoping to find an affordable electric and an amp. He'd been taking lessons for a while and was getting pretty good. Kate sighed. Speaking of noise...

"See you tomorrow, Brayle," she called after her daughter's friend.

James had already forgotten the girls had been in the room, until they returned and began a friendly disagreement about which movie to watch first; he rolled his eyes and retreated to his room, mumbling something about "guess I'll do it later." He would have to listen to his music and read, or play his dad's old acoustic since he and Claire didn't have the internet in their bedrooms.

Kate would have liked to have stayed to watch the girls enjoying their movies and each other, but she knew that, even though they really wouldn't mind her presence, she should really let them be. She, too, went to find something else to occupy her Friday night. Maybe Alan would want to take a walk.

* * *

Joni was heading off to work soon and wanted to see Emma and her two friends before she left. Kate watched from the doorway of Line Dried Laundry as her friend talked to the girls before sending them off to the rummage sale. Kate would have been standing there with Joni, but she couldn't leave the shop. She smiled. Claire and her friends were in very capable hands. Joni brushed Emma's hair back from her face. For good measure, she mothered Claire and Brayle too, tugging Brayle's collar straight and laying a hand on Claire's shoulder. From some people these caresses would be unwelcome and intrusive, but Joni Leonard had an effortless way of making everyone feel at ease. She put a hand on her hip and tilted her head, looking each of the girls in the face.

"Now make sure you're polite. You're representing our church, *and* you're representing Jesus." She smiled at them. Joni's voice was warm honey, somehow there was always a bubble of laughter murmuring under her words. Even now, giving instructions, Joni's manner was open and kind.

Joni was one of those people who was always in motion. Not in a jittery nervous energy way that set people on edge, but in fluid leans and easy graceful gestures. No one would ever describe Joni as fat, but her body was pleasantly curved and attractively rounded. This only added to her huggable charm. Her hair was the same coppery bronze as Emma's, only Joni wore it short, combed away from her face and falling in a natural, but flattering style. Brayle and Claire thought their friend's mother was beautiful. Not movie star beautiful, but everybody's mom beautiful.

She lifted her chin looking at them with loving pride. "Now have fun. And remember who you are and Whose you are."

With one last affectionate swat on Emma's bottom, she sent them on their way.

* * *

Emma, Claire, Melody, and Brayle bounced along Main Street chatting happily and keeping their eyes peeled for a lunch option to strike their fancy. The difficulty was which delicacy to choose. The four friends were on a break for lunch from the fundraiser. They had been working hard, were all very hungry, and everything looked good. The smell of apples was drifting wonderfully through the air, mingled with cinnamon, autumn leaves, and elephant ears. The girls were wearing their matching orange t-shirts Pastor Josh had chosen. The shirts were patterned to look like rippling water with the name of their youth group, *Brushfire*, on the front, and on the back, their theme: *Spread the Word.*

"How about apple dumplings?" Emma suggested. The other three nodded enthusiastically. Claire was glad someone else had said it. She felt a little guilty having dessert for lunch, but, hey, it was apple festival. This was a special occasion.

They wound their way to the stand that was reputed to be the best and got in line.

"Wow, I am having a *bad* hair day," Claire commented as she tried to smooth the flyaway strands of soft brown hair into a ponytail. She readjusted her glasses and shrugged. "That's as good as it's gonna get," she joked at herself. Then she laughed as

Emma and Melody rolled their eyes at her in opposite directions as if they had choreographed it.

Brayle snorted, "I would *love* to have straight hair for just one day!" she rebuked. Now it was her turn to receive the eye roll, but she continued. "When it's humid, my hair gets all frizzed out and I look like a scarecrow!"

"Scarecrow? You're definitely ugly enough to be a scarecrow. All of you are, actually."

The girls spun around. Lindsay and Dena had sneaked up behind them in line. They often used this tactic in order to catch people unaware and gain access to intimate conversations, thereby collecting information to use as weapons.

"My Uncle Billy is a farmer; maybe you could stand in his cornfield and be ugly." She made a spitting noise at them, a hybrid of a snicker and a derisive snort. "Scarecrow. Makes sense. Everyone always knew you didn't have any *brains*. It explains a lot actually. No wonder you're so stupid." Lindsay seemed particularly pleased with herself. Apparently she considered this latest insult especially witty.

Dena, of course, laughed like she had never heard anything so humorous.

Emma bristled. "Well I guess it's better than the alternative," she looked Lindsay in the eye, "I'd rather be a scarecrow with Brayle than be the lion and the tin wood man like you." She stepped back and looked back and forth between Lindsay and Dena with mock indecision furrowing her brow. She pointed at each of them. "Now which of you is the coward and which one needs a heart?" She smiled and waved a hand. "Oh, never mind, girls, you can both be both."

Again there was laughter, but this time it wasn't Dena. It wasn't even Brayle, Melody or Claire who, impressed with their friend's quick thinking were speechless. James and his friend, Nate, had appeared out of nowhere, and they and the old man selling apple dumplings out of his booth were all enjoying a good laugh at Emma's slight on Lindsay and Dena.

The girls suddenly realized that there was now no one in front of them in line; still nobody moved. The old man spoke, smiling. "Worse yet," he chuckled, "ya might could be a wicked ol' witch!"

Lindsay hadn't noticed James and his friend approaching. She hadn't had time to put on the mask she wore for James. When she *did* notice him laughing at her, she turned scarlet with rage. Dena looked at her leader in fear as this time all four girls, along with James and Nate, bent double with laughter at the man's joke. In an attempt to regain some dignity and reassert her authority over her favorite victims, she stepped around them to the counter. She tossed her head.

"I want an apple dumpling," she commanded the old man imperiously. "She does too." She jerked her head at Dena.

The man squinted. He shrugged apologetically. "Sorry. Fresh out."

Lindsay drew herself up to her full height. With one glance at the fresh dumplings, waiting to be sold and enjoyed, she spun on her heel and stomped away, dragging Dena with her. Her pride was too bruised to award James with one of her dazzling glances. She pretended he wasn't there and that he hadn't seen her defeat; pretended he hadn't laughed at her.

"Good for you, girlie," said the old man, twinkling a smile at Emma.

"What are *you* two doing here?" Claire asked James.

He shrugged, still chuckling, "Getting some dumplings."

Before anyone could recover from this episode there was another interruption.

"Brayle! BRAYLE!"

Brayle sighed. "What, Brayce?"

Brayle's younger brother, Brayce, trotted up to his big sister, panting. "I've been looking all over for you," he accused. "Where have you been?"

Brayle stared at him. "We've been working. You knew I had the rummage sale today."

"Oh. Right. I forgot. Well, anyway, Mom wants you."

Claire and Emma saw a shadow pass over Brayle's fair features, "What's wrong?"

He scratched his left calf with the toe of his right sneaker. "She needs you to watch Bry and Branda."

"I still have work to do after lunch!" she objected.

Brayce spread his hands in self-defense and shrugged. "I'm just doing what she told me to do!"

She sighed. "All right, let's go." She began to walk away.

"Aren't you even going to eat anything?" Melody asked, indignant over the whole situation. Claire frowned her agreement. Emma looked like she was angry, but was trying not to show it.

"Nah, I'd better go."

The three girls let James and Nate go ahead of them in line. They ordered the food they had waited for all year but, after all that had just happened, when they sat down to eat, they didn't really enjoy it much.

*   *   *

People could hear her for blocks. It wasn't the first time Brandy Robinson had made a scene in public. Unfortunately, it wasn't the first time she had done it at the expense of one or more of her children.

Brandy was usually pretty, with a thin frame and hair like her daughter's, but at the moment she was screeching with rage. Many people probably would have found her much more attractive without the excessive eye makeup and if she wore clothes that were more suited to her age. As it was, most people didn't see past the overdone image she put on, and the attention it did draw was, for the most part, negative. She was drawing attention now, but for a very different reason than her looks.

Passersby watched while they pretended they weren't watching as Brandy made her oldest daughter wish she could turn herself invisible. Brayle ducked her head, feeling the stares of the strangers around her, her eyes stinging from anger and hurt at her mother's words.

"...really too much to ask for a little help? I mean I bend over backwards taking care of you four all by myself, and I wake up and you're gone and they're whining always wanting something. Way to go, genius, didn't you know I'd need you around to take care of them today?"

The rant went on, peppered with curses and accusations. Brayle knew that she would have to wait for her mother to run out of steam and then she would be sweeter, pouting and apologizing to get Brayle to do what she wanted.

The Valley Without Her

She hated it when Mom acted this way. It wasn't just the pain of hearing the poisonous words, it was the shame. People were all around. She could feel their pity. It burned her skin. Brayle could guess what they were thinking: *that Mama doesn't care about her own daughter.* Some thoughts she didn't even have to guess. She could hear the murmurs. A very round grandma with a teased beehive clucked to a pale woman with long silvery hair, "Such a shame. Poor thing."

The lady with long hair nodded mutely. This only made Brayle feel worse. There was even a guy down the street with a camera who was taking snapshots of the festival. *Great. Just peachy.* He was far enough away that Brayle dared to hope he wasn't capturing this heartwarming moment on film.

When her mother's tirade finally came to a close, Brayle risked a quick stop back to the rummage sale to tell her friends and Pastor Josh she had to go. There was plenty of disappointment to go around. Claire and Emma gave her hugs, promised to call her later and Brayle left for home. As the distance grew between her and her friends, she recognized the pale-looking woman who had witnessed her mother's tantrum. Brayle ducked out of sight before the woman could meet her eyes and remember her. She didn't think she could stand another moment of pity.

* * *

In spite of everything, the youth group was having fun. Emma wasn't kidding when she told Pastor Josh that she and Claire could make fun out of anything. At the fundraiser, though, they didn't have to try very hard. There were people from all over. There was a pack of college freshman boys who didn't buy anything, but teased the girls, proposing marriage to each of them in turn, just to see them blush. There was a beautiful woman, wearing sunglasses and expensive-looking clothes, who Serena declared was a celebrity disguised as a regular person. There was a young mother who had adopted a handful of cute little kids from as many countries. It reminded the teens of the children's song about Jesus loving all the little children of the world. The lady was delighted to find several matching pairs of sandals that had been donated by the Schmit family who had quadruplets. They were visited by a sweet elderly couple that held hands and, for some inexplicable reason, bought every soup ladle they had out. Everyone laughed at Drew when a man in a baseball cap entreated him to try on a lady's pink raincoat covered in fat-cheeked duckies because he was, "'bout her height."

Pastor Josh felt like a policeman directing traffic, a personal shopper, and a bookkeeper all rolled into one person. Frank and Anna Lopez, his youth sponsors, had had to leave early to see their daughter, Mia compete for (and win!) the Apple Blossom Queen crown, so he was on his own. He talked to the people who came to shop; he directed the kids as they refilled the tables, and helped people, if they needed it, carry their purchases back to their vehicles (no extra charge); he kept a close eye on the cash box, and he politely asked a mouthy woman with bleached hair to leave when she had shouted at Emma for the price of a handmade quilt being too high. He was so proud of his teens. Not only was their fundraiser going really well, but they were showing God's love through their helpful kindness. It was a madhouse; kids were coming and going, calling out to each other for help ("Hey, Serena, we have any more tablecloths like this one?"), answering people's questions and even trying on the funky hats that Widow Perkins had donated, but there was a method to the madness and everyone was doing a good job and having a good time. He tried to keep tabs on who had been doing which job the longest, and to be fair about giving breaks. The sun was beginning to set. He glanced at this watch.

"Claire! Emma!" They looked around at him. "Why don't you two go take a quick break."

They nodded happily at him. They waved their understanding, not bothering to try to make themselves heard over the noise and ambled away to stretch their legs.

"I feel really bad about Bray having to miss out again," Claire confided.

Emma's face clouded, "I know. This seems to be happening a lot, doesn't it?"

"She acts like it's no big deal, but I can tell she's upset when stuff like that happens."

"Maybe we should—" Emma stopped when Claire yanked on her elbow.

"Let's go this way," she mumbled. Emma followed Claire's gaze and saw Lindsay and Dena half a block away, browsing at a fussy little stand selling cosmetics. She grimaced at her friend as they turned as one down a side street.

Pastor Josh glanced up in relief when he caught a tiny glimpse through the forest of bodies, strollers, toys, clothes and more clothes. *There they were.* The second he let Claire and Emma leave they had a sudden rush of business. Not only did there seem to be two people for every teen, every one of them seemed to require help of some kind. *Do you have one in my size? Do you have one in blue? Are there only six of this place setting? Can you tell me where they sell the bacon apples? Can you tell me what time it is?* It was enough to wear him out, and that was no small feat.

He joyfully helped every person he could reach and tried to keep an eye on his kids as they tried to do the same. He was so proud of them he thought he might bust. At last the crowd dwindled and it came time to pack up what little was left, clean up, and go home. Pastor Josh was about to gather his kids around him to tell them what an outstanding job they had done and to announce the day's earnings when Claire appeared at his side. Her face was crinkled in confusion.

"Where's Emma?"

He looked at her. Now it was his turn to crinkle. "I thought she was with you."

"No, we left here together, but then I went to talk to Mom for a minute and she said she was coming back here. I thought she got here before I did, but there were so many people..."

"She didn't come back with you?" Pastor Josh asked slowly.

"No! Didn't you see her?"

"I thought so..." *Claire....He had only seen Claire.*

Claire was stumped. "But that was a long time ago."

"Almost an hour." He tried to keep the anxiety out of his voice. He could tell Claire was worried and he didn't want to frighten her any more than she already was. This was difficult because he was frightened as well. "Come on, we'll ask everyone. Someone's seen her."

Now he did gather the teens, but instead of sharing good news with them, he calmly (he hoped) asked if any of them had seem Emma.

"Yeah," Ben offered. "She was here helping me with the man who wanted to buy his daughter that old bike."

"But that was before!" Claire trebled. "That was before we left together." There was a low murmur of dismay through the group. The sound was like a bathtub being filled on the other side of the house. The group had broken into spontaneous little interviews. Everyone wanted to be told by someone that they had seen Emma not five minutes ago selling a sundress to a middle schooler. No one got their wish.

Pastor Josh raised his hands to restore order, "Now just wait, hang on, HANG ON! She can't be far, we'll find her. Everyone break into pairs and go in different directions. Stay together." His voice took on an unfamiliar sternness, "*Stay together* and look around. If you don't find her, meet back here in fifteen minutes. I'll wait here in case she comes back here before any of you find her out there."

He watched his kids wander off in different directions, Claire and Melody were huddling close together, looking like little girls as they went. Pastor Josh could read the logo written on their bright orange shirts, standing out in the gathering darkness. *Spread the Word.* He stared at the bobbing letters on the backs of the kids. *Yes,* he thought, *spread the word. Ask everyone you see.* He began searching the immediate area, trying not to let the terror that was crouching in his stomach crawl up into his throat and strangle him. *We'll find her.* He prayed as he walked the short distance to the church van and around the perimeter of the tent where they had spent the day. He prayed as he looked in the van, in a clump of trees that shaded one corner of the tent and even under the tables that hadn't yet been taken down and loaded up. He prayed.

One by one the pairs returned to him staring at him round-eyed. None of them spoke. None of them asked about the success of the rummage sale. None of them made jokes or goofed around. And none of them had found Emma.

Chapter 3

He was afraid that the trail was cold before they even knew anything had happened. Detective Doug Palmer hated these cases. They had constructed a time line of Emma's day. They had interviewed every person they could see. That kid pastor had told him that a woman had shouted at Emma earlier in the day, but he didn't think she'd wanted to hurt Emma. Palmer had a description of the woman, but there was no sign of her anywhere. The old man who sold apple dumplings shook his head sadly. He had remembered Emma and her friends, but hadn't seen them since just after noon. Yes, she had stood out to him. No, he didn't have a criminal record. Yes, he had been right here with his dumpling stand all day. Was there anything he could do to help that nice little girl? Palmer took down his information and told him he would be hearing from him.

He talked to as many people as he could, he even stopped an old couple as they were tossing armfuls of ladles into the trunk of their expensive luxury car. They hadn't noticed Emma. They'd been to the rummage sale put on by that youth group; yes, but they were sure the girl who had spoken to them was blonde. Melody, the lady thought her name was. The problem was that events like these were big, all-day things. People coming and going from morning till night and from who-knew-where.

Now he stood in the dark giving instruction. The festival's evening activities had been canceled. Dozens of people were there, all of them more than willing to help. People from the church that the girl attended had shown up as soon as they had heard what had happened. Local businessmen and parents of kids who went to school with Emma had left their warm homes, pulled on coats, and awaited his directions. There were quite a few cold-looking kids in orange t-shirts with their parents—one girl was dressed in a formal gown and wearing a crown on her head and a sash that declared her the Apple Blossom Queen. She stood there with her parents, wearing her father's jacket over her dress, looking beautiful and miserable. All of these people were ready to search for Emma Leonard.

They were going to split into little groups and search the area. They had all expected to be home by this hour, but many of them stayed hoping there was something they could do to help. It was late. It was dark. He had sent out the proper alerts, posted the girl's description, talked to her friends and the pastor, Pastor Josh McMillan his name was, who was now pacing around the area like a man searching for his car in a parking lot. He had spoken with the girl's parents who were now talking to a police officer. The image of Emma's mother, crumpling in despair on the sidewalk was seared into his brain. The sound of her heart-wrenching wail still rang in his ears. Twenty-five years on the job and he never got used to that part. The cries of the mothers stayed with him, merging together in one horrible harmony of agony. He rubbed a hand over his eyes, trying to banish the ghosts. "All right everyone, let's go."

* * *

They had their instructions. Ruth Daniels watched as the people scattered in all different directions. She wished she were searching, too, but there was no way she could handle that much walking. Instead she posted herself at a central location and manned a little table with coffee, cocoa, and water. One of the vendors donated hot cider. Already she could hear people calling out for Emma. They were shining their flashlights into car windows and up into trees. The voices of the people calling for her were like a chorus of crickets, only instead of it eliciting nostalgic summertime memories it was a horrid sound. They were pleas with no answer. Ruth set her chin and prayed. That detective man had gone over to the poor Leonards, bless them, and was asking questions, questions, questions. She heard him tell them that they would be making up fliers with Emma's picture and description and posting them everywhere.

Periodically a group would come back and offer information and she would tell them what she knew. The news was always the same. No one had seen any trace of Emma. After more than two hours, the detective called it quits and sent them home. Some said they wanted to keep looking; they kept searching. Palmer was taking Joni and Greg home himself. After that, he had a lot of work to do and he wanted to get started. They should all get some rest, he told them. Ruth thought that this was an odd thing to say. She doubted that any one of these people would sleep tonight.

* * *

After Ruth talked with Alan, Kate, and her good friend, Sherry Albert, the women agreed to meet at Joni's. Sherry took Ruth with her in her car. Kate drove the Leonard's car. They arrived at Greg and Joni's house within seconds of each other. Kate glanced at her watch, and was surprised to see it was going on midnight. She put her hand on the knob and walked in without ringing the doorbell. Detective Palmer was already gone. The

Leonard's beagle, Tesla, named for Greg's admiration of the inventor, greeted them nervously. His tail was oddly curled and Greg always called it his "Tesla Coil." Whenever people asked him about this he would simply shrug and say, "Look it up." Tesla seemed to sense that something wasn't right and whined to be petted. Ruth patted him on the head as they passed.

They were not the only ones to have this idea, showing up to offer help, but Kate assessed the situation and acted. After walking through the front entryway past the dining room, the three women found Joni sitting on her living room floor in front of her couch, staring at the wall, still wearing her scrubs, and not listening to Julie Burish who was gibbering at her, "You're a good mom, Joni, and don't think for a minute that this means you aren't. This could've happened to any of us, even me! No one thinks you've done anything wrong and feeling guilty is just a waste of time, so we're just going to—"

"Julie?" Kate interrupted the well-meant, but inappropriate monologue.

Julie looked around at the three women framed in the arched doorway of the Leonard's living room.

Kate wrung her hands and shifted her weight. She shuffled her feet against the pretty cream-colored carpet, the carpet Joni usually didn't allow anyone's shoes to defile. She formed her face into childish helplessness.

"We need someone to plan meals for Greg and Joni for a few days; they're going to be busy with talking to people, and then when Emma comes home...*and* we need to alert everyone to pray, and there's Joni's Sunday school class tomorrow. Well," she sighed helplessly, "what do *you* think we should do?"

The Valley Without Her

A gleam came to Julie's eyes. *A project.* Julie flipped her shiny shoulder-length honey-colored hair.

She smiled at Kate indulgently, "I'll take care of all of that," she soothed. She spoke to Kate as if she were a wet-behind-the-ears freshman instead of a woman fifteen years her senior.

Kate sighed with a relief she didn't have to fake. She could feel Sherry and Ruth relax on either side of her as well.

"Oh, thank you so much." Kate gushed.

Julie rushed out of the room like a superhero. She grabbed her husband, David, who had been standing uncomfortably nearby.

Julie's heart was in the right place. She was loving and compassionate, but she was also a pushy control freak and Kate knew that if she couldn't handle Julie's exploits right now, Joni most certainly couldn't.

As one the three women moved to Joni. Sherry and Kate curled up on the floor on either side of her as Tesla laid down and rested his muzzle on Joni's lap. Ruth pulled a soft armchair closer to the three women (and the little dog) and settled silently into it. In younger days, she would have plopped there on the carpet with the other ladies, but she was creeping up on seventy and her plopping days were over.

Kate took Joni's hand. "Where's Greg?" she asked her.

Joni's tone was flat and lifeless. "Outside."

The friends looked out the sliding glass door to the patio where they saw Joni's husband, Greg, standing in the backyard. He stared into the sky as if he were waiting for a meteor shower.

They understood. He didn't want to be around people right now. They did wonder a little, though, what he was doing with his thoughts. Greg attended church with his family, but it was unlikely that he was praying right now. They'd been praying for him for years.

These women had been friends for a long time. Sherry had given them advice when their kids were babies and the weight of the new responsibility threatened to overwhelm them. Ruth had been going to Hillside Church longer than any of them and they could all remember her warm welcome when they had started attending. The three women knew that Greg's parents had passed away several years ago and Joni's mother had died as well. Joni's father was in a nursing home with Alzheimer's and didn't recognize Joni or her sister, Jennifer, who lived in London. Friends were the only family Greg and Joni had right now.

Sherry gently rested her hand on Joni's shoulder. No one spoke. No one asked questions. No one prayed. Not out loud, anyway. Kate watched her friend. She wanted to cry. She wanted to scream. She wanted to run outside and drag Greg into the house and make him put his arms around his wife. She wanted to run around yelling Emma's name until she couldn't speak. Until it hurt. She didn't do any of these things, though. She sat with her friend and held her hand. Sherry and Ruth both had their eyes closed. Both women murmured silent prayers, pleas to the throne of heaven. For a long while, no one moved. They were sentries sitting together with their cherished friend. They kept vigil over Joni and breathed, hoping by their presence to keep at bay at least a little of the fear that gnawed at the edges of everything.

A little after 2:30, Greg came through the door. He didn't seem to realize he was shivering. Joni continued to stare at nothing. Kate and Sherry stood and pulled Joni to her feet as Ruth bent herself creakily out of the armchair.

"Thanks," he whispered, not meeting their eyes.

He put his arm around Joni and led her away and up the stairs toward their bedroom, although, Kate suspected, the room they were headed for was most likely Emma's. Ruth wordlessly led the way out of the house. They locked the door behind them.

* * *

When Kate walked through her own front door, as she had anticipated, her family had not gone to bed. She found the three of them huddled together in their pajamas on the living room couch. Their faces were lit softly by the warm light coming from the electric candle lamp. Alan had removed the cushions of the couch and pulled out the sofa bed. She left them only long enough to take a sixty-second shower and pull on some pj's. Claire, trembly-chinned and puffy-eyed, was curled up against Alan with her head on his shoulder and James was draped over the foot of the bed, lying on his side. He stared at the floor. Alan held his free arm to her and she melted into his embrace, curling up in the space not occupied by James. Alan kissed her forehead.

"Are Greg and Joni doing okay?"

"No."

They all instinctively gathered closer together. Kate reached across Alan's chest and ran her fingers though Claire's hair. James, then Claire, then Alan drifted off, Claire still gasping soft little sobs, whimpering in her sleep like she did when she was a baby. Finally, Kate, too, succumbed to slumber, her family safe around her, all four of them sleeping fitfully and dreaming of copper-haired Emma.

* * *

Amie M. Johnson

Scott Fischer sat quietly in the pew, frozen and wide-eyed. *Boy, did I pick a whopper of a day to visit this church!* He was new in town, about to start his new job at Barton Construction the next day and he was looking for a church to attend. Hillside had seemed like a good choice but, apparently, they were in the middle of a crisis. He had briefly attended the festival that everyone was talking about, the festival where this Emma girl had gone missing, but he had left after only about an hour. It wasn't really his thing. Although his work was in construction, his hobby was photography, but he preferred waterfalls and moose as his subjects to little kids with balloons and ladies in sunhats eating candied apples. Unfortunately, sun-hatted ladies were a lot easier to come by than moose.

Scott stayed seated but let his mind wander. He didn't want to draw attention to himself, but he knew it was probably inevitable. He was tall and broad shouldered with black hair and dark eyes; he wouldn't be able to melt into the crowd when he was a head taller than most of the people here. On top of that, he was new. New people got noticed and smiled at and invited to small group meetings and coffee. On the other hand, today everyone here was preoccupied with a tragedy and may not give him a second glance. Scott considered himself a Christian and hoped God was pleased with his life, but he didn't feel comfortable getting involved in complicated situations. Maybe this place wasn't for him. As soon as he could, without drawing attention to himself, he would leave and put this whole mess out of his mind.

***

Pastor Ward's hands were shaking. He gripped the sides of the lectern, looking out at his fold. The people looked exhausted, both from sorrow and from staying up all night. He had never seen the pews of Hillside Church so packed on a Sunday morning.

He had never been more at a loss for words. Pastor Ward gave them the best he could think of.

"Let's pray..." and they did. Not only Pastor Ward, but Pastor Josh prayed. Helene Smith, the preschool teacher; Bruce Montgomery, the high school soccer coach; Ruth; Sherry; Alan; Wayne Norton, the mail carrier; Anna Lopez; and Julie and David Burish all prayed, too. Even a few of the teens were among those who stood and prayed for the Leonard family. There was no sermon, no music, just prayer warriors in battle. The service went a little long and Pastor Ward and Pastor Josh invited everyone to come back later that night, and the next night, to pray again. Monday night, however, would be a special candlelight vigil held in the high school auditorium and they would be inviting other churches and posting notices around town. Everyone was welcome. They encouraged everyone to continue to pray and fast, if they were able and wished to. Everyone wanted to do anything they could to bring Emma home safely.

***

Pastor Glenward "Ward" Franklin was weary. He loved the Lord. He loved his people. He loved his job. He missed his wife. Especially times like these. *Especially,* especially now. Pastor Ward shifted his, not-as-fit-as-I-used-to-be weight in his office chair. He rubbed his chin; there usually wasn't as much stubble there, but right now nothing was usual. He was tired. He thought even his hair was tired, what was left of it. Even the ring of silvery-white circling the back of his head felt heavy today. Boy, did he miss his wife. Mollie Brown would have known what to say to the woman sitting in front of him. Brandy Robinson was looking at him as if he could wave his hand, say a few magic words, and make her fears vanish like a morning fog. Her too-thin frame looked childlike, as she slumped in the chair.

Amie M. Johnson

He knew what he'd *like* to say to her. But that wouldn't do. No. He wasn't that man anymore. In the past he would have verbally shaken this woman, given her a dressing-down for her poor choices and objectionable behavior. God had dealt with this flaw in his personality with His own loving shakings and dressings down. "Spiritual spankings" Mollie had called them. Now he would try to answer this woman's questions with Christ's love and do all he could to help her. He was breaking to pieces inside. Oh, how he missed his wife.

Mollie Franklin was one of a kind. Mollie with her hair twisted artfully into a bun and her scent like baby powder and freshly baked bread. She used to hide little notes for him to find: love notes, notes of encouragement, often written on little scraps of paper with a grocery or to-do list printed neatly on the other side. Mollie Brown had a way with words. She had a way of speaking right to the heart of a matter. She could scold you, tell you the truth, help you figure it all out, and make you feel as loved as a child, all in the same breath. Children loved her. He had watched the most cantankerous of babies melt into coos and smiles in Mollie Brown's pleasingly plump arms. She could get the angriest of couples holding hands and laughing together by the end of a tension-charged marriage counseling session. She could call a wayward loved one to the carpet for his flaws and bring him around to grace without stirring up defensive anger. She made it seem so easy. These gifts of hers were a few of the reasons she had been given the nickname "Mollie Brown" after the legendary survivor of the *Titanic:* the unsinkable Molly Brown.

Mollie did not sink when she was diagnosed with breast cancer. She battled the disease *and* the treatment and came out a survivor, who, as time went on, would counsel other women with the same disease, keeping their heads above the frigid waters of despair. Mollie did not sink when bitter church attenders took out their life's frustrations on him and, subsequently, on her, but instead loved them back around to the peace of God. Ward had wanted to throw in the towel and leave these few to their own devices, leave Gardenville, find a new pastorate and move on. Mollie had told him they were the lost sheep that Jesus would have left the ninety-nine to find. As usual Mollie was right.

Mollie didn't sink when their oldest son, Paul, nearly drowned at the age of ten, or when their youngest, Adam, told them at dinner one evening that he wasn't sure he believed in God. Both sons were now pastors of their own churches. Their two daughters, Esther and Merry (born on Christmas Eve), fought like cats and dogs during adolescence and still Mollie Brown did not sink. The two sisters were now best friends and spoke nearly every day. Mollie *nearly* sank when she miscarried a baby girl between Esther and Adam. It was the only time Ward had ever heard her express any doubt in God's plan. Still Mollie rallied and leaned on Him to bring her through the months and years to come, stronger and braver than before.

None of those crises could keep the unsinkable Mollie Brown down for good. But the drunk driver could. Mollie was coming home after visiting Merry and her family when a man sped at eighty miles an hour right through an intersection and hit Mollie's car. She died at the scene before the emergency teams arrived. Ward would soon find out that a teenage boy named Jake who had witnessed the accident got out of his car and braved his way into the wreckage to see if he could help Mollie. Jake had never met her, but he held Mollie's hand as she died, promising to pass on her last words to her husband. "Tell Glenward I'll see him at home." The young boy may have thought that Mollie Brown didn't know what she was saying, but Ward knew. Mollie was telling him that they would see each other again in heaven.

A few days later at the graveside service after her funeral, Pastor Ward watched them lower the love of his life into the earth next to their baby's little marble headstone bearing just one date and the name Elizabeth Mollie Franklin. So sank his unsinkable Mollie Brown. The man who had hit her, Ray Crawford, was shattered by remorse from what he had done, although he had never met Mollie. Crawford was shaken to his core and vowed to turn his life around. Sentenced to prison for his crime, he sought help there and the chaplain introduced him to Jesus. Ray would tell anyone who would listen about his new faith and eventually began to disciple other inmates. He became Mollie Brown's last rescue. Even in her death, she could change someone's life.

Pastor Ward missed his wife. All of his musings lasted no longer than a few seconds and Brandy Robinson still looked at him with the same woebegone expression she had had on when she walked unexpectedly thought his door. Mollie Brown would have known what to do.

He took a breath. "How can I help you today?" he asked her kindly.

Brandy wrung her hands and fidgeted uncomfortably in her chair.

"Well," she began, "I don't know..." She avoided his eyes. "Me and my kids came to the candlelight thing the other night for that girl..."

"Emma." Pastor Ward supplied. It hurt him to say her name, and again he tamped down his vexation. He knew full well that Brayle and Emma were friends. *Why didn't she?*

"Yeah..." she seemed to wilt a little in her chair. "The thing is, well, what happened to her? I mean, she was with Bray before and then she was gone." She ventured a glance at him, swallowing hard. "Didn't anyone see what happened? I mean, you know, she was just a kid..." her voice trailed off.

Pastor Ward felt a rush of compassion for her. "You're afraid that what happened to Emma could happen to Brayle or one of your other children? You're afraid your children aren't safe?" he asked kindly.

She looked relieved to have her own feelings put into words. "I guess, yeah."

"You know what, why don't we schedule an appointment for a week or so from now? That way you'll have time to think about what you'd like to talk about with me, how I can help you. Would this time next week work for you?"

Brandy nodded.

"Good. I want you to make a list of questions you want to ask me. Anything at all. How's that sound?"

She nodded again, but knit her eyebrows in confusion. He knew she expected him to put her mind at ease right this moment, but he also knew this would be a marathon, not a sprint. She needed to be willing to put in the work, and he needed to know if she was going to follow through.

"Good," he said again, smiling at her. "I'll have Judy call you in a few days to make sure we're still on."

"Who's Judy?" she asked bewildered.

"My secretary; she spoke to you when you came in."

"Oh. Right."

"So you write your questions and I'll see you next week, all right?"

"Oh...okay." She rose from her chair and picked up her purse. She started for the door. She paused and turned to look at him before she exited the room.

"Uh...thanks."

She was gone.

Pastor Ward sighed, still missing Mollie Brown.

Chapter 4

Detective Palmer was a big man. He had trouble finding clothes that fit him. Some people probably thought he wore the same suit every day after day since all of his suits were identical. He didn't care about his clothing; he had more important things to think about. He sat in his small uninteresting office looking over reports from the officers who worked in the areas surrounding Emma Leonard's disappearance. Nothing. A few petty crimes, maybe some neighbors calling to tattle on each other. One ambitious rookie had pulled over a middle-aged woman on the interstate several miles from Gardenville when he noticed her taillight was out. She had promised to have it fixed as soon as she arrived home.

Palmer took a sip of his coffee and nearly spat it out. It was cold and tasted like it had been made last Thursday. He set it aside and forgot about it. Palmer ran a hand through his hair. He would have been proud of his full head of dark hair, silver at the temples, if he had ever given it much thought. But concerning his appearance, his hair was no more important to him than his clothes were.

Again he picked up the time line he had pieced together from the information given to him by the people who had been with Emma that day. It was fairly straightforward since Claire Thomas had been with her nearly every minute. The two girls had separated at around six o'clock in the evening, intending to meet up again at the fundraiser their youth group was sponsoring. The Thomas girl returned, assuming that Emma had preceded her, at about 6:20. There were lots of people there, over quite a large area; the kids had been very busy with their fundraiser and Claire didn't notice her friend's absence until much later.

They had parted ways just down the block from a little store owned by Claire's mother, Kate Thomas. From there, Emma would have turned east and headed back to her group. They had interviewed all the people working along that street and came up with nothing. *What happened after the girls' parting that kept Emma from reaching her destination?* Palmer leaned back in his chair and looked at the water-stained ceiling. He intended to find out.

***

"What do you think about going back to school tomorrow?"

Claire looked up and then back down again. She shrugged. "I guess."

She could tell mom was surprised that she hadn't made more of an argument. But, really, what difference did it make? She really couldn't feel any worse. It was Wednesday and Mom had let her come along with her to work today. James had wanted to go to school, but Claire had taken her mom up on her offer to tag along to the shop. Dad had had to go back to work right away to help train the new guy—Scott, she thought his name was.

Claire loved Line Dried Laundry. The way the bell above the door tinkled when she came in. The pretty lace curtains in the windows that she had helped Mom sew. She loved the invitingly creaky wood floors, making sounds like grandma's old rocking chair when she walked across them. She loved the smells. There was the dusty scent of antiques and the sweet aroma of whatever was the on the menu for the day, and the piney floor cleaner that Mom always used.

Claire had hoped to draw solace from all of these things, wrapping herself in the place like a down comforter. It didn't work. Today, instead of being comforted by the familiar surroundings, she felt them mocking her. Claire picked up the piece of butter pecan fudge from the batch her mom had made. Usually it was her favorite treat from the store. She took a small bite. It tasted like mud. She could feel her mother's eyes on her. She could feel her chin tremble. There was no one else in the store. Even Marty wasn't there, but on her lunch break. Even though it was only twelve thirty, Kate moved to the door and put up the cute little "closed" sign made out of an antique school slate. She came back to Claire's table and held her as they both cried.

* * *

"You know what, Judy; I'll call her myself." Pastor Ward decided it would be best if he handled his accountability call to Brandy Robinson in person. Some people needed just a simple reminder, but he suspected Brandy would need a lot of personal care and encouragement. Something nagged at his brain. He knew she was going to need something else: special attention, but what was it he was supposed to do?

"All right, then," Judy replied, "anything else before I go?"

Judy looked at him with sadness behind her smile. He hadn't seen a true smile on any of his people's faces since they found out about Emma. Not that he blamed them. He felt the same.

"No, I think that's all for today. Thanks, Judy."

She nodded her good-bye and left.

Pastor Ward dialed Brandy's number and waited. After several rings there was a change in sound and he could tell the phone had been answered. It had possibly been answered by Peter Pan's Lost Boys during a particularly nasty battle with Captain Hook, by the sound of it.

"'Lo?" a too-loud child voice breathed into the phone.

"Well, hi there!" Pastor Ward answered. He instinctively felt grandfatherly toward little ones, especially ones who *needed* a grandfather. "This is Pastor Ward; who am I talking to?"

"Bwy," the voice answered.

It must be the boy, Brylyn. He thought to himself. *Poor little guy can't say his name.* "Is your Mama there?" he asked kindly.

"She seepin,'" said the puppy-voiced babe.

"Hmm," he was concerned but kept his tone light, "Is someone there watching you?"

"Bway." He said simply

"Oh, your big sister, Brayle's, there?"

"Yeah, her here."

"Good, can I speak to her, then, please?"

"OK." Presumably, Brylyn put down the phone to search for his oldest sister. The pirate battle that had been going on during their conversation became louder when the little boy's face no longer blocked the phone from the noise. The sounds weren't alarming, just chaotic, underlined by the noise of cartoon sound effects and a blaring radio. He waited patiently for Brayle, listening to the drama on the other end.

"...where my...can't find..."

"Look under...there yesterday..."

"NO!...only...blue one..."

"...Brayle said...blue..."

"No, no, NO!...*pink* one."Again the mayhem was muffled.

"Hello?"

"Brayle?

"Yes."

"Brayle, this is Pastor Ward. I'm calling to talk to your mother, but your little brother told me that she was resting so he found you."

Brayle sounded embarrassed, "Oh. Yeah. Um, would you like me to have her call you back?"

"That would be just fine, thanks." His heart ached for his girl. He knew she had much too much resting on her young shoulders.

"Pastor Ward?" Brayle's voice sounded so sad he thought it might break him in two.

"What is it, child?" *That's what she was, just a child, but with an adult's worries.*

"Do you think...do you think Emma will come home?"

"I hope so. I pray so."

"Me too," her voice was still small. He thought she was going to ask him another question when there was a muted sound of a voice lower than the others in the background. Brandy had woken up.

"Oh," Brayle said, "here's Mom."

"Thank you, Brayle," he replied.

But she was gone. "Hello?" Brandy said drowsily into the phone.

"Hello, Brandy, this is Pastor Ward, I'm just calling you to remind you of our meeting in a few days and was wondering if you'd written those questions for me yet."

For a while she said nothing and he thought she may even hang up on him, but then she answered.

"Guess I haven't," she mumbled, "written anything down, I mean."

He had suspected as much, "That's all right; you still have time to do that. Are you still planning on meeting with me?"

"Yes."

Oh, Father, thank You. He realized he had been holding his breath. "Good. Good. Well, you write those questions, and I'll see you then, all right? Do you remember the time?"

She did.

"Good," he said again. "I'm looking forward to our visit." He meant it.

They said good-bye and he began making notes to himself, planning his time with Brandy Robinson, something still itching at the back of his mind.

* * *

Youth group had never been this subdued, not even on a Sunday night, which was usually more low-key than Wednesday night. The kids sat in pairs and trios, talking softly together on safe subjects. Each of them looked like they had lost their best friend. Claire Thomas had. She and Brayle sat together with Melody, none of them speaking. Before Pastor Josh had started the meeting, during the time when kids were arriving, Melody had quietly asked him to pray for her. She'd been having nightmares. He himself was riddled with guilt since Emma had gone missing during an event that he had planned. He said a silent prayer that he would be able to help these kids in some way. He felt he was in way over his head.

Pastor Josh got their attention. He had planned to give a simple lesson and then let the kids take the lead. He wanted to pray with them, and then let them ask any questions they wanted. He did this from time to time. He got all sorts of questions, from "How do you *know* you're saved?" to "Does God think *The Far Side*® is funny?" The latter inquiry had actually launched a great discussion about heaven and hell.

Tonight, though, was much different. They didn't ask him anything out loud, but they looked at him, hoping that he would have answers. He looked at the faces he loved, painted in varying states of distress. Of course, he couldn't tell them what had happened that night, just over a week ago, but he could see it on each face. *Why?* He knew they were struggling, wondering *how* such a thing could happen and right in front of them. They were scared.

"We don't always understand why God allows bad things to happen," he said to them. "Sometimes we never get to know. Most of you remember Pastor Ward's wife, Mollie Brown."

They nodded at him, knowing where he was going.

"She was an amazing woman of faith. She blessed many lives and God used her to bring glory to His name." Pastor Josh paused, taking a moment to compose himself as he was flooded with memories of Mollie and of Emma. There were even a few scenes in his mind starring both of them. There was Mollie Brown and Emma in the Christmas program playing the innkeeper's wife and her granddaughter. They had stolen the show. He tucked away the images and continued. "Mollie Brown's not with us anymore, but that doesn't mean she's really gone. Emma's not with us right now," his voice broke, "but it doesn't mean," he took a breath, "it doesn't mean she's gone. We'll see Mollie Brown in heaven someday, and right now we're going to pray that we see Emma real soon."

And so he prayed. He prayed for Emma and her family. He prayed for Pastor Ward, knowing he missed Mollie, and then Pastor Josh prayed for each of his kids by name. As the teens prayed silently along with him, they felt a peace settle over them. They were still walking in the dark. But they were not alone.

* * *

Monday morning Joni looked around her kitchen at the food and letters and even flowers that people had sent. Julie had been true to her word and taken care of everything. *So much food.* She may never cook again. She may never eat again either. Greg would wander aimlessly around the house and if he happened through the kitchen, he might grab something as he passed by. A chicken leg, a carrot stick, once even a few scalloped potatoes. He just reached for the gooey slices like they were finger food and walked away. A minute later, he was rinsing his hands in the bathroom sink, looking confused, like someone who had just woken up to find they had been sleepwalking.

They were suffering. Even poor Tesla sniffed around the house, looking for Emma. He kept going to her room or sitting by the front door, wagging his funny tail when the knob began to turn, thinking Emma was going to walk in. Inevitably she didn't, and Tesla would pout in his puppy dog way and go in search of his playmate somewhere else. Joni's sister had called and offered to fly home, but Joni told her no, there was nothing Jennifer could do and Joni didn't know if she could stand to see her sister going through all this pain, too. Joni didn't know it was possible to hurt this much. She and Greg had both been told by their employers, the hospital and the garage, that they could take as much time as they needed. She felt as grateful as she could with no room in her body for any feeling, emotion, or thought other than razor-sharp grief.

The talks with Detective Palmer did little to help. He had called nearly every day and met with them again one day so they could approve the flier with Emma's picture and information. After that meeting, Greg had left the house and ran around the neighborhood like a jogger. Only he wasn't running for exercise, he was trying to get away from the terror caused by seeing his daughter on a missing person poster. Joni suspected that he was also, in a way, looking for Emma even though it made no sense. She herself had run to the bathroom and was sick for a few hours after the men left the house. At that meeting with Palmer, Joni had noticed that he looked thinner and older. She knew he was working hard on finding her daughter and the sight of him as stressed as he was added to her despair.

Sometimes Joni thought she might be losing her mind. Early one morning she got out of bed, dressed, brushed her teeth and told herself she should eat breakfast. The thought of food made her feel ill. She looked at the clock, thinking she would eat later in the day and was stunned to see that it was eleven-thirty. After a split second of weird relief that it was nighttime and not actually pitch dark outside at eleven-thirty in the morning, Joni began to feel the cold fingers of hysteria clawing up her limbs. She had dozed for only a short while and then got herself out of bed thinking that she had lain there all night long. It was as if time itself were terrorizing her, dragging along, stretching out the empty seconds. Every moment they didn't know where Emma was or what was happening to her was a perfect torture, and time was gloating. That night Joni didn't bother getting back into the sweats she had worn to bed, but went to Emma's room and laid fully clothed on the bedspread in a tee shirt, jeans, and socks. Greg was there. He had fallen asleep at Emma's desk, looking at her yearbooks. He said almost nothing, but she knew that Emma's disappearance was killing him. She had found him one night looking for their daughter in the tree house he had built for Emma when she was eight. She hadn't played in there for at least a year, but there he was standing on the ladder, barefoot at three a.m., whispering her name into the empty space. She convinced him to come down into the house. His lips were blue. Joni doubted her husband could feel his feet. Maybe that was the point. Maybe he had wanted to be numb.

Chapter 5

"You sure you want to do this?" Alan studied his daughter carefully as she sat in the passenger seat of the truck. He and Kate had decided to keep Claire home for the rest of the week. It was now Monday morning and her first day back at school since Emma's disappearance. Even though James had ridden the bus to school, as usual, Alan wanted to drive her to school and spend a little time with her. During the past week, James had been uncomplainingly getting Claire's assignments from her teachers and bringing them home for her.

"No," she answered, adjusting her glasses, "but I need to."

"Good," he said, pinching her nose. "I love you, Honey."

"I love you too, Daddy."

She opened the door to get out, but turned back around and flung herself into his arms. Alan returned her hug and patted her dark hair. "It's okay," he said, "you're going to be just fine."

He watched her go, keeping his eyes on her retreating back until she reached the doors and entered safely into the building.

He eased his truck out of the parking lot and turned off onto the highway and headed to the main workshop that served as home base for Barton Construction, the company Alan worked for. He was worried about his kids. He wasn't surprised that this was a very difficult time for Claire, but even James wasn't himself. The night before James had sought him out in the garage and started asking questions. Alan went over the conversation in his head as he drove.

He had been putting the lawn furniture into the overhead storage area.

"Dad?"

"Hey, you come to help?"

James gave a half smile, but he was distracted, "Uh, yeah... Dad?" he began again.

"What is it," Alan had asked, even though he had an idea what would be the topic of his son's question. He was right.

"Well...what do you think happened to Emma? Do you think she's, you know...okay?"

James was asking him if he thought this girl that he had known for most of his life was still alive. Alan secured the ladder and climbed up a few rungs, thinking hard. This wasn't any easier with his son than with his daughter. Even though he knew Claire was having a hard time just getting through her day, it was difficult for him to see James trying to make sense of a senseless situation. Usually James had no interest in anything more serious than his grades, and this tragedy had shaken his simple little world.

Alan prayed for wisdom before he answered. He reached down and James handed a lawn chair up to him. "I don't know what happened, Buddy, we're all wondering that. I'm praying for Emma and her family and trying to trust God. I know He loves her, even though something bad has happened."

James was still struggling with his thoughts, he held a piece of the picnic table in his hands, staring at it but not seeing it.

The Valley Without Her

"Yeah but, do you think she...I mean, I don't think Emma would run away or anything..."

"No. I don't think so either," Alan said softly.

"So someone had to take her," James handed his dad the table piece but didn't look at him. "Someone who would steal a kid wouldn't be a good person, you know...What if...?" his voice trailed off. He didn't want to say it. He turned around to grab another lawn chair.

Alan wanted to get his son's mind off of these dark thoughts. James was right. It was unlikely that Emma's circumstances were ideal, but those concepts were too much for a fifteen-year old boy to carry around with him.

"Hey, you know what, I really want to get these all put away before dinner. You think you could get the other ladder and help me with the table top?"

James knew that his Dad was not snubbing him, but trying to give his mind somewhere else to settle. He understood what Alan was trying to do, and a faint look of gratitude passed over his young face.

Alan didn't want to leave his son with no encouragement at all, though. He watched him as he took the ladder down from its place on the wall. "Just keep praying. In times like these it doesn't seem like much at all, but really it's the best thing you can do."

After they had finished, they went together into the house for dinner. The family had had a quiet meal, all thinking about the same thing and none of them talking about it.

Alan arrived at work; there was so much to do today. The new guy, Scott, was still learning the ropes. Alan grabbed his hard hat and his lunchbox, still thinking about his kids, hoping that he was helping them in some way. Wishing he could shelter them from the pain they were going though, from the evils of the world. Wishing he could have done the same for Emma.

*** * * ***

    Claire and Melody sat together at lunch looking somehow diminished without their friends. Usually they sat with Brayle and some of the other girls from youth group, but today Brayle was absent. She missed a lot of school, having to stay home with the twins if they got sick or if her mom needed extra help. Emma's absence was, of course, pronounced. Today it was just the two of them. They could feel the stares and hear the whispers of their peers. Some were merely curious, many sympathetic and only a very few were contemptuous. Even if this last category had bothered the two friends, the girls would have rightly assumed that these people were masking their fear with something else in order to make themselves feel a little more in control in this frightening situation. As it was Claire and Melody *didn't* care about the stares and ignored them and their own lunches, as they talked softly together in the crowded lunchroom. They were not very surprised and almost welcomed a confrontation when Lindsay Glass plunked herself down in an empty chair at their table.

    However Lindsay didn't come for a battle. Even more bizarre, she didn't come with her maidservant, Dena. Claire and Melody stared at her as she took a huge breath and began chattering at them.

    "Oh, hey, girls! I just wanted to come over and tell you, hi. Um...I was wondering if you had Mr. Buchanan for English. I have him for my first class and we're supposed to write a sonnet before Friday, and I'm such a ditz at poetry." Lindsay rolled her

The Valley Without Her

eyes at herself. She laughed a forced, fake laugh. "Have you ever written poetry? I'll bet you're *way* better at it than I am. You're both, like, honor students or whatever." She didn't wait for them to respond, but instead changed the subject and kept going. "Oh, have you been to that cool new clothing store downtown? It's called "You're So Clad" and I love it. I go there, like, all the time. You should check it out; you'd like it."

She went on. Claire and Melody weren't really listening. It was just so *weird*. All of it. The look on Lindsay's face like she were some sort of nervous makeup consultant on her first sales pitch, the endless babbling that held no hint of insult or scorn, the complete lack of Dena Roberts. They each surreptitiously looked around for Dena, wondering if she was absent from school. Nope, there she was. They spotted her not far away. She was looking at them in a way that was meant to seem like she wasn't looking at them. Her expression was odd. She looked...angry? Her face was hard to read and only added to the strangeness of the situation. Claire and Melody glanced at each other and communicated with only their eyebrows.

What in the world?

Beats me!

Eventually, the soliloquy ended and Lindsay shrugged with a sigh. "Well, talk to you later," she chirped. And then she was gone.

For a moment the two just sat in silence and blinked a few times.

"What..." Melody faltered

"...just happened?" Claire finished for her, knowing the look on her face was as astonished as the one on her friend's.

They stared at one another for a moment, then both girls burst out laughing. It felt so good to laugh. They hadn't had a good laugh, hardly a smile even, in over a week. After a few seconds, their giggles died down and, though neither of them mentioned it, they each felt a little guilty for being happy for a moment. Had they betrayed their friend by having a good time when she may be suffering right now? They both jumped when the bell rang, signaling the end of the period and they got up to dump their scarcely touched meals into the trash.

"What do you think...?" Melody began

"Was that crazy or what?" Claire said.

"Do you think she wants us to do her homework for her? She talked about that sonnet she has to write." They headed down the hall to stop at each of their lockers to get their books for their next class which they were thankful to have together.

"I thought of that too, but she talked about lots of stuff. I mean I think she did; I wasn't really listening."

Melody nodded, "And what about Dena? Have you ever seen them *not* together? She looked mad or something. I mean, I always thought that Lindsay hated us and Dena was kind of riding her coattails."

"I know! I thought it looked like Dena was mad that Lindsay would be nice to us. So weird."

"Well, whatever," Melody shrugged and tossed her blonde hair, "I don't plan on being all chummy with either one of them any time soon."

"Yeah, me either," Claire frowned. "You don't think..." she slowed to a stop and people had to move around her to keep from bumping into her.

Melody stared at her apprehensively "What?"

She bit her lip. "You don't think it was just Emma, do you?"

Melody looked puzzled.

"Like it was just...Emma...Lindsay didn't like and now that she's not here..."

Melody turned pale. "That's awful," she whispered. "Let's just stay away from both of them, okay?"

Claire took a deep breath. "Deal."

They again started walking down the hall.

***

Once again Pastor Ward sat in his office looking across his desk at an uncomfortable looking young mother. Brandy Robinson wasn't very old at all. In fact she was really too young to have a daughter Brayle's age. Brayle had been born when Brandy was only 16. He surmised that this was the beginning of the reason she had trouble knowing what it took to be a proper parent. While he knew many parents who had started young and were now flourishing in the role, for Brandy this was not the case.

Pastor Ward tried to make her feel at ease. He knew she felt out of place here, but was still seeking answers. He quietly thanked God that she had kept their appointment. He smiled kindly at her. "I'm glad to see you again."

"Um. Thanks." She fidgeted. "Me too."

"Have you brought any questions you would like to ask me? Did you make the list we talked about?"

"Uh, no, actually. I couldn't think of what to say." She looked like a kid who hadn't done her homework. He supposed that was what she was, in a way. He had expected it. Really the assignment, while helpful if she had completed it, was really just a way to keep her involved.

He waved a hand at her to let her know it was all right.

"Well then, Brandy, maybe you can answer a few questions for me so that I know better how to help you. How will that be?"

"Oh. Um...okay." She gave a small smile. "Fire away."

She was loosening up. This was a good sign.

"Can you tell me why you came to see me? What made you seek me out in the first place?"

"Well...I guess it was, you know, that Emma girl. Bray's friend. She went missing and Bray was upset and my kids were scared...I was scared."

"Well, I can understand that," he said softly, "Emma is very special to a lot of people. I pray every day that she'll return to us soon and unharmed."

Brandy nodded, not saying anything.

"So, what do you think brought you here?"

She looked at him now, confused. "Well, what I just said," she answered, "I'm here because of that girl that didn't come home..."

"No, that's not what I meant," Pastor Ward answered patiently. "I mean what was it that made you choose to come *here* specifically and not, say, to the library for a self-help book."

"Oh. I don't know," she thought for a moment. "I guess it was the kids. When they come here, they seem happy. Like, peaceful and," she scratched her head, "like they aren't as worried about stuff."

"I'm glad to learn that your children find encouragement here. Do you think that that encouragement comes just from the people they meet when they walk through the doors or do you think it's more than that?"

She began to look uncomfortable again. She shrugged. "I suppose it's God, you know, but I've never been very religious."

"You know what, neither have I." He said thoughtfully.

She looked at him, confused. "But you're a preacher."

"Yes, but to be religious is to be about following rules. 1 John 4:18 says "Such love has no fear, because perfect love expels all fear. If we are afraid, it is for fear of punishment, and this shows that we have not fully experienced his perfect love." Following God is about being in a relationship with Him. He wants us to obey Him because we love Him and want to please Him, not because we're always afraid of what will happen to us if we don't. It's not all about *rules*, you see."

Brandy gave him another half-smile.

"So what were you hoping would happen when you came to see me? What are you wanting to see change?"

"I don't know, it's hard to explain. I just don't want to feel scared like this anymore. I don't want my kids to be scared. My twins are four and they ask me things and I don't know what to tell them."

"Yes, I can understand that. I don't have all the answers either, but I know that God does and I try to trust Him and lean on Him." He paused, praying and gathering his thoughts before going on. "What are you willing to do, Brandy, in order to bring peace to your family?"

She made a face. "What do you mean? Don't you just say a prayer for us or give me something to read or something?"

"It's really not quite that simple," he told her. "If it were, we wouldn't ever have to really trust God, and He wants us to trust Him completely. He doesn't just change our circumstances so that we no longer have problems of any kind, but instead He wants us to tap into His strength and wisdom so that we may face the challenges we encounter."

"I'm not following you."

"Well, it's like being a parent, in a way. It's impossible for you to make the world safe for your four precious children, so you must equip them to protect themselves, teach them right from wrong, and how to make wise decisions. So what are you willing to do? Can you think of ways that you could help your children yourself? Would you be willing to do things differently if it meant something better for your children?"

"Wait...you think I'm a bad mom?" She accused.

"Oh, I didn't say that at all," he answered, "I'm only asking you about what you're willing to commit."

"This was a mistake," she said getting up from her chair. "I thought you were going to help me, not tell me I had to change my whole life."

He stood too, not pointing out that he hadn't said anything of the sort.

"I'm sorry if I've upset you—" he began, but she cut him off.

"I'm not upset; this was just a mistake. I'll figure it out myself. Sorry to waste your time."

She left abruptly. She was definitely angry. He was sure it had more to do with being defensive than his actually saying something that had insulted her. Brandy needed a lot of improvement and she knew it; she just didn't like hearing it. He supposed, too, that she wanted to do better but was overwhelmed by the task.

Pastor Ward settled back into his chair, once again praying and thinking. Although he had done what he believed he was supposed to do during the conversation with her, he knew he was still missing something.

"What is it, Lord?" he asked aloud, rubbing his chin. "What is it You're trying to tell me?"

Chapter 6

Greg grabbed his lunch box from the employee fridge in the break room and looked around for a place where he could sit by himself. Ever since he had come back to work, every day had seemed like some sort of crazy interview where they asked questions they didn't want to ask but thought they had to, and he answered questions he didn't want to answer but felt like he should. He knew on some level these guys cared about what had happened to his family, but some of them hadn't said more to him than "could ya hand me the socket wrench?" in the ten years he'd worked here at Miller's Garage. Now almost everyone wanted to talk to him every day, while shuffling their boots and inspecting their dirty fingernails.

He didn't think he could put up with it right now. He headed outside to eat his lunch under the oak tree in the back. He sat down on the far side of the tree and opened his lunch before he realized it was cold out here and that he had forgotten his jacket. He had also forgotten to wash the grease from his hands. What difference did it make? He half shrugged, shaking his head and took a bite of the sandwich that one of the church ladies had packed for him. He supposed he was grateful for all that they were doing for him and for Joni. None of it mattered, though. Emma was the light of his life and she was gone. He would probably never see her again.

The Valley Without Her

All the coworker questions and church lady casseroles and people telling him they were praying weren't going to make a bit of difference. He knew they meant well, and he didn't go out of his way to be rude, didn't have the motivation, but he couldn't bring himself to do much more than acknowledge them either. He was almost glad that his parents weren't around for this. They hadn't been all that involved with him and his brothers in the first place. Greg hadn't had a happy home life and had left the day he turned eighteen. He hadn't spoken to either of his brothers in well over a decade.

He finished his sandwich and began eating grapes with his dirty fingers. Of course, Joni would disagree with his opinions about prayer. At least the old Joni would have. She wasn't the same anymore. It was as if someone had taken Joni away, too. The spark that had always lit her up from the inside had gone out. Her voice was flat, even her hair was flat. She'd lost weight. She had really believed in all that stuff that they preached at that church they went to. It was all right, he supposed. Before, anyway. He didn't really buy into it, even then, but Joni and Emma had loved going there and it made them happy when he went with them. He loved his girls and it was a small sacrifice to make. Now he wasn't so sure. Wasn't going to church and praying to God supposed to protect you from the horrible stuff that had happened to his family? He drank his bottle of water in three gulps and leaned back against the oak. He had to acknowledge the people who wandered in and out of his life. There was really no avoiding them. As for God, if He wanted Greg's recognition, then He was going to be disappointed. Greg really hadn't been that enthusiastic about God in the first place and now he had nothing to say to Him at all. Greg realized he had been taking his wife and daughter for granted. He had known he was a lucky man to have two such amazing women in his life, but he had rarely shown it. Maybe God was punishing him. Maybe he didn't deserve them, so God took them away. Whatever the case, he was alone. Emma was gone and now Joni, in a way, had left, too.

It was cold. He felt almost as cold on the outside as he did on the inside. He still had ten minutes left of his break, but he stood to go in anyway. It would be warmer in the garage and it would take the bite off his hands and face. But it would do nothing for the chill he felt inside.

* * *

Detective Palmer scanned the information he had printed off about Gardenville and found what he was looking for: the town's newspaper, *The Grapevine*. He smirked, *cute*. Palmer read for a moment before finding the paper's phone number. He looked at the clock on the wall and shook his head. It was too late to call today. Tomorrow he would call and request all the pictures they had taken of the apple festival. He had come up with nothing so far in his search for the Leonard girl. He was interested in finding the woman that kid pastor had told him about, the one that had yelled at Emma about the price of a quilt, but he'd had no luck. He hoped that there would be something in the paper's photos of that day that would give him some kind of a clue about what had happened, give him any new information at all.

* * *

Alan, along with the other guys on the crew, had been working with Scott Fischer for a while now and got the impression that the younger man was starting to get comfortable with their ways. He was a fast learner and easy to get along with. Now that every second didn't need to be crammed with the transferring of information and Fischer was familiar with the ins and outs of the job, they could talk about more than just work. They were driving to a new site, just the two of them in the truck, when Alan struck up a conversation.

"What do you do with your time when you're not installing bathtubs?" Alan joked.

"I like taking pictures," Scott offered.

"Really? Huh, I don't know anything about photography," Alan told him.

"It's just a hobby. I took a class when I was a kid living in Michigan."

"So that's where you're from?" Alan asked cordially. He felt bad that he didn't know much about this new guy. Fischer was probably in his early thirties, and Alan had gathered that he was alone here and didn't know many people.

"Oh, I'm from everywhere I guess. My folks split when I was a kid and Mom moved around a lot. She passed away about five years ago and I guess I never dropped the habit. I'd like to find a place to stay for good, though. Got to settle down sometime, I guess." He shrugged. It was one of those things he didn't give much thought. It wasn't of immediate importance.

"Well, this is a pretty good place to live," Alan told him. "I've lived here all my life and it's a good community. I go to a great church. You go to church?" He'd been meaning to invite him, but there was so much going on, both at home and here at work.

"Well," Fischer hemmed, "yeah, usually. I was hoping to find a place to go. I visited one place before I started working here, but they had a lot going on and, I don't know, maybe it just wasn't the right time."

"What do you mean?"

"Well, you probably heard about that girl, you know that one that went missing?"

Alan wasn't expecting to have this subject sprung on him from out of nowhere. It felt like a kick in the gut. He gripped the wheel and focused on not driving the truck into the ditch. He pulled himself together before he responded. "You visited Hillside Church?" He asked, his voice strained, though he tried to sound calm.

"Hey, yeah, how'd you know?"

"That's where my family attends. Emma Leonard was," he cleared his throat, "is a good friend of my daughter's. Claire was with her right before she went missing. It's been really hard on her. Well, on all of us, to be honest."

Scott turned in the seat to look at him. "Oh, man, I'm sorry. I didn't know." He fidgeted; serious subjects had always made him uncomfortable. "Do they know anything?" He asked because he didn't want to be rude. It wasn't that he didn't care, but he wished they were talking about something else.

"No," Alan sighed. "Nothing yet." Alan shook his head as if to clear it. "So wait a minute, the Sunday you visited was the day after it happened?"

Scott merely nodded, looking out the window.

"Wow." Alan didn't know what to say, except, "Well, why not give us another try? It really is a great church."

Scott turned now to look at him. He really didn't want to get involved in such a big deal, but for some reason he still heard himself saying, "Sure, why not?" He looked back out the window, now feeling obligated and hoping he wouldn't be sorry.

***

The Valley Without Her

Joni paced around the house with a can of furniture polish and a dustrag. She needed something to do, something to occupy her mind, but there wasn't a speck of dust to be found anywhere. Not even a dirty sock in the hamper or a toothpaste smudge in the sink. The ladies from the church had been over every day to clean and bring meals. They had watered the houseplants, walked Tesla and brought in the mail. Kate had even been handling the Leonard's bills, doing everything but signing the checks. She would sort the mail, find the bills, throw out the ads for faster Internet and open anything important, and then tell Joni or Greg about the contents. Kate wrote out the checks, handed them over to Joni to sign, then placed them in their envelopes, addressed and sealed them. She even put them out to be picked up by the mail carrier. Joni was so distracted by her grief that she only remotely noticed such activities until moments like these when she was looking for something to do. Greg had gone back to work, and now Joni thought that he might have had the right idea. She put away the cleaning things, sat down at the kitchen table and gazed around her spotless, empty home. The silence pounded her ears. Tesla trotted up to her and pushed his cold nose into her hand. She scratched his ears absently.

The nagging thoughts she was always trying to keep at bay came creeping up like crouching cats. *Where was her precious daughter? What was happening to her?* Not knowing was excruciating. Her sweet Emma could be dead or was maybe even experiencing something worse than death. What if...?

She stood abruptly, startling Tesla.

"I have to get out of here," she said to the silence.

She grabbed her keys, not even taking the time to find her coat despite the chilly day. She dashed out of the house and got in her car, headed she didn't know where. Maybe if she kept moving she could escape the poisonous thoughts that were chasing her, biting at her heels like wild dogs. She tried to pray, but the words wouldn't come. At the moment God seemed as elusive to her as Emma did.

* * *

Pastor Ward was talking with Pastor Josh when it hit him. Mollie Brown had always claimed that the best ideas came to her at the oddest times. She would walk into the living room in her bathrobe with her wet hair all twisted in up a towel, and announce that while she had been in the bath she realized that Caroline Parker would be the perfect person to take over the third grade Sunday school class. She had been asking for a way to get involved and Widow Perkins had been doing it for so long and really needed a break. Children loved Caroline. Why hadn't she thought of it before? There were times when she would dash back into the house while hanging clothes on the line to write down some idea that had suddenly come to her. She had always been amused by those moments and now Pastor Ward was having one of his own. One corner of his mind marveled at how often he was reminded of her.

He clapped a hand to his forehead. "Oh!" he sat for a moment while Pastor Josh looked at him. "So *that's* what You were getting at, Lord? Really? Hmm."

Pastor Josh was used to his mentor praying out loud at unexpected moments. The first couple of times this happened he was taken by surprise, but found the habit to be refreshingly honest. Pastor Ward was open about his walk with God, and his spontaneous conversations with Him included others in His blessings and encouraged them to be bold in their relationships as well.

"What's happened?" the younger man asked. "Can I help?"

They had been discussing an upcoming event. Hillside Church got together annually with other local churches for a special night of prayer, singing, and fellowship, followed by a huge potluck dinner. It was coming up next month and the men were planning their part of the evening.

Pastor Ward told Pastor Josh about his visits with Brandy Robinson and how he had felt the beginnings of an idea. It had been over a week since she'd left his office in a snit and ever since he'd had a nagging feeling that he was missing something. He told Pastor Josh about the idea that had just been whispered into his mind as they had sat there talking.

"Wow, really?" Josh asked. "Not that I'm questioning if it's the right thing to do, or anything it's just...wow," he said again.

"I know," Pastor Ward agreed. "That's probably why it took me so long to realize it."

"I think it's great," said the younger pastor clapping his hands once and rubbing them together as if he were about to build a barn or chop down a tree.

"Yes, I think so too. It must be from the Lord—I never would have come up with it on my own."

Pastor Josh's face fell slightly, "Do you think she'll do it?"

Pastor Ward rubbed his chin. "I do. Maybe not right away, but I think she will."

"What about Brayle's mom? She walked out didn't she?"

"Yes, but I have a feeling the Lord is working on her even as we speak. I've been praying and—"

He stopped midsentence when the phone rang.

"Hello, Hillside Church, this is Pastor Glenward."

"Um...Pastor Franklin? This is Brandy Robinson...I'm sorry, I just, um. Would it be okay if you talked to me some more? I've just been thinking about stuff and I shouldn't have ran off like that and, I'm—I'm sorry."

"I understand; it's quite all right." Pastor Ward was grinning. Pastor Josh got the message. He shook his head, a smile growing on his boyish face.

"You know what, I have something I need to work out, and I'll get back to you, all right? There's a...resource...I'd like to get lined up for you. In the meantime, we can meet again. How's that sound?"

"Yeah, that sounds good, thanks," she answered, still sounding sheepish.

"Good. I'll be in touch very soon." He kept his tone warm, hoping she knew there were no hard feelings. If only she knew. He wished that her storming out of his office was the worst behavior he'd ever witnessed in one of his people.

"Okay, well, thanks. Bye, then."

"Goodbye, Brandy."

He hung up and smiled at his friend. "Well, do you want to pray before I make the call or shall I?"

Pastor Josh laughed out loud. "Praise God!"

They both prayed, but when Pastor Ward picked up the phone to call Joni Leonard, there was no answer. She must have gone out.

Chapter 7

Melody's mother, Lisa, leaned over the railing and hollered up the stairway, "Melody, phone! I think it's Brayle!"

Melody was glad to hear it. It was Thursday and she and Claire hadn't seen Brayle since Sunday.

"Thanks, Mom!" came the shouted answer from upstairs. Melody picked up.

"Hello?"

"Hey, Mel, it's me."

Her mother had guessed right; it was Brayle. Her voice sounded weird. Right now, though, everything was weird. Melody was still having nightmares and had been asking her little sister, Charlotte, to sleep in her room with her. Charlotte was six and was tickled pink to be staying with her big sister.

"Oh, hey, Bray. What's up?" Melody snuggled down against the pillows on her bed. Right now, in the day time, listening to her friend's familiar voice, she felt safe. She knew, though, that when it got dark, when it was time to close her eyes the comforts would fizzle out like a song giving way to static on the radio and she would be hounded again by savage fear.

"You will never guess who just called me." Brayle said, sounding dazed.

Melody gasped. She shot up to a sitting position, her whole body feeling tingly.

"Emma?!"

"Oh!" Brayle was taken aback. "No!" Her voice melted into sadness. "No...Not Emma."

Melody could tell that Brayle was sorry she'd started the way she had. Both for Melody and for herself. She felt light headed. Melody had had a sudden rush of adrenaline and then a major disappointment. She flopped back down onto her bed, her head spinning.

"No, not Emma," Brayle said again. "It was Lindsay, Lindsay Glass."

"Um...what?"

"Yeah. You know, horrible Lindsay?"

"Yeah...What did she want?"

"Well, that's the thing, nothing really. She was, like...*nice.*"

Melody nodded, knowing her friend couldn't see her nodding. "I know! She came and talked to me and Claire at lunch on Monday. We were really freaked out."

"Mm-hmm, Claire told me. I called her, too. So...what do you think?"

Melody was silent for a moment before answering. "Claire wondered if it was because of..." she didn't want to say it.

"Yeah, she told me," Brayle answered, knowing what her friend meant and saving her from having to repeat it. "She was always really nasty to all of us, though."

The Valley Without Her

"That's true," Melody breathed her relief. It was a funny thing to be relieved about, knowing that *all* of her friends had been harassed by this bully. She thought some more. "Did Lindsay mention Dena?"

"No."

"I don't know, Bray, but I don't like it."

"Yeah, me neither. Claire said the two of you decided we should keep staying away from her. Dena, too."

"Yep. We did." Melody was still nodding, still knowing it was futile for communication.

"I think so too," Brayle said. She sounded relieved. Melody understood. Even though they hadn't the foggiest idea why their archenemy would suddenly decide to play nice, it was good at least to know they all had the same opinion about how to handle it.

* * *

Julie Burish pushed her cart through the aisle of the local supermarket, looking over her menu for the week and the shopping list she had made from it. She liked being organized and disliked having to come back to the store for one or two items. Her house, her kids, her kitchen and her life were neat, clean, and orderly and that was just how she preferred it. She was sure there were times when her fastidious nature frustrated her family, but it was worth it to her if it meant having everything done properly. It gave her such a feeling of accomplishment to have everything in order.

Now that she was helping the Leonard family, it was almost like taking on a whole other household. The other ladies from church were doing their part, too, though and together they tried to be as much help as they could. Julie paused in the baking aisle, trying to choose between semi-sweet and milk chocolate chips when she saw a familiar group rumbling up the aisle like a tornado.

She watched them out of the corner of her eye. It was that mother with all the kids. She thought she knew the oldest girl's name, Brittney or Bailey or Brindy or something like that. She attended the youth group at Hillside and was friends with Claire Thomas. She'd been friends with Emma, too, Julie thought. She shook her head as the family came closer, making a racket. *Such a shame.* She eased her cart away in search of something else on her list. She didn't really want to have to make small talk with the woman in a tank top, pushing the cart full of sticky-faced twins. Julie had a habit of speaking her mind and she was pretty sure her thoughts would not be welcome. *Someone ought to tell her what's what, though. That woman could use a good lesson in parenting.* She headed for the produce section pushing the family behind her out of her mind.

* * *

Joni walked through her front door and sighed. Tesla came charging down the hall and jumped at her. He was happy to see her, but she could tell by the decrease in energy when he had spotted her that he had been hoping for Emma. His reaction was just one of the reasons that it was hard for her to walk through the door. She had taken so many things for granted. Coming home after running errands to find her home full of noise with Emma and her friends draped around the living room, laughing over even they didn't know what. Coming home from work to find Emma asleep on the couch because she'd wanted her to kiss her goodnight. So many everyday things that, while she had always loved them, she had never realized their value.

The Valley Without Her

She had spent the afternoon with Kate at her shop. Halloween was around the corner and Kate, although she never went for the spooky stuff, always decked out Line Dried Laundry with autumn colors and harvesttime treasures. They had set out pumpkins and mums and spent some time stringing leaves to make garlands and then hung them up around the store. Kate had made little wreaths out of grapevines, accented with cute little bows made of gingham and jute. The place looked fabulous and smelled like cider. Joni just wished she could have really enjoyed the time with her friend and their eye-appealing, nose-pleasing accomplishments—the way she used to.

This wouldn't do. If she didn't get busy doing something, she'd go mad. Maybe it was time to go back to work. She nodded once, decisively. She'd call them today and tell them she was returning.

She reached for the phone, but was startled when it rang the moment her fingers touched it.

"Hello?"

"Joni! This is Pastor Ward; I've been trying to catch you."

"Oh, sorry. I didn't know. I went out and decided to visit Dad. I hadn't been to see him in a long time. He, of course, didn't know that, but I still feel bad. Anyway, we turned off the answering machine. We were getting too many unwanted calls after..."

"I understand; it's quite all right. And how is your father?"

"Not too good. He's shutting down, I think." Her voice sounded small.

"I'm sorry to hear that." He paused before continuing. "So how are you holding up, Joni?"

His voice dripped with compassion. She knew her pastor was asking because he cared, not because he thought he had to.

Joni pinched the bridge of her nose and squinted her tired eyes shut. "Not too good, either," she told him, "I think I need to go back to work like Greg has. I need to be busy, I think."

"Well, I think I may have something for you to do. Would you like to meet with me so we could talk about it?"

Joni was surprised, but also just a little intrigued. She couldn't help but think, *Why in the world would he trust me with anything right now?* "Well, sure I guess so. When?"

"How about tomorrow?"

"All right. Where? Kate's place? We just worked on it and it's...nice." Just trying to work up any enthusiasm at all was exhausting.

"Well now, that sounds just fine," Pastor Ward's voice smiled through the phone. "How about lunchtime?"

"Okay. Tomorrow is Kate's potato soup." *As if I'll be able to eat anything,* she thought. Nothing had tasted right since it had happened. Not even such delicacies as were found in Kate's shop.

"Oh, that's one of my favorites." he told her. "I'm looking forward to it."

"Yeah, I am....well...I'll be there." She said. It wasn't that she didn't want to meet with him, but to say that she was looking forward to it, too, would have been less than true. She was hardly even curious. She may never look forward to anything again.

* * *

The Valley Without Her

Pastor Ward hung up the phone and smiled. He knew he could have asked Joni to meet with him right then and she very likely would have been available, but he wanted to spend adequate time in prayer before speaking with her. This was a delicate situation and he wanted to be sure to handle it carefully. He also knew that she wasn't being rude in her reticence; this was just one more manifestation of all the pain she was enduring. "God, help this child of Yours," he prayed aloud. He picked up the phone to call young Pastor Josh. He would also speak with Judy, Ruth, Lucinda Perkins, Kate and possibly a few others, though he wouldn't give them many details. He wanted to fight this battle in prayer and he wanted some of his warriors fighting by his side. The Lord must have a reason for giving him this plan and he intended to follow his orders, hopefully helping everyone involved, and that through it, God would be glorified.

* * *

She stared at him. They sat at a table by the front window; they could watch the people passing by outside. He waited for her answer as he enjoyed some of Kate's delicious potato soup. Marty brought them a basket of the homemade rolls that came with the meal. They reminded him of Mollie Brown, which made sense because she was the one who had given Kate the recipe for them. It hadn't escaped his notice that Joni had hardly touched her food. She was growing thinner. Her eyes had lost their sparkle. He was concerned about these things, but not surprised.

"Are you sure?" Joni's voice was tired. There wasn't a hint of the ironic humor that would normally have accompanied such a question. It was just a request for information, flat and neutral, like a telephone survey.

Pastor Ward sipped his tea, "Quite," he answered. "The Lord has been rather adamant, in fact." He rubbed his chin.

Like Pastor Josh, Joni was familiar with Pastor Ward's intimate references to God. He spoke about Him in the manner that people spoke of friends. This familiar trait gave her a moment's glimmer of warmth in her spirit.

She gave him a shadow of a smile, then became sober again, "But why me? Kate would be better, don't you think? Or Julie. Julie would probably love to do it."

Pastor Ward kept his face serene, but suspected that they were thinking the same thing. Yes, Julie Burish probably would jump at the chance to mentor Brandy Robinson, but he doubted very much that Brandy would welcome Julie's style of leadership.

"No, I don't think that would do," he answered conversationally. He could have been talking about the weather, but still he earned another shadow of a smile from Joni. She even rewarded him with the palest of chuckles before turning away. He knew she hadn't meant to be rude in mentioning Julie.

At that moment, Kate came to their table to check on them. Pastor Ward had given her a little more information than he had some of the others so she knew what the two were discussing. She had overheard their last exchange.

"I think it's a great idea," she put in. "You, not Julie," she added in case there had been any question. There hadn't. "Just my opinion," she smiled at her friend. She placed a plate of ginger cookies for their dessert on their table and left them to talk.

"I don't know, pastor, I mean I can hardly even get out of bed in the morning. Don't get me wrong; I'd love to help you out. I'd love to help *her* out, and of course there's poor Brayle, and the other kids but..."

He picked up a cookie. "What makes you think I'm only thinking of them?"

"What do you mean?"

"This would be for you, too, Joni."

"Me? How?"

He leaned back in his chair. "After Mollie Brown died..." He cleared his throat. "After Mollie died, there were times that I thought I would die too. Sometimes the only thing that helped was to get involved in someone else's life. It's such a blessing to bless someone else, child, and I think you could do with a blessing."

Joni looked at her hands, fiddling with her napkin. "Yes," she whispered.

"Will you think about it?"

She didn't look up, but nodded. "I'm just not sure if I can do it. I don't know if I have the strength." She ventured a glance into his eyes. He was smiling confidently at her.

"Well, of course you don't." Pastor Ward leaned forward as if sharing a wondrous secret. "That's really the best part, you know. You will do it with *Christ's* strength and we will see His glorious might."

She sat for several quiet moments, thinking. He watched her patiently waiting for her answer, sipping his tea.

"Can I have some time to think about it?"

He patted her hand. "Take all the time you need."

* * *

Pastor Ward was not asleep when his phone rang at one am. He reached for the phone next to the chair where he sat praying with his Bible in his lap.

"Hello?"

"Oh, Pastor, it's Joni. I'm sorry I just now realized how late it is. Did I wake you?"

"No, no, I was awake. Are you all right?"

"Yes, well, no, but I mean that's not why I'm calling."

"Of course. What is it you need, then?"

For a moment, she said nothing and he almost *almost* lost hope.

"Pastor Ward," he heard her take a deep breath, "I'll do it."

After they hung up, Pastor Ward laughed. "Praise God!" he said. "Praise God."

Chapter 8

Emma ran. She kept stumbling, her legs tangling in the impossibly tall grass. It was dusk. The air was muggy. They were everywhere, chasing her and laughing, their voices harsh and mocking. She crouched in the weeds and tried to untangle her feet but the tendrils seemed to reattach themselves as she tore at them. She heard her name, a jeering whisper in her ear. She didn't stop to look at who or what it was, she just ran. At least she tried to, the tangles of weeds and maybe it was her clothing, kept tripping her up, keeping her from reaching safety. The brambles scratched at her face. There were trees ahead. She could see them in the moonlight. Somehow Emma thought if she could just reach them she could hide and finally be safe. The voices were getting louder, closer. She could feel faceless pursuers tracking her, hands grabbing at her. The trees seemed so very far away. Emma was crawling now, for what seemed like years, but felt a tiny ember of hope as she finally reached the woods. She could still hear the voices, but now felt that maybe, just *maybe*, she could escape them for good. She wriggled herself into a big hollowed out tree, trying to quiet her breathing. Her heartbeat pounded in her ears, so loud that surely they could hear it. She clenched her teeth and her eyes, hearing footsteps outside her hiding place. She felt something tickle her face and she screamed. Small hands were shaking her. She couldn't get away from them.

"Sissy?"

Melody opened her eyes. She was gasping and drenched in sweat. Her legs were tangled in sheets and blankets. Charlotte was sitting on her bed, leaning over her—her sweet six-year-old face worried and white, puffy with sleep.

"Sissy, you were yelling again. Are you okay?" Charlotte's voice sounded afraid. As if she had been the one to have the nightmare.

Melody reached for her baby sister and pulled her close. "I'm sorry, Lottie Lou; did I scare you?"

"It's okay," Charlotte gulped.

Melody felt guilty. She knew that it scared her sister when she heard her have one of her nightmares, and as much as she drew comfort from having her close by, she thought maybe she was being selfish. Maybe it was too much of a responsibility for this sweet little girl. She was about to tell her so, tell her little sister that she would be fine and it would be okay if she wanted to go back to sleeping in her own room again.

"Sissy?" Charlotte began.

"Hmm?"

"I'm going to stay with you till you aren't scared anymore." It wasn't an offer it was a statement of fact. It was as if Charlotte had known what Melody was going to say. Maybe she did.

Melody pulled her closer and nuzzled the top of her sister's silky, baby shampoo-smelling head.

"I love you, Lottie Lou." she murmured into Charlotte's hair. She could feel her heart rate returning to its normal cadence.

Charlotte yawned. "I love you, too, Sissy." her breathing began to slow and deepen. "Emma's going to be okay," she whispered sleepily.

Melody snuggled her sister even closer, wishing she could know for sure if what her little sister said was true.

* * *

Pastor Josh had debated with himself whether or not he should cancel the annual harvest costume party. He had actually given it a lot of prayerful thought and decided that it would be good for the kids to do something fun. They had all been on edge since the apple festival (as he preferred to call it in his mind, instead of "Emma's Disappearance"), and he hoped that some normality would be healing for them. Claire rarely smiled anymore. Alan had confided in him that she was plagued by guilt, thinking it was her fault since she had been with Emma immediately before it happened. Brayle seemed even more stressed than usual and Melody had dark circles under her eyes, which told him she still wasn't sleeping. James and the other guys tried to joke around and make things seem lighthearted, but inevitably their smiles fell, the masks cracked and their faces went back to the worried expressions they all wore now. Not that he blamed them. He'd had his share of sleepless nights too.

He looked around at the party. The kids were talking and sometimes almost laughing in their goofy costumes. There had been rules, of course, about what they could wear: nothing inappropriate, gross, scary, or skin-baring. The last of the list had elicited a loud complaint from Ben, saying that he had planned on dressing up as a mermaid and now what was he going to do with his costume and how everyone was going to be so disappointed. Ben had actually gotten a decent laugh out of that one. Pastor Josh really didn't expect too much trouble with this bunch, but just to make it a little easier on them, and himself, he made up a theme and offered prizes for the best costumes. This year the theme was "outer space" and the kids were dressed as astronauts and Martians. Serena dressed as a sci-fi movie character and Nate was dressed in his street clothes, but wore a pointed helmet he had made of foil and kept warning everyone that they'd better put a helmet on, too, or "they" would be able to read their minds. John wore a suit and stood next to a refrigerator box that he had painted bright blue. Everyone was having fun and that was what he'd hoped for.

Frank and Anna Lopez claimed that it wasn't ethical for them to be judges in the contest since Mia was involved, but, really, Pastor Josh suspected, they just wanted to laugh at him while the kids all tried to butter him up in hopes of being chosen as the winner. Pastor Josh always gave a big bag of "the good stuff"—excellent Halloween candy as the grand prize and most of the kids hoped to be the one to nab it.

They paraded in front of everyone, one by one, silly and in character. Melody had painted her face green and Ashley was dressed as Mr. Spock. In the end, Pastor Josh decided that Drew had earned the prize. He wore all black and covered himself in white Christmas lights. He plugged himself in and said he was the Milky Way. It may have been a hint at the type of candy he hoped to win, but anyway Pastor Josh thought it only fair to reward the kid who had chosen a costume he couldn't sit down in. He announced Drew as the winner and rewarded him with the large bag of candy. Instead of the gloating and taunting that usually accompanied the winning of the grand prize, Drew smiled and began handing out the loot, sharing with everyone, even the adults. To Claire he gave a huge bar of chocolate and Pastor Josh watched her face soften into a genuine smile. Yes, it had been a good idea to have the party.

* * *

Alan sat on the floor next to Scott. He leaned against the wall. "Hey, haven't had much of a chance to talk lately, huh?"

Scott shook his head. "Been pretty busy." He took a sip of his coffee. They were on a break and this was the first time they'd had a chance to talk without distraction since their conversation in the Barton Construction truck. They were on a site, adding a sun room and a new master suite onto an already very large home in the country.

"We've missed seeing you at Hillside. Well, I doubt any of us noticed that first time you came, but I'm sure you could forgive us for that. Still, you should give it another try."

Scott nodded, a little embarrassed. "Yeah, I know. You know how it is, you get out of the habit and it's easy to let it slide."

"Yeah, I know what you mean. Mollie Brown, Pastor Ward's late wife, always used to say 'You can always find a reason *not* to do something, but if it needs done you've got no excuse.' That one always got me." He smiled at the younger man.

Scott chuckled, "She sounds like a handful." He became more serious, "What happened? Cancer?"

Alan looked at him. "Maybe you should ask Pastor Ward. It's quite the story."

Scott smiled and gave him a suspicious glance. "You just trying to wrangle me into going to your church again?"

Alan laughed. "That too!"

* * *

"So, I trust you already know one another?" Pastor Ward looked back and forth between the two women. Both were quiet. Wary. He had chosen to meet with the two of them at the same time before simply throwing them together. This way, he hoped, they would be a little more comfortable together in the neutral territory of his office.

"We've met a few times." Brandy said simply.

"I think we've talked on the phone a couple of times, too," Joni said, "when our girls were making plans together." She looked away from the other two, the casual mention of Emma stirring up emotion. She cleared her throat and looked at them again and offered a quick smile. "We don't really know each other well, though."

"No matter," Pastor Ward said. "You'll surely get to know each other as you spend more time together. Why don't you tell one another a little about yourselves? Joni, why don't you begin?"

"All right," she thought for a moment. She looked at Brandy. "Well, I'm a nurse. I've lived here all my life. My husband, Greg, is a mechanic at Miller's Garage. We were high school sweethearts. After I graduated from nursing school, I came back here and we got married. I worked at the hospital for several years before we had Emma. I stayed home with her until she got a little older. We always wanted lots of kids, but..." her voice trailed off. She looked at the wall.

"Thank you, Joni." Pastor Ward did not intend to be rude in stopping Joni. He knew that she had reached painful territory and wanted to save her from reliving those things just now. Although he believed that Joni's testimony would be of value to Brandy, he wasn't going to force anything and this wasn't the time. Joni would share her past when she was ready. He looked at Brandy. "Would you like to tell Joni a little more about yourself?

The Valley Without Her

Brandy shrugged. "Okay. Um, well, I grew up all over. My mom and dad were never married, but I had a stepdad." She looked at her hands. "He wasn't, um, he didn't treat my mom and my sisters and me very nice, and eventually Mom left him. I met Brayle's dad when I was in high school and had her when I was sixteen." She gave Joni a grim laugh, "He broke up with me as soon as I told him and started going after another girl the next week. Even though she was one of my friends and everything." She sighed. "Then when I was working at the convenience store, I met Brayce and the twins' dad. He was separated and going to get a divorce, but then when it was almost final, he went back to his wife. They don't have any kids. He doesn't come around though. Brayce hardly remembers him. The twins don't remember him at all." Brandy seemed to come to herself and realize that her story sounded bleak. She sat up a little straighter in her chair. "I like music, you know singing and stuff. I like to sew. I made all the curtains in my house."

Pastor Ward listened. He shook his head. This young woman had had more than her fair share of troubles. Seeing these two together reinforced what he already knew. God was going to do great things in the lives of the women sitting in front of him. He was going to use them to bless each other.

* * *

Sunday morning Scott Fischer slipped into a pew at the back of Hillside Church. He had intentionally showed up a little late, not wanting to attract a lot of attention. Still Alan Thomas looked around when he came in and gave him a friendly smile. He'd probably been watching for him. Now he'd have to talk to him after the service. Alan knew he had seen him and it would be rude if he ducked out, the way he'd been planning to.

He turned his attention to what the pastor was saying. He looked at his bulletin. Pastor Glenward Franklin. *Wow. With a name like that you were either going to be a pastor or a professor of some brutally boring subject like world civilizations. I'll bet this sermon is going to be dry as sawdust.* He had yet to hear a sermon from Pastor Franklin. The one time he had visited this church, there hadn't been a message, but instead they had all prayed for that Emma girl. He didn't have high hopes, and was already building up excuses in his head; he would simply tell Alan that this place wasn't for him and then he could move on. He wasn't sure he wanted to go to church with a coworker anyway. Too much familiarity.

He tuned in to what was going on. The announcements, prayer, and music were over and the pastor was already speaking.

* * *

"Beloved, Jesus meets you where you *are*. I don't know where this notion came from that a man had to get himself all fixed up *before* he met Jesus. I know, and I hope that you know, that that's just not possible. That's why we need Him.

Jesus meets you *where you are*. When our children are little we tell them about Jesus walking on water. We tell them about Noah's ark. We tell little children the story of King Nebuchadnezzar's furnace and three young Hebrew men being saved by the fourth 'Man' there in the flames with them that today, we know was Jesus. We tell them about Daniel and the lions. Do you see? We choose those accounts for their story-like quality and for their great potential for teaching simple truths. Now, I'm not saying that as adults we have nothing to learn from these accounts, but we use them for children because they meet a child *where he is*. We don't talk to little children about sacraments and sanctification. They're still on what the Bible calls 'spiritual milk.'"

The pastor paused, letting his words sink in before he continued.

"When my son, Adam, was about sixteen, he told us one night as we were sitting at the supper table that he wasn't sure he believed in God anymore. Now we had raised him in a godly home. He'd been to Bible school and Sunday school and to camp. His devoted mother, my unsinkable Mollie Brown, had prayed and shared Jesus' love with our four children and they were all past spiritual milk and onto 'solid' spiritual food when our boy told us he wasn't sure about God. Now, maybe he was just hoping to shake us up a little. A little tired of the scrutiny he endured being a PK, as we affectionately call pastor's kids, and thought he'd take it out on his family. I'll admit I was angry at first. Mollie, though, she was upset, but she didn't show it. She prayed. And God started meeting that boy right where he was. He was with his friends one day and thought he'd impress them by telling a racy joke, and my son lost his voice just like that right in the middle of telling it. Adam still couldn't talk after a day or so and he had to give a speech for a class he was taking; the day came and still no voice. He wrote his teacher a little note and walked up to her desk to hand it to her and he said, 'Here this is 'cause I lost my voice.' The teacher just looked at him a minute and he realized what he'd done, and went back to his seat with his little tail tucked between his legs."

Scott found himself chuckling along with everyone else.

Pastor Franklin continued, "It's okay that I'm telling stories on him because, well, he's not here right now."

Again there was a friendly rumble of laughter in the pews and Scott realized he was not only listening to this man's words, but actually enjoying himself.

"There were other things that happened to my son that week he spent as a moderate atheist, but my point is, that the Lord met Adam *where he was.*"

He picked up his Bible. "If we look in John, in chapters three and four we see Jesus having two very different conversations with two very different people. Now there are a few similarities—both conversations were private and both of them were about spiritual matters, of course, but let's focus for a moment on the differences.

In chapter three, Jesus is talking to Nicodemus who was a Pharisee. These guys meant serious business when it came to religion, and I mean with a capital 'R.' They had rules about what to eat, what to wear, how many steps you could take on the Sabbath, you name it. And they knew the Word like no one else. The Pharisees knew the Scriptures backward and forward. Or I suppose you could say they knew it forward and backward."

Another chuckle from the people in the crowd who got the joke.

"When Jesus was talking to Nicodemus he spoke the most famous words in the Bible. John 3:16 says, 'For God loved the world so much that he gave his one and only Son, so that everyone who believes in him will not perish but have eternal life.' Now I'm sad to say that some people take this verse and define the word *believe* to mean 'know it to be true.' As in 'I believe Jesus is God's Son. End of Story. No more requirement of me.' But we know that that's not all there is to it. Jesus was speaking to Nicodemus, a teacher of the Law. Not the Samaritan

The Valley Without Her

woman at the well whom we meet in chapter four. You'll see what I mean in a moment.

"To the woman, Jesus spoke about *personal* things. Jesus told that woman what was going on in her own heart and her own life. He didn't bring up the old Scriptures and complicated theological mysteries to this lost soul. He talked about everyday life and the way to life eternal. He met this outcast woman *where she was* by sparking her interest, talking about what she thought she wanted, and then telling her what He knew she needed. He changed her life.

"He changed Nicodemus' life, too. Jesus casually mentioned to this Pharisee a snake being lifted up in the desert. While the average Joseph may have needed it explained that Jesus was talking about the cure for snakebites that God gave to Moses for the Israelites back in chapter twenty-one of the book of Numbers, Nicodemus knew exactly what Jesus was talking about, and he was on the edge of his seat—just like the Samaritan woman had been when Jesus told her he could give her living water. Jesus had the answer Nicodemus needed too, and he met that Pharisee *right where he was.* Jesus knew that Nicodemus knew about the bronze snake. He knew that Nicodemus knew that the Isrealites couldn't merely *believe* that the snake could save them, but that they had to *do* something to get the cure. It required a response—not merely an acknowledgment.

"We know that Nicodemus was changed because we are told in John, chapter nineteen, that Nicodemus was among those that prepared Jesus' body for burial. Pharisees didn't touch dead bodies. Jesus *changed* that man's life by meeting him *where he was*—as a teacher of the Law. We learn in chapter four that the woman at the well went and told everyone she knew about what Jesus had said to her. This woman had been avoiding people by going to the well at the hottest part of the day, when she hoped no one else would be there, instead of in the early morning like the other women did. Jesus changed this woman's life. A lowly soul with three strikes against her: A woman, a Samaritan and a known sinner. Jesus changed their lives, meeting them *where they were* and He does the same for you and me."

* * *

Scott listened as the Pastor spoke a little longer. He tied up his message, said a prayer, led one last song and dismissed the people. Scott had liked the sermon. Really liked it. Instead of ducking out, like he'd planned to do, he went to find Alan. He wanted to thank him for inviting him to Hillside and ask him if he would introduce him to the pastor.

Chapter 9

Detective Palmer sank into his chair and immediately wished that he had made himself some coffee before he had sat down. He got back up, grumbling at himself, at the dark cold morning and at the world in general. While others of his cases had been a piece of cake, the Leonard case was only taunting him. He didn't like being taunted. He didn't like to lose. He made himself a strong cup of coffee, burning his fingers and grumbling some more, and sat back down at his desk. He sipped carefully, not wanting a burnt tongue to go along with his burnt fingers, as he glanced through his mail. Palmer opened a large bulky envelope without looking at the return address. He got crank mail all the time and was expecting to pitch whatever this was into the trashcan. He was wrong. When he sliced open the envelope, several pictures fell onto his desk. There were pictures of dolled up teenage girls wearing formal gowns, pictures of little kids riding ponies, of young bucks trying to knock over milk bottles with baseballs, of a quaint little storefront with a sign that read, Line Dried Laundry (the 'y' looked a little funny. *Oh, it's a clothespin. Clever.*) and pictures of apples, apples, and more apples. He smiled his first smile of the day and his best one of the week. *The Gardenville Grapevine* had sent him their pictures of the apple festival.

* * *

Thanksgiving had been a bleak affair this year. Even with the usual traditions and amazing food, everyone was thinking of Joni and Greg and, of course, of Emma. The Thomas family had invited them over for dinner but they refused. Break was over, school had been back in session for a week and Christmas was just around the corner. Ordinarily this was when everyone was up to their ears in excitement about the holiday and everything that came with it. Some of the girls from the Hillside youth group sat together at lunch one dreary Wednesday and tried to induce enthusiasm in one another by pretending to be passionate about what was coming.

"The Christmas program is going to be really good this year," Mia smiled. "Julie Burish and my mom are singing a duet." The girls all nodded and murmured their approval. Julie and Anna both had exceptional voices and the whole church always considered it a treat when the two of them sang together.

"Yeah, and I think the little kids are going to—"

"Hey, girls!" Lindsay Glass had appeared out of nowhere.

Serena forgot what she was going to say. She forgot she had been speaking at all for that matter. There were no seats left at the table, so after Lindsay's chipper little greeting, she turned and noisily dragged a vacant chair from another table and scooted it as close as she could to theirs. The girls took this opportunity, as her back was turned, to close their mouths, as every one of them stared at Lindsay as if she had just jumped over their table in an aerial somersault.

Lindsay squeezed herself in between Ashley and Melody and sighed dramatically. She still seemed nervous. And strange. "Wow, what a crazy week, huh? I love Christmas and stuff, but it's always so hectic, you know? Are you guys going to any parties? I have, like, five of them this year at different family members' houses."

Brayle found her voice. She was making a small effort to be polite, but mostly she was just fishing for information. "Are you going to any parties with Dena?" Things hadn't changed since that first time Lindsay had plunked herself down at Claire and Melody's table, much like today. The girls still hadn't seen Lindsay and Dena together. In fact the two seemed to be avoiding each other. When Brayle mentioned her name, every other girl at the table but Lindsay turned to see where Dena was. She was sitting with another group of girls but removed, as if she weren't really with them. Dena seemed to know that Lindsay was talking to them and her mouth was pressed into a thin line. Once again her expression was difficult to read, but it wasn't happy.

Lindsay's face froze, and for a split second there was a shadow of the old Lindsay and the other girls' wariness intensified. If Lindsay noticed each of the other girls instinctively leaning away from her, she didn't let on.

Her smile drooped a little, but then she hiked it back into place. "Oh, well, um...no. She doesn't really talk to me anymore." Lindsay tried and failed to look pitiful and martyr-like. No one at the table felt sorry for her. "I guess she thinks I shouldn't be friends with you guys. Dena thinks it's still like it was back when we weren't getting along very well."

Under the table Melody actually pinched her own arm. *Is this another one of my bad dreams? 'Cause what she just said is all kinds of wrong.* Not only were they not really friends with Lindsay, as she had just attempted to make it sound, but saying that she hadn't gotten along with them implied that the conflict between them had been a two-way street instead of the hunter-hunted situation that it truly was. Furthermore, "not getting along" was an extravagant understatement. Lindsay Glass had inflicted abject misery on nearly every girl here; at best she had been extraordinarily rude. Melody looked at each of her friends one at a time. Claire was withdrawn, as she usually was during uncomfortable situations; Brayle looked angry; the other girls' faces ranged from fear to frank confusion. It was almost funny. She looked away, avoiding her friends' eyes so she wouldn't laugh.

Lindsay was still talking. The girls all sat uncomprehendingly until she again flitted unexpectedly away. In the loud silence of her absence, the girls stared at each other. Before they could discuss what had just happened, the bell rang and they had to go their separate ways.

* * *

Judy stuck her head in the door of Pastor Ward's office. "Pastor, Joni's here. Do you have time?" Judy knew that Pastor Ward would drop whatever he was doing to speak with Joni, but she still thought it best to be respectful and ask him before she sent Joni in to see him.

"That would be fine, Judy, thank you. I thought she might come around this afternoon."

Judy smiled and disappeared. He heard her telling Joni to go on in. Joni entered the room looking like a battle weary soldier and fell into one of his guest chairs.

"How did your first meeting with Brandy go?" he asked her.

Joni shook her head. "I don't know. Not as good as it could have, I guess. She doesn't seem to trust me and I just didn't know what to say. Maybe I'm not ready for this."

"I'm sure it seems like it," he told her, "but just give it time. I suspect this will be one of those paths that the Lord lights one step at a time. Will you give it another try?"

"Oh, I'm not giving up," Joni answered, her voice flat. "I'm just not sure if I'm going to be of any help."

Pastor Ward studied her as he rubbed his chin. "You're forgetting that you're not in this alone. You have your pastor and your church behind you, and most importantly, you have God carrying you right now. I know it may not seem like it right this moment, but He is with you."

* * *

Joni wanted to scream. Although he hadn't mentioned her directly, Joni knew that Pastor Ward was talking about Emma. No, it didn't seem like God was involved right now. She wanted to believe she was wrong about that, but with her heart so full of sorrow, there just wasn't much room left for faith.

* * *

Joni walked through her front door and again experienced the blow of emptiness. Tesla loped over to her and licked her hand as she petted him. He wagged his funny tail and she could read it in his eyes: *Today? Is she coming home today?* Joni felt her heart break in half yet again. She dropped her bag and fell to her knees. Joni wrapped her arms around the little dog and cried into his fur. He knew he had his answer. Tesla whimpered his understanding and kissed Joni's face.

She sighed, picked up her bag off of the floor and stood up. Her house, as usual, was so clean that that TV detective with OCD would be willing to eat off her kitchen floor. She couldn't let them do this anymore. She needed to do things for herself. She was going to lose her mind if she didn't.

A few phone calls later, Joni had stopped the food and cleaning help and told the hospital she was coming back to work. Some of her friends had tried to talk her out of it, but she had insisted. The church ladies she spoke to had ordered her to tell them immediately if she needed anything at all, from a meal to an aspirin, whatever it was, just let them know. She would be starting back at work after the New Year. Joni wondered vaguely if she had made the right decision. *Who cares? What difference does anything make anyway?* The last call she made had been to Brandy, arranging another time to get together. They had decided to wait until after Christmas. Rather, Brandy had suggested it and Joni went along. That didn't really matter to her right now either. Pastor Ward may have high hopes for his new mentoring project, but hope was something Joni could hardly remember the meaning of.

She ran herself a bath and was settling in to the water when she realized that she hadn't discussed any of her decisions with Greg. For a moment she was concerned, but that, too, she quickly tucked into the little box in her mind labeled "apathy." She and Greg hardly spoke about anything. He was wrapping himself in a cold cocoon and every day it was more impenetrable than the day before. This distance between them added to the ache in her soul. She had tried to shove her husband's aloofness into the "apathy box" too, but it was just too big to fit. Joni pulled at her wet hair until chunks of it came out in her hands. *What more was God going to take from her?*

* * *

The Valley Without Her

Outside the bathroom door Greg stood staring. He was debating going in there and talking with his wife. His thoughts were sluggish, each word in his mind coming to him as if through thick mud. *Maybe she needed him. But what would he say?* He reached for the doorknob. His hand felt heavy. A cruel voice hissed in his brain. *You don't have anything to say to her. What good could you possibly do? She's alone and you're alone and you'll only make things worse.* Greg dropped his hand and turned away.

* * *

Joni opened her eyes and looked at the alarm clock. Six a.m. She turned her head and was unsurprised to find that Greg wasn't in bed. She knew it didn't have anything to do with her; he often fell asleep in odd places. She assumed that this was because he would keep himself occupied with looking at Emma's yearbooks or albums or even old kindergarten art projects until he simply ran out of steam and crashed from exhaustion wherever he happened to be at the time. Joni tried not to take it personally because she knew that Greg dreaded the hours he would spend lying awake in the quiet, being tormented by the monstrous thoughts that now hunted them both, but still she felt rejected.

Joni lay there for a moment, concentrating on breathing. She had woken because she had suddenly been sideswiped with fear. It took all of her willpower not to panic. It would hit her out of the blue, these moments of terror. While every moment of every day was like a stroll through hell, an anguish that she donned every morning like a backpack full of nails, sometimes the fear would jump out at her and leave her frantic. She waited for the industrial-strength anxiety to pass and her spirit to return to the usual cold dread of depression. Slowly her heart stopped pounding and she sat up. Something felt off.

Joni untangled herself from the bedclothes and put her feet on the floor. She was cold. The house seemed empty and unfriendly. Something scratched at Joni's mind. It wasn't the same blood-chilling fear she had suffered a moment ago, but an uncomfortable nagging. Like a sharp insult remembered for days after receiving it, even when it wasn't at the forefront of thought.

Joni shivered and made her way down to the living room. Tesla greeted her when she reached the bottom of the stairs. She began looking for Greg and found him sleeping at the kitchen table. He'd been working on a model car, a jeep that he and Emma had started together when she was twelve, but had never finished. She let him sleep. Something was still wrong. She went to the living room and turned on the TV. There was a movie on, one of her favorites: *A Christmas Carol*. And then she understood. It was Christmas morning. *How could she forget Christmas?* The panic that she had felt not fifteen minutes ago came back with a vengeance and Joni collapsed on the living room floor. Tesla was there whining, wanting to help.

Greg was in the room before Joni realized that she was screaming. He fell down next to her and grabbed her.

"Where is she?" she sobbed.

"I don't know." Greg was crying now too.

"It's Christmas and we didn't even know it. We've never forgotten Christmas. She should be *home* for Christmas. Where is she? Where's my baby, what's happening to my baby?"

"I don't know," he wept, "I don't know, I don't know, I don't *know…*"

It was as if these past few months Joni and Greg had been in a poisonous fog, it was deadly and noxious, but blinding and numbing, as well. When Joni realized that the two of them had completely forgotten Christmas, forgotten the cookies, the nativity, the tree, the presents, the music, the little Santa hat with ear holes that they always made Tesla wear, all of it, it was as if a light were turned on. Even with all the holiday hype that greeted them everywhere they went, they hadn't thought to do anything celebratory themselves. They had, of course, been feeling Emma's absence keenly, but now, in this moment, on Christmas morning it was so *real,* so permanent.

On the television, Scrooge was running amok with yule-tide glee. Joni detached herself from Greg, picked up one of Telsa's tennis balls that was lying by the couch. She threw the ball as hard as she could at the TV. The silence that followed offered no comfort

Chapter 10

"Hey, Pa-paw, guess what!"

Ward smiled into the phone. He loved talking on the phone with his grandchildren. He missed them very much. It was a shame they all lived so far away.

"What?" He asked Micah, his four-year-old grandson. Whatever was coming it was sure to be priceless. All of his grandbabies were beautiful and angelic geniuses, of course, but Micah was *funny,* even when he wasn't trying to be.

"I'm getting a puppy!"

"Really, now?"

"Yep! On'y guess what. I on'y get a puppy for a few minutes then he had to go home."

"You're only getting a puppy for a few minutes?" Ward wasn't sure what Micah meant. He could hear his son, Paul, in the background trying to set Micah straight. Ward couldn't make out what Paul was telling Micah and the little boy was obviously not listening to his dad.

"Uh-huh, cause really the puppy lives with Aunt Shirley and she goin' to have a baby that day." Even though Micah pronounced her name something like "Shully" he knew who his grandson meant.

The Valley Without Her

Ward chuckled. "Are you sure?" He had met "Aunt" Shirley several times. She was sweet and loving and all the children, and some of the adults, in his son's church called her Aunt Shirley. She was a stout woman with snow-white hair and little round glasses. She was at least sixty-seven years old and looked exactly like Mrs. Claus. There was absolutely no way she was having a baby.

"Yep!" the tale continued "On'y guess what, her friend Betty goin' too, on'y Daddy won't let us have Miss Betty's kitty like we have Aunt Shirley's puppy."

"Why not?" Ward asked because he wanted to see what the little boy would say.

"'Cause Daddy say Miss Betty make him want to have a upchuck."

Ward was laughing so hard tears were streaming out of his eyes and he could hear Paul shouting in the background.

Between gasps he managed to ask his grandson a question, "Is Miss Betty going to have a baby too?" He'd met Betty as well. She was older than Shirley by at least ten years.

"No," Micah answered earnestly, "just Aunt Shirley. Miss Betty not fat like her."

"*Give me the phone!*"

Ward thought he might fall out of his chair.

"Dad? DAD! It's not funny!" Paul had wrested the phone away from his son.

"Oh." Ward sighed. "Yes it is. You've got it coming, you know." He was still chuckling softly. "So you're watching Shirley's puppy because..."

"Her granddaughter had a baby last week and she wants to visit her and she asked us to keep her puppy for a few days. Betty Jacobs is going with her," Paul explained. "The kids are excited about the dog. Especially Micah."

"Yes, I can see that. And Betty? I didn't know the two of you had a falling out." He laughed again.

"You know I'm allergic to cats! Don't encourage him, Dad! We told him that cats make me sick. I don't know how he got it turned around that *Betty* was the one who would make me sick. And I *never* said anything about...about...*upchucking,* he just assumed it." Paul sighed. "What am I going to do with him?"

"Enjoy it. It'll be over before you know it."

"He's going to get me in trouble."

Ward could hear the smile under the exasperation in his son's voice. He knew Paul could see the humor in what his little boy had said in innocence.

"Oh, he was only talking to his old granddad, and anyway those ladies wouldn't care about what he said. They love him like he's one of theirs. Besides, I needed a good laugh. I don't mind telling you it's been a while."

"Oh, Dad, I'm sorry. Have you heard anything new about the girl?"

"No. That poor detective's just wearing himself out. I saw him the last time he spoke to the Leonards, and he looked like he hasn't been sleeping well. He came down here personally just to tell them he's working on some leads, but I think he's grasping at straws. God's going to have to be the one to bring Emma home."

"Do you think she'll come home?" Paul asked his father. There was a long pause.

"I believe anything is possible," Ward said. "I know the odds are not good, but I know who holds the world in His hands, too. I refuse to give up hope."

"You sound like Mom."

"I'll take that as a compliment." He sighed again. "I miss her," he said simply.

"Yeah." his son agreed. "You know what I was just thinking about the other day? The little notes she used to write to us."

"I think about those notes all the time."

"Remember that time that she barged into Merry's sixth grade classroom because she'd written Merry a note on the back of her shopping list and wanted it back?"

"I forgot about that one! Tell me."

"Well, Mom had written us all notes that day and put them in our lunches, but Merry's had Mom's list on the other side so she came into school to get it. Just sailed into the room. She went through Merry's lunch and dug out the note, then went over to Merry's desk and *rewrote it for her* so she would still have one. She apologized to the teacher and waltzed out like it was nothing. Merry said she thought she'd die of embarrassment, but she told me years later that she'd liked it. It made her proud for her whole class to see how much her mom loved her. I don't think a lot of other kids were getting notes in their lunchboxes."

"No, I don't suppose they were," Ward said softly. He was thinking of Brandy. Joni had called him to tell him that they were meeting again. He had been praying all day.

"Thank you for telling me that story," he said to his son.

"Sure." Remembering was bittersweet for both of them.

"I should go now. Give Rachael and the kids my love."

"I will, Dad."

They said good-bye and Pastor Ward went to his chair to get his Bible and pray for Brandy and Joni.

* * *

Joni knocked on Brandy's front door and waited. She wasn't sure they heard her, but then the door swung open and Brandy greeted her. Joni was pleased to see that Brandy was wearing less eye makeup. Joni had made some gentle suggestions to her and Brandy was beginning to look more like herself, and not as if she were trying to appear younger than she really was. Brandy had welcomed suggestions and the change was very becoming. Tonight Brandy wore a simple long-sleeved sweater that was the same green as her eyes. Even her hair looked a little softer, her curls not so teased and hair-sprayed. All she had needed was a little guidance. Brandy had merely been doing what she had always done, grooming as she had when she had been a teen. She hadn't been trying to conceal her age; she had simply needed some tips.

"Hi, sorry, I hope you weren't waiting."

"No, I just got here." She attempted to give Brandy a friendly smile. Smiling was hard for Joni even when she meant it. She and Greg had had one of their updates from Detective Palmer earlier that day. The man had tried to sound positive and optimistic, but he had had no good news and their spirits were especially low after they hung up with him.

"Well, let's get going then," Brandy said lightly, reaching for her coat.

"What about the kids?" Joni asked her.

"Oh, Brayle will watch them." Brandy reassured her.

"You know what, why don't we take them with us and let Brayle have some time to herself?"

Brandy looked skeptical, "Well, I don't know..."

"Don't worry, we'll find something at my house for them to do." If Joni had to insist, she would. She wasn't going to leave all this responsibility on Brayle's shoulders and hoped that she would be able to broach that very topic with Brandy soon.

"Are you sure?"

"Positive. They'll need their coats. It's cold."

Brandy went in search of winter wear for her three youngest when Brayle appeared.

"Hi, Mrs. Leonard." Brayle looked shy, like she didn't know what to say. Joni shook her head a little. *Even now, she thinks she needs to be responsible for* me *instead of herself. We'll see about that.*

"Hello, Brayle." Joni smiled at her, more easily than before. "There's been a little change of plans."

"Oh, you're not getting together now? Where's Mom?"

"No, she's still coming with me, but we're taking the kids with us." Joni watched as it dawned on Brayle what she had just said.

"You're taking them with you? All three of them?" Brayle looked like she was trying not to look excited.

"Yep. You've got the house to yourself." Joni knit her eyebrows at Brayle. "No parties."

It took Brayle a second to realize that Joni was making a joke and then she smiled. Joni guessed that Brayle's moments to herself were few and far between. She gave a small laugh.

For Joni it was all worth it just to watch the tension ease out of Brayle's cute freckled face.

"Have fun."

* * *

Have fun. Brayle's smile faltered just a little. The last time Joni had told her to have fun was the last time she had spoken with her own daughter. Joni didn't seem to make the connection though. In fact, there for a minute, Joni had seemed like her old self. It was wonderful even if it didn't last very long.

The next moment the rest of the family noisily returned and made plans about who would sit where in Joni's car. As they left the house, Joni seemed to be waiting on Brandy to say something and when she didn't she turned back and looked at Brayle.

"Now lock all the doors after us. Don't answer it if someone knocks and you don't know who it is, and keep the phone with you. Call my house if you need anything all right?"

Brayle smiled. "Got it."

Brandy looked relieved and grateful that Joni had thought to say it and a little annoyed that she hadn't thought to say it herself. She hugged her daughter. "Have fun," she told her. And the five of them left Brayle in peace.

* * *

With Brayce settled in the den with Tesla and a stack of kid-friendly DVDs and the twins coloring happily at the kitchen table, Brandy and Joni sat on the living room floor next to a cheery fire in the fireplace. They were looking through a stack of books that Joni had grabbed off of her bookshelf. This was as good a place to start as any.

The Valley Without Her

"Wow, your house is way cleaner than mine. I mean you saw what it looks like. I'm embarrassed." Brandy looked it. Joni wanted to help her in this area, too, but wanted to do it without adding to her discomfort.

Joni shook her head. "My house isn't perfect." She nodded toward her duct-taped TV. "In fact for a while some of the ladies from Hillside were helping me out a lot—cooking and cleaning and everything. Our church always does that kind of thing when someone..." Joni cleared her throat. "Um...when someone needs help."

Brandy could read between the lines about what Joni didn't want to say, but at the same time she was intrigued by what she *had* said.

"What do you mean, they help out? Why?" While she wanted to steer Joni away from the painful topic, she was truly interested in the answer.

"Well, you know what it's like when one of your kids gets sick. You know you can't make it better. You can't fix it and make the problem just," Joni took a breath, "make the problem just go away so you do the things you *can* do. You rub their tummies or sponge their foreheads." Joni looked away and Brandy could tell she was remembering. "Read them stories, you know, you let them know you're there." She looked back at Brandy and gave her a sad smile. "Love takes some of the hurt away."

Brandy nodded. "That sounds nice."

Joni took a deep breath. "Well, I thought maybe we could start with some books anyway and," she reached into the middle of the pile, drew one out and handed it to Brandy, "this one may help you with housekeeping stuff."

"*The House that Cleans Itself?* Well, I like the sound of that," Brandy laughed.

Joni nodded, "It's by Mindy Starns Clark. She usually writes fiction, but this one is about housekeeping. I've found lots of good ideas in that book."

"I can borrow it?" Brandy looked surprised.

"Sure, that's why I pulled it out." Joni turned her attention back to the stack. "Oh, this one's really good. I thought maybe I'd borrow Kate's copy, and you and I could read it together and talk about it."

Brandy took the book from Joni. "*Captivating?* What's this one about?"

"It's about spiritual and emotional things, specifically about women. It's by Stasi and John Eldredge." Joni nodded at her reassuringly. "You'll like it." She picked up another book, this one a little thicker than the others. It had an attractive cover. "Oh, I forgot I had this one." She held it in her hand for a moment, frowned and shook her head, and then turned and tossed the book into the fire. Brandy looked at her, bewildered.

Joni shook her head. "You don't want to read that one, trust me." It was a book that someone had given her a few years ago. While she agreed with the basic principles of the book, she felt that the author abused the Scriptures, twisting their meanings to make them prove his points. "Some people have gotten some good out of it, but personally, I don't think it's worth it." Her old self never would have just burned a book like that, especially not a gift, but things were different. She was different.

She turned her attention back to Brandy who seemed to trust Joni at her word, and didn't mention the book that was now burning merrily in the fireplace.

The Valley Without Her

"I want you to know that I'm not perfect. Obviously. You probably think I'm a terrible mother." Joni's voice broke. She was surprised to feel Brandy's hand soft and warm covering her own.

"Don't say that." Brandy whispered. "I might have thought it at first, you know," she looked at Joni apologetically, "only at first! But then I thought it could have happened to any of us. It could've happened to me." She withdrew her hand and looked away. "I want to be a better mom. My kids deserve a better mom." Her lips trembled. Joni could tell that it hurt Brandy to say what she had just said out loud. She felt such compassion for this young woman, and compassion felt really good. Pastor Ward was right. This was going to be good for both of them.

The two women talked a while. Nothing too heavy, they just got to know one another a little better. Joni learned that Brandy had been an excellent swimmer and won all kinds of awards before she had had to quit school to have Brayle.

Joni told Brandy about growing up in Gardenville, and how when she was a little girl she had had a crush on Greg and would write him love notes even though he kept yelling at her to stop, only to find out years later that he had kept every single one of them. He still had them in a shoebox under their bed.

They talked about their favorite and least favorite foods, Joni hated peas and Brandy was allergic to poppy seeds. They talked about places they wanted to visit and places Brandy had lived. They didn't talk about their children.

After a couple of hours the women decided it was time to pack up the kids and go home. Brayce had fallen asleep in Greg's chair with Tesla draped over him and the DVD was offering the movie's menu. The twins had joined him in the den and both were asleep on the floor. Joni told Brandy to leave their papers and crayons on the table. She'd get them later.

They were all quiet as they drove back to the Robinson's house. The kids were tired and the two women were lost in thought. With a quick goodbye to a refreshed-looking Brayle, Joni got back in her car and drove home. After she got ready for bed she picked up the phone. When he answered she kept her conversation with him short.

"Pastor Ward? You were right."

"It was God, Joni. He wouldn't let it go."

Joni didn't know what to say. "Good night, pastor."

"Good night."

Joni went to her bedroom where Greg had barricaded himself for the night. He was asleep. She had been wondering what he'd been doing, but when she looked more closely she saw an old shoebox on the bed next to him. He'd been reading the notes she'd written to him all those years ago.

Chapter 11

Joni got out of bed and shivered in the cold January air. Greg had already gone to work. She had wanted to talk to him about the notes he had been reading the night before but it was too late. The comfort that she had gotten from her time with Brandy the night before was seeping away and again in its place came the ache.

Joni made her way down the stairs into the kitchen and thought she might try to force down some breakfast when she realized that she hadn't cleared up the kitchen table from the night before. The twins' creations still littered the table strewn with a rainbow of crayons.

She picked one up of the drawings and looked at it. *How in the world?*

* * *

"So, have you figured out we're not a bunch of loonies and decided to make Hillside your church?"

Scott looked sideways at Alan. "Yeah, I think I like Hillside well enough, but the jury's still out about whether or not any loonies go there." Scott's expression made it clear that Alan was the one in question.

"Well, if there are, then you'll fit right in!" Alan smiled.

Scott laughed, "You have no idea."

Once again it was just the two of them in the Barton Construction truck on their way to a new job. They were remodeling a big old house and putting in a shiny new state-of-the-art kitchen.

"So what did you think about the message on Sunday?" Alan asked.

Pastor Ward had spoken on God's faithfulness that day. He had told them that God delivered Shadrach, Meshach, and Abednego from the flames, and while He didn't keep them from having to go into them in the first place, He was right there with them, physically present and visible to everyone there, not just watching from a distance.

"Yeah, it was really good. I like how he always gives stories and examples and stuff like that. Hey, is your family going to that concert thing?" Scott did like Hillside. He liked the pastor and the people and he really liked the potlucks they had every so often, but he still wasn't comfortable talking about personal things with people. It was just the way he was. Even his sister, Macy, had a hard time getting him to talk to her about anything serious, and he was as close to her as he was to anyone.

Alan recognized a rebuff when he saw one and graciously let it go. "I don't know yet. We'd like to. The kids really like that comedian what's-his-name, and they could use something fun like that." Although he hadn't meant to, Alan realized he had circled back around to another serious topic. Scott would know that Alan had alluded to Emma Leonard and he knew that that subject always made him uncomfortable. He supposed because of all the emotion that everyone had tied up in it. He had learned that that was the sort of thing that made Scott squirm. He tried to make the conversation light again. "So what about you? Are you going?"

They stayed on risk-free subjects until they reached their destination. Alan knew that Scott didn't exactly dislike him, but it seemed that he'd rather have his privacy than a good friend.

* * *

Ever since she had been a little girl Claire had loved field trips. School presented a lot of stress and the days her class took a trip somewhere offered a short reprieve. Some of the freshman English classes were visiting an art gallery today, and later Claire and her classmates would write a paper comparing and contrasting the exhibits that they had observed.

Melody pointed to a huge painting that hung on the wall. "How," she scoffed, "is that art?"

Claire studied the work her friend had indicated. It was a solid black background with a white stripe across the top and an orange stripe across the bottom. She leaned in to read the title. *Orange and White on Black.* Claire rolled her eyes. "It's not, I mean I could do that with a paint roller."

Melody looked at her. "What are you going to write about it?" She indicated the notebook in Claire's hands. They were supposed to be taking notes about what they saw.

Claire shrugged. "I don't know. Maybe I won't talk about this one at all. I think they just put stuff like this up on the wall to make people feel stupid."

"Yeah," Melody agreed, thinking, her eyes narrowed. "Like... like they want us to think that they know something we don't."

Claire gave the painting one last disdainful glance, "Let's go find something good."

They left the room in search of something more interesting. Somewhere in this huge building there was supposed to be a room full of fountains. The girls were looking forward to that. Today it was just the two of them out of their group of friends. The other Hillside girls either weren't taking English this semester or their teachers didn't participate in this particular outing.

They talked quietly as they wound their way through the rooms of sculptures and mobiles, chatting and taking notes. They entered a beautiful room displaying exhibits made of stained glass. There was only one other person in the room and the two friends didn't notice her until she turned and looked at them.

It was Dena Roberts. For a moment no one moved or spoke. Claire and Melody hadn't interacted with Dena in several months and had no idea what she was going to do. They didn't realize that they had huddled together slightly, as if Dena might charge at them. Dena did move closer to them, but slowly. *What was she going to do to them?* Always in the past it had been Lindsay who had sought them out and bothered them. Being approached by Dena on her own, was unprecedented. They studied her closely as she came nearer. She didn't have that determined hateful look that Lindsay had always worn when she was about to pounce.

Dena opened her mouth to say something to them. Claire and Melody were almost glad that the suspense was about to end.

"Hey, girls!"

The Valley Without Her

Claire and Melody each jumped and then spun around in an about-face. It hadn't been Dena who had spoken. Lindsay had come up behind them before Dena had said anything.

"This place is *so* boring. I wish we could've gone somewhere fun like the mall or something."

"Huh?" Melody said. *Wow I sound intelligent,* she thought.

It didn't faze Lindsay. As she usually did of late, Lindsay merely babbled on about no-one-knew-what while the girls stared at her. She was saying something about that clothing store again. "...We should go together sometime don't you think?" Lindsay's tone was friendly, but there was a steely glint in her eye. She wasn't looking at them though. She was looking past them. When Claire and Melody noticed this, they looked behind them to see Dena's reaction, but she was gone. She had left through the door on the other side of the room, and they were left to wonder what she had been going to say.

* * *

Joni sat at one of the tables at Line Dried Laundry and waited for Kate to have a free moment to talk to her. She sipped the tea that Marty had brought her and leafed through the papers in front of her.

When the busyness died down, Kate came over to Joni's table in a quiet corner of the shop and sat. "What is it? What's wrong?"

Joni slapped the stack of papers down in front of Kate. "Look at these," she told her.

Kate picked up the colorful stack and began looking at the papers one at a time. She wrinkled her brow.

"Where did you get these? Did you do them?"

Joni snorted at her friend, "You know I can't draw a straight line. No, Brandy's kids did these. Her twins who just turned five last month."

Kate looked more closely at the artwork in front of her. They were what she would expect a five-year-old to draw: Rainbows, animals, cars and trucks, princesses in towers, there was even one of a pod of whales.

"Brandy's twins did these?"

"Last night at my kitchen table."

The women looked at the drawings again. The subjects were typical five-year-old work, yes. The talent was not. These drawings were good. Good wasn't the word. They were *impressive.*

"Wow," Kate whispered. "You should do something. Brandy needs to get them into classes or..."

"I know." Joni said. "I thought so, too."

Just then the bell over the door dinged and they looked up to see that Claire was home from school.

"Hey, Mom," Claire said, "James went on home; he has a lot of homework to do."

Joni felt a momentary stab of jealousy when Kate kissed her daughter's cheek in greeting. She felt a tiny measure of relief from it when Claire came around to her side of the table to receive a hug from her as well.

Claire noticed the pictures on the table that they'd been looking over and picked up one of Brylyn's depicting a very cute snowman in a plaid scarf. "Wow." She said, "Who did these?"

The Valley Without Her

"Brayle's little brother and sister," Kate told her, watching her face for her reaction.

Claire's eyebrows shot up. "The *twins* drew these?"

Joni nodded. "I saw them drawing them. They're theirs."

"Wow." Claire said again. "These are better than some of the stuff we saw today at the museum."

Chapter 12

"I don't know," Melody said to the others after youth group one Sunday night. "I still don't trust either one of them."

"Yeah," Claire murmured. "I don't like it at all."

"Tell us again. What did she say?" Mia asked.

"Well, that's the thing, Dena didn't say anything," Melody answered. She pushed her blonde bangs out of her eyes. "She was about to say something to us, but then Lindsay came in and she disappeared."

"Well, what do you *think* she was going to say," Ashley wanted to know, "like what did her face look like?"

Claire thought, "I don't know. Serious maybe?" She looked at Melody for validation of the adjective.

"Yeah," Melody said slowly. "Well, she wasn't all smiley anyway. It's hard to say, you know, Lindsay was always the one you had to watch; she was the diva and Dena was the backup singer."

The other girls laughed at the analogy.

"I know what you mean," Brayle said. "Since Dena never did anything by herself, we don't know what to think of it now that she *is* doing something herself."

"I have a theory," Mia told them. They were all ears. "I think it's a trick. I think they're doing some sort of divide and conquer or bait and switch or...what's it called?" She clapped her hands and pointed at them, "Good Cop, Bad Cop!"

The other girls nodded at her. "Yeah, that makes the most sense," Melody agreed, "but why? What was wrong with the old system of just making us miserable directly?"

"Yeah," Mia said, "I mean, what's the *point*?"

"I still think we should just avoid both of them," Claire said decisively. When it came to Lindsay, Claire had always opted for avoidance and she saw no reason to stop now.

It seemed to be a popular solution. The girls again agreed that neither Lindsay nor Dena was someone to be trusted.

* * *

"So how are the talks with Brandy going?" Kate asked Joni after church. People had clumped together into little groups after the service and some of the ladies were catching each other up with their weeks. Kate was glad to have something easy to talk with Joni about, though she wanted to be careful to keep things general and not too personal. She didn't want to be gossiping about Brandy or talking behind her back. Brandy had been attending Hillside, but very little. Kate had noticed some differences in Brandy and was hoping that the get-together that Pastor Ward was planning would encourage her to be more consistent.

"It's going really well." Joni sounded a little surprised, but pleased, too. "Brandy can be really sweet. I think all she really needs is a little confidence.

"Well, at least, she's stopped dressing like a working girl." Julie added bluntly. For a second no one spoke. While it was true that shopping with Joni had made a positive difference in Brandy's appearance, the ladies were a little startled by Julie's bald way of putting it. Brandy may have dressed a little young for her age, but it was not as bad as Julie had just made it sound. Joni had confided in Kate that she had discreetly directed Brandy toward more modest clothing on an outing together, telling Brandy, truthfully, that such-and-such an outfit was more flattering. All she had needed, it seemed, was some guidance in this area. Brandy had simply been doing what she had always done. Joni had no intention of discussing these details with everyone here, and especially not Julie. She steered the subject back on track.

"Actually, I just remembered, Kate, I need to borrow a book so she and I can read it together."

"Sure." Kate was glad there was something she could do, even if it was something small.

"I think it's a great idea." Anna smiled. "I think you'll both get a lot out of it." Her dark eyes sparkled at the thought of all the possibilities. "Where will you begin?"

"I thought we'd start with the basics like—" Joni began

"Oh, you're going to teach her about proper grocery shopping, and menu planning!" Julie's interruption of Joni was not a question, but a command veiled as a suggestion. "Most people don't have that skill." Julie shook her head. Her isn't-that-a-shame tone was light, but the bossiness of her words was impossible not to notice.

Joni was momentarily flustered, having lost her train of thought when Julie again commandeered the topic.

"Well, I hadn't considered that a priority with—"

"No! It's only the nutritional welfare of small children and the financial responsibility of meal planning in a family who obviously needs it." Julie smiled in an attempt at polite sarcasm.

Kate felt her temperature start to rise. She didn't like it when Julie got this way, and she could tell by the expressions of the other women standing there that they weren't impressed either. Anna's eyes were now smoldering, although, Kate knew, she was far too gentle a person to give Julie a piece of her mind as Kate suspected Anna was longing to do. Sherry stared at Julie as if she'd never seen her before. Ruth's face was hard to read. Joni looked about the way she always did. Depressed and not herself. But Julie wasn't finished.

"All I'm saying is that Brandy Robinson has a lot of room to grow. The Lord entrusted her with precious children, and she's not living up to her responsibility. I see what I see, and sometimes I speak my mind. So maybe I don't have much of a filter when it comes to—"

"Now I'd like to know what you mean by that." This time it was Ruth's turn to interrupt. She, being slightly shorter that Julie, was staring up at her with a stern look on her face.

Julie smiled indulgently at the older woman who needed her to explain the trendy expression.

"Oh, that just means I say what I—"

"I know what you think it means, girly; I'm not as senile as you'd like to believe."

This time Julie was actually surprised by Ruth's interruption and was now staring at her with her mouth open. For that matter, so was everyone else.

Ruth waved her hand in the air as if she were scribbling on an invisible chalkboard. "You've got this imaginary red marking pen and you go around correcting everyone's lives with it, saying out loud whatever proud nonsense flies into your head and excusing that rudeness by saying you've got no "filter." Well, as I see it, as long as you're calling things by what their names are and telling it like it is, why don't you just call it by its right name. You call it filter, but I believe the word you really mean is *manners.*"

Julie gasped. It wasn't as if no one had ever pointed out her bluntness to her, but it had never happened in church before. And not in front of people whose respect she expected to have.

"It seems to me you *do* have yourself a filter, as you call it, 'cause you just used it for yourself. It's not your place to tell Joni what to talk about with Brandy Robinson. The pastor told me that God handpicked Joni for the job," Ruth put her arm around Joni, "and I think the good Lord knows what He's doing, and He doesn't need your advice any more than Joni here does."

If David Burish had known what he was stepping into, he never would have chosen that moment to come and get his wife to take her home. Kate saw his face morph from bland expectation to acute apprehension in less than a second.

Laughing would be a very *bad thing right now.* Kate looked at the wall. Even though there was no clock there she said, "Oh! Look at the time, better get the kids!"

It didn't matter much as everyone except Ruth, Joni, and Julie had all said some other nervous version of Kate's deflection at the same moment she did. David steered his wife away from the others as Anna went in search of Frank and Mia while Sherry bolted out the door.

The Valley Without Her

Kate looked at the two women, the older with her arm still around the younger. "Joni. Are you all right?"

Joni almost laughed. "I can't even remember what 'all right' feels like." She looked at Kate. "But Julie doesn't bother me." She turned on Ruth with wide eyes. "You!"

Ruth looked a little regretful, but Kate sensed she wasn't really sorry. "I just thought that girl needed to hear it." She sighed. "I sure did when I was her age."

* * *

Across the room, Pastor Ward was blissfully unaware of Ruth's confrontation with Julie as he chatted with Scott Fischer. "So will that night work for you?"

"I'll double check, but I think so," Scott answered, smiling. "Do I need to bring anything?"

"Just yourself." Pastor Ward was relieved to see Scott's enthusiasm. He had sensed Scott's standoffish nature and was afraid that he would decline attending the event.

Once or twice a year, Pastor Ward hosted a small dinner for new attendees. He knew that if a visitor was going to turn into a member, personal connections were vital. In the past the gatherings had taken place in his home, but since Mollie was gone, he no longer did it this way. For one, he wasn't much of a cook, and since it had been such an important event to Mollie, it was difficult for him to plan them without her. Pastor Ward asked different families in the church to host the parties; and that way, too, the new people could connect with some of the regulars. He loved this ministry and was always glad when it came around each year.

"Good." Pastor Ward said, rubbing his chin. "Good. Then it'll be you and Irene Holland. She was recently widowed and has been coming with Lucinda Perkins—have you met Widow Perkins?"

Scott laughed. "The hat lady? Yeah, she's fun. When I met her, she told me to stand up straight and then gave me a peppermint."

"That's Lucinda!" Pastor Ward smiled. "The Downing family will be there. Simon and Noelle they have two children, and I've invited Brandy Robinson, but I'm not sure if she'll be there. She's only attended once or twice. Have you met Brandy?"

"I don't think so, no. I have met Simon, though."

"Good, you'll know someone besides just Alan and me then." The Thomases had agreed to host the dinner this time. Pastor Ward thought they would be a good choice since they had connections with a few of the new people. Although, since Scott was so determined to keep to himself, having him visit a coworker at home might be a bad idea. Pastor Ward hoped it wouldn't backfire and scare Scott away for good. It wasn't that he supported the younger man's reluctance, he just knew that people were best won over gently and gradually. This, too, was something that the Lord had taught him the hard way.

***

Two weeks later a small group of Hillside Church members gathered at the home of Alan and Kate Thomas. There were ten people including the two Downing kids: Natalie who was eight, and Kyle who was ten. Their parents, Simon and Noelle, had been invited to Hillside by a colleague of Noelle's. Irene Holland had called Pastor Ward asking for Kate's number so she could call her and insist on bringing dessert. Alan had felt a secret twinge of dismay at this, being so familiar with his wife's skill in desserts, but was immediately comforted by the sight of the gorgeous chocolate and caramel trifle that Irene carried with her when she arrived. Brandy Robinson was there by herself. Joni had offered to host a movie for her and Kate's kids during the dinner. Kate tried to talk her out of it at first, but soon she realized that Joni really wanted the kids over, most likely welcoming the distraction of a noisy house for the evening. Pastor Ward had been worried that Scott wouldn't show up, but he was there right on time and actually seemed to be looking forward to the evening.

Pastor Ward made the necessary introductions, taking care to include the children, and made sure that no two people had not met. When it came time to acquaint Scott with Brandy, he couldn't help but notice a spark of interest in Scott's eyes. He smiled a little more warmly and held Brandy's hand a touch longer than he had the others'. Brandy was looking very pretty in an oversized sweater and jeans, and if she noticed Scott's interest she didn't show it. Brandy was polite, but no more enthusiastic than she had been when she had met Irene Holland. Pastor Ward looked around and caught Kate watching. She looked away, but he glimpsed a small smile on her lips. *It wasn't his imagination. She had seen it, too.*

Throughout the meal, Pastor Ward noticed the glances that Scott gave Brandy. He noticed Kate noticing, too, although they seemed to be the only ones. Alan and Simon had found common ground in their love of old cars and were talking shop. Irene had the children entranced with stories about her years as a trainer of service dogs. Brandy and Noelle made polite conversation about nothing in particular, but seemed to be enjoying themselves very much. Pastor Ward and Kate both sampled bits of each conversation and covertly watched Scott watching Brandy.

Once in a while he would join in on her talk with Noelle, but mostly he just looked at her. Kate had a hard time hiding her smile. Eventually Noelle caught on, too, and turned away from Brandy, engaging Kate and Pastor Ward in a new conversation in a socially graceful way that was neither rude to Brandy nor made it obvious what she was doing. Noelle's plan worked and it left Brandy and Scott to talk together relatively alone.

* * *

Although it was impossible not to overhear what they were saying, everyone left the two of them to themselves as they enjoyed the evening together. After dessert, which was so good it made Alan want to cry, everyone spread out a little to talk. Simon and Alan went to Alan's den to have a friendly debate with each other about the '55 pick-up vs. a '69 muscle car. Irene took the kids into the living room followed by their mother. Pastor Ward and Kate went into the kitchen, leaving Brandy and Scott at the dining room table.

"Well, I didn't see that coming!" Pastor Ward helped gather the dirty dishes as Kate loaded the dishwasher.

"I didn't think of it either. What do you think?" Kate asked him.

"Well, it could be a very good thing..."

"But?"

"I'm not sure I should say anything."

"It's all right, I know what you're thinking. He's a little reluctant to really get involved in anything complicated and Brandy's life isn't exactly simple. You're probably a little concerned that when he realizes what's involved he'll run and she'll get hurt."

The Valley Without Her

Pastor Ward just smiled at her.

Kate stopped what she was doing and looked at him. "I've got a good feeling about it," she said to him "and I think we're all due for some good feelings, don't you?"

* * *

Brandy and Kate had dropped off their kids at Joni's and then driven back to Kate's together in Kate's car in order to save room for others in the driveway. On the way to Joni and Greg's house, Kate took the opportunity to ask Brandy about the evening.

"So," she tried to keep her voice casual, "you have a good time tonight?"

"Mm-hmm." Brandy looked out of the window.

Kate glanced at her. *Was that all she was going to say?* Kate tried to think of a way to draw Brandy out without being pushy or nosy, but Brandy seemed to know what she was thinking and cut to the chase.

"There's no point, Kate. I always mess everything up, so I'm not going to get my hopes up. Scott was nice and I could like him. But I've been hurt too many times, and I'm not looking to go through it again."

Kate was a little taken aback but not entirely surprised. Of course Brandy had reason to be cynical, but still...

"But you never know, maybe—"

"Maybe not." Brandy cut across her. "Things like that don't happen for people like me. Just let it go, okay." Her voice had no edge, and held no spite, just resignation.

"I'm sorry you feel that way, Brandy," Kate said, "but I know that God has plans for you—you and me and everyone else. You just wait and see."

Kate dropped it, as Brandy asked, but she had no intention of forgetting this night. She wouldn't meddle, no, that never helped anything. But she was sure going to pray that God would soon prove Brandy wrong.

Chapter 13

With Valentine's Day around the corner, Kate had Line Dried Laundry looking good. Her decorations were pretty and festive without being sappy or over the top. Garlands made of off-white and pale pink lace hearts graced the walls, and the table centerpieces were vases made out of glued together valentines that had then been filled with artificial flowers. She had a little table set up in the corner by the window where people could make a valentine and either hang it up on the wall or give it to someone. Mostly little kids participated, but sometimes people made them for their kids, spouses, or sweethearts. It was fun to watch faces light up when a valentine was delivered.

Joni and Brandy weren't making valentines, but they were enjoying the new dessert on the menu. Kate had gotten the trifle recipe from Irene Holland and it was quickly becoming a favorite. As they enjoyed their food and coffee, they discussed the book that they were reading together. Joni could already see differences in Brandy and always felt a measure of comfort when they were together. It gave her something to think about other than horrible fates for her daughter. Going back to work had been a good idea, too. She had to stay focused on what she was doing when she was at the hospital and it offered a small vacation from the dread she lived with every moment of the day—if not completely, then at least by degree.

Brandy was talking about what they had recently read. "This book is good, but it's kind of hard to read, you know? Like it's not really for me—all that stuff about God wanting to know me and stuff. It's like I'm not really worth all of that."

Joni nodded at her. "I feel that way, too, when I read it. Kate says the same thing."

"Really?"

"Yes, and I think that's why we need books like this," she pointed at the open book in front of her, "God loves us so much, and when we start to acknowledge that, then it changes the way we see ourselves and it changes the way we live. Make sense?"

"Maybe. A little."

Joni let it go for now. She would try again later. Both women were a little subdued today. For Joni, this was another holiday without Emma, and she and Greg hadn't even talked about doing anything special together for Valentine's Day. Joni knew that Brandy was feeling guilty for snapping at her children after the party. Meeting Scott and sensing his interest in her had shaken her up, and she had taken it out on her kids and now she felt badly about it.

Joni noticed the baby steps Brandy was taking, but she had learned that it was best not to push Brandy, but to let her notice God working. Joni had drawn Brandy's attention to her twins' artwork and their considerable talent. Brandy had known that the artwork was good, but hadn't realized that not all five-year-old kids could do what hers could. When this was pointed out to her, she was delighted and it was easy for Joni to point out to her that God had blessed her little ones with this gift. Now

The Valley Without Her

Joni planned to wait for another opportunity to point out God's faithfulness to Brandy. She was sure that He was going to come through for Brandy again, even though she secretly doubted if He were going to do the same for her.

While the two women sat quietly, each lost in her own thoughts, James, Claire and Brayle came into the store. James made his way to the counter, most likely to sweet talk his mother into giving him a sample of the dessert special, and the girls made their way over to their table.

"Wow, what's that?" Brayle asked as they sat down.

"It's a new dessert that Kate just added to the menu," Joni told her.

"Yeah," Claire added. "Mom got the recipe from Mrs. Holland after that new people party."

Joni watched Brandy's reaction at the mention of the party where she had been introduced to Scott Fischer. Kate had told Joni about Scott's obvious interest in Brandy and about her gloomy reaction to it. Brandy's cheeks flushed ever so slightly, but if Joni hadn't been watching for it, she never would have caught it. She wouldn't bring it up now, in front of the girls, but she intended to ask Brandy what she thought about Scott soon. For now, she gave her attention to the girls.

"So how was school?" she asked them.

Claire and Brayle exchanged dark looks. "Lindsay Glass tried to talk to us again today after school." Claire told them. "Brayle said something about having to leave and we got out of there."

"This is still going on? She still hasn't picked on any of you or..." Joni asked.

"Acted like her old self? No." Brayle frowned.

"Who are you talking about?" Brandy asked.

Once again Brayle looked embarrassed that her mother was uninformed about something that the other moms knew all about. Joni could read it on her face and wondered if she was making a difference for Brayle by meeting with Brandy as she was.

"You know, Lindsay." Claire answered. "She was always calling us names and sometimes she even made Melody cry."

Brandy narrowed her eyes. "Oh, yeah, I remember Brayle talking about that. So now she wants to be friends?"

"No." Brayle said firmly, "She wants us to *think* she wants to be friends, but really she has some other evil reason. We don't know what it is, but we're all a little freaked out."

"Pretty much," Claire agreed. "It could have something to do with James, I guess," she said thoughtfully. "She's liked him forever."

"Huh?" James asked loudly from across the room.

Claire didn't even bother turning around when she answered him. She knew that out of what she had said, he had caught his own name and nothing else.

"Nothing," She called flatly. James turned his attention back to his snack.

"But why would that make a difference now?" Brayle asked, "It's never kept her from being a nightmare before. It still gives me the creeps."

Claire sighed. "I know."

Joni had heard plenty about this Lindsay girl and understood why the girls were reluctant to warm up to her. There were countless times that Emma had come home wounded by some new cruelty of hers. But people changed. Maybe she was tired of being mistrusted by everyone and wanted to build bridges. She thought it was probably best not to say this to the girls though.

"Well, we'd better go, Bray. We need to go pick the twins up and Brayce is home by himself." Brandy said.

Brayle nodded. "Well, see you tomorrow, Claire. Bye, Mrs. Leonard." Brayle bent to give Joni a hug, and Joni relished the feel of her arms full of sweet, young girl. She closed her eyes and just for a moment, she might have been holding Emma. She blinked away tears and hoped no one noticed. They did notice, but they understood, too.

* * *

Pastor Ward was pleased to see that Brandy Robinson was attending service this morning. She was irregular in attendance and today made three weeks in a row that she had made it to Sunday morning service with her kids. Scott Fischer was here, too, and while that wasn't really unusual, he was encouraged still, for he had been a little afraid that Scott's general apathy would cause him to give up coming to church altogether. The pastor suspected that Brandy had something to do with Scott's enthusiasm, but for the moment it didn't really matter, he was just glad that they were here.

* * *

"If something is wrong then it's wrong. If it's the wrong thing to do then that means it's wrong for *you,* and there isn't a special set of circumstances that make you an exception to God's law.

"You notice that we don't find the word *unless* anywhere in the Ten Commandments, because God offers no clauses for sin. God said, 'Do not commit adultery.' He didn't say unless your spouse is abusive and unloving or no longer treats you properly. Jesus told us to love our enemies, to love our neighbors as ourselves. He didn't say that under special circumstances that it would be acceptable *not* to do these things, although, to be honest, it would make sense to me if He had. Wouldn't it make sense if the Lord had said it was okay to be rude to people who mistreated us; or that if someone wronged us, we could retaliate? At the very least, treat them with the same attitude with which they were treating us? No. He said to *love*."

Pastor Ward noticed uncomfortable looks on some of the faces of his people. A few of the teen girls were giving each other glances from across the aisle as they sat with their families, and Ruth Daniels looked repentant as well. He didn't know why the girls were feeling convicted, but he had heard about Ruth's scolding of Julie Burish. The Burishes were in church today, but since Julie's clash with Ruth, they had not interacted much with anyone. He said a short silent prayer for his people.

"Taking things into our own hands doesn't work, beloved," he continued. "We don't know better than our Master, and there are reasons for His rules. When we don't obey them, there are consequences. That's why He gives us parameters, because He knows what's good for us and wants us to have the best life possible.

"For most of us, it's not in our nature to be submissive. We don't want to be accountable to anyone, and many try to find ways to justify this rebellious attitude. People are fond of saying not to judge and quoting Jesus saying 'he who is without sin can throw stones,' but I want to point out to you today that in the moment Jesus spoke those words there were *actual* stones that were about to be thrown. A woman was about to be murdered for something that she *did do.* Jesus didn't tell the people that they were wrong in their judgment of the adulteress' actions; in fact he must have agreed, because He told her to stop what she was doing. He didn't stop them from thinking she had done something she shouldn't, He kept them from causing her harm. The truth is, that if you make bad choices, people are going to judge you. If you claim a special set of circumstances that exempt you from God's laws, then it won't do you any good to cry that people shouldn't judge. People will, even when they shouldn't. You really don't need me to tell you this. If you found out that I was stealing from the church treasury for my own selfish reasons, you would, of course, get rid of me, but you would also think badly of me, and me telling you that Jesus said 'don't judge' would not change that. When we make bad decisions, it changes the way people see us and we lose their respect, and respect is a very, *very* difficult thing to get back once it's lost."

* * *

After the service, a few of the youth girls gathered together, each looking miserable. Mia's dark eyes clouded as she spoke what everyone was thinking. "Well, I guess we don't have any excuse for not being friends with Lindsay." Mia said the name as if it tasted bitter in her mouth. The others nodded.

"So what do we do?" Melody asked, looking a little afraid, her fair skin paler than usual under her blonde hair. "I mean I really don't want to walk up to her and strike up a conversation. I have enough nightmares already." Her friends nodded sympathetically. They all knew that Melody was still having bad dreams. Though not as frequent as they used to be, she still dreaded going to sleep at night in the event she might wake up with her heart pounding in terror.

"Let's go ask Pastor Josh what he thinks. Maybe we won't have to do *that*," Brayle said. "Maybe we can just wait and see what she does. Let her make the first move and then we'll just...I don't know...respond instead of avoiding her like we have been. Who knows, maybe we'll get lucky and when we go back to school tomorrow, we'll find out that she gave up on us and went back to Dena."

None of them really thought they would be that fortunate, but Brayle's plan was better than nothing.

* * *

Ruth tried to find Julie after the service. Although she still stood by the things she had said, Ruth was afraid that she had hurt Julie and for that she was ashamed. Yes, Julie needed to be held accountable for her rudeness, but Julie had feelings and Ruth hoped she hadn't gone too far. Unfortunately, the Burishes had left immediately after the service, so there was no chance for her to clear the air. Joni had told her that Julie was still teaching Sunday school for her like she had been since Emma disappeared, and that knowledge provided Ruth with some comfort. At least Julie and her family hadn't left the church and didn't seem to be preparing to do so. Still she felt bad. She would have liked to have talked with Pastor Ward about it, but that young man, Scott Fischer, had already pulled him aside. It seemed she wasn't the only one who had been smitten by today's sermon. In fact, a few of the teen girls looked repentant and were talking to Pastor Josh. The Lord must have known what He was doing when He gave the pastor this morning's message.

Chapter 14

Greg wasn't paying attention to what he was doing. For the second time this week he had nearly caused himself a major injury at work because he wasn't keeping his mind on the task at hand. He was starting to come apart at the seams. He didn't like mystery, and he didn't like loose ends. Greg liked problems that had solutions and when he came up against a challenge with logic, he methodically chipped away at it until it became smooth. This was the biggest problem, the biggest challenge, he had ever faced and there was no logic, no method, and no reasoning. There was nothing he could do and he felt useless and lame. Although Detective Palmer still made regular reports to them—never with any good news—he had called the detective himself in order to try and force the man to make some progress in the search for his daughter.

Palmer seemed to have been expecting it, and for five minutes patiently explained to Greg all that was being done to bring Emma home. He knew that Greg knew all of it already, but just needed to be reminded. He told Greg about the fliers with Emma's picture that were going to be distributed over even more territory; he encouraged him not to give up hope. None of it had made him feel much better. The fact that people were working hard on Emma's case only meant that she was unreachable. It wasn't because the detective was incompetent that his daughter was still missing. She simply couldn't be found. Thinking of her as *still missing* was just about all the hope he had. The alternative was too monstrous even to consider.

* * *

There were, of course, things that Detective Palmer had *not* told Greg. There was no point in depressing him with details of worthless clues and dead ends. For instance, he had not told Greg how bitterly disappointing he had found the photos sent to him by the newspaper, *The Grapevine*. They had turned up absolutely nothing. He set them aside, thinking he might look at them later if he got desperate, but he might as well throw them away for all the good they did. He didn't tell Emma Leonard's father this, though. The man was hanging on by a thread as it was.

* * *

Two weeks had passed since Pastor Ward's sermon about judgment and not making excuses, and the Hillside youth group girls were starting to relax. They had spoken to Pastor Josh after the service, and he had given them a little perspective.

He had assured them that while they needed to be friendly to Lindsay, they didn't have to let her have any control over them or what they did. In fact, he told them, it would probably be wise for them *not* to go along with most of the things that Lindsay wanted to do, but instead to include her in what they were *already* doing. The girls agreed that this was a better way. But not much better. For two weeks the girls felt like they were waiting for lightning to strike, and just when they were beginning to breathe easy, it happened. It was lunchtime again when Lindsay swooped in and began jabbering one of her peculiar monologues at them. Only this time, the girls steeled themselves and resolved to respond instead of just staring at her like a herd of frightened deer.

The Valley Without Her

Lindsay was babbling on about this weekend's basketball game and when she stopped to take a breath Mia took a chance.

"You know, Lindsay, we were wondering..." Mia began. Lindsay looked surprised to be addressed by one of the girls—surprised and a little apprehensive. An actual two-way conversation with this group was new territory for her, too.

"We were wondering if you wanted to come to our youth group sometime."

Lindsay looked around the table at each face as if she expected them all to burst out laughing at her.

When no one did, she found her voice. "Oh. Um, I don't know. Church really isn't my thing. We could do something else though, are you going to the game?"

No, none of them were, and the girls each felt a weight lift off her shoulders. Doing the right thing hadn't been as awful as they thought it was going to be. Ashley even pushed the issue a little, telling her when meetings were and assuring Lindsay that youth group was always a lot of fun.

Lindsay stammered some excuse and left as quickly as she had appeared. For a moment, the girls just looked at each other and finally Claire spoke.

"Well, that wasn't so bad."

"Yeah, I think *we* actually scared *her* this time," Brayle said.

"Not that I'm ready to trust her or anything," Melody began, "but I still feel bad."

"What do you mean?" Mia asked.

"Well, I'm kind of glad that she didn't want to come to youth group. We mentioned it and she scampered off, and I was relieved. That's awful." Melody tossed her hands helplessly. "I mean, I'm *glad* that someone doesn't want to come to church."

"It's not really that simple," Claire said reassuringly. "She's given us lots of reasons not to trust her. Yeah, maybe it's not the greatest thing that you're glad she didn't fall all over herself to join up; I think we all felt the same." She looked at the others who nodded guiltily. "But at least we tried. It's a step in the right direction anyway."

"I guess so," Melody said reluctantly. "I just don't think I'm ever going to trust her or want to be her friend." She sighed. "Why does it have to be so hard? It's like nothing will ever be the same again." Her voice began to tremble and the other girls at the table could all feel the familiar sadness gathering around them like darkness. Then Melody said softly what each girl was thinking.

"I miss Emma."

* * *

Pastor Ward had had no idea what impact his words would have the Sunday he had preached about accountability. Pastor Josh had told him that even some of the young girls had been concerned about their treatment of a classmate who had been bullying them, but was now suddenly, and inexplicably, friendly. He could understand the girls' suspicion of the mean girl, but agreed with Pastor Josh that there was no excuse to be rude to her for past deeds, and that Jesus had said to love our enemies.

Scott Fischer had found him after the service, wanting to make an appointment with him, and Ruth Daniels had called him the next day. She was torn by what she had said to Julie Burish and wanted him to help her sort it all out. Pastor Ward could see why Ruth was troubled. Julie had been hurting people's feelings for years with her sharp words and there was plenty of biblical foundation for someone like Ruth to reprimand her. On the other hand, Ruth was not compassionate at the time, and was very worried that she had embarrassed Julie, and worse, hurt her feelings. He had advised Ruth to talk to Julie, but Ruth was having a difficult time getting her on her own. She wanted to talk to her face-to-face, but Julie and David had been grabbing their two little ones, Jeremy and Lily, and bolting for the door after every service. He had advised Ruth to give it time. Julie couldn't hide from her forever. Pastor Ward knew that it was probably Julie's ego that had been bruised more than her feelings, and suspected she just needed time to get over it. She had needed one of Mollie Brown's so-called spiritual spankings and, predictably, it had stung.

And then there was young Scott Fischer. He had felt convicted by the sermon too, and came asking questions. Pastor Ward had gently explained that there was really no place for apathy in his relationship with God. Spiritual apathy would spill over into every other aspect of his life and that was not being a good steward of the gifts and blessings God had given him. He loaned the younger man one of his copies of a compilation of books by C.S. Lewis. Pastor Ward drew his attention to *Mere Christianity* and told him it was a good place to start. Scott had seemed genuinely enthusiastic about reading the book and Pastor Ward took that as a good sign.

He then cautiously broached the subject of Brandy Robinson with Scott. He didn't make a habit of getting in the middle of such things, but this time he felt the circumstances were special. There were a lot of past hurts in Brandy's life and there were her children to be considered. A relationship with her was not to be taken lightly.

"So I hope that I don't sound too much like a protective father, but frankly, I think the circumstances may call for one," Pastor Ward began.

Scott looked at him curiously.

"May I ask—what are your intentions with Brandy?"

"Oh!" Scott was surprised (and maybe a little embarrassed). He blushed. "Intentions? Well, I don't know. I just met her. She seems nice." He smiled softly. "She's pretty."

Pastor Ward nodded. "I can see how you could be interested in her, but it's important that you understand that things are different with Brandy. She's been hurt in the past; she's working on improving her life, and she has four precious children. Although she does not need my permission to have a relationship, I feel obligated to protect her."

Scott looked only slightly offended. "Well, I don't plan on doing anything to hurt her," he said.

Pastor Ward rubbed his chin. "No, you may not *plan* to hurt her, but Brandy's life is somewhat complicated and, if you'll forgive me, complications are not something you enjoy facing. All I'm asking is that you take into consideration the big picture when it comes to Brandy. If you decide she's worth a little extra work, and I think you'll find that she is, then go for it. Ask her to dinner. I think it would be good for her."

"I see what you're saying," Scott answered. "I'll think about it."

"Good." Pastor Ward smiled. "I'm looking forward to seeing how it turns out."

Scott thanked him for the book before he said good-bye. Pastor Ward could tell that the young man had a lot on his mind.

The Valley Without Her

When the door closed behind Scott, Pastor Ward prayed aloud. "Please give this young man the wisdom to make the right decision, Father, and then give him the strength and courage to act on it."

* * *

Joni had learned how to go through the motions. She walked, talked, sometimes ate, and, most recently, worked. She knew that she wasn't the person she used to be. Even her own voice didn't sound the same to her anymore. She used to laugh easily, and now it took all her strength to just summon a smile. It was as if vital parts of her character had been amputated and she was stumbling around like a zombie, not actually dead, but not really living either. Her beautiful daughter was missing. Her husband, though she saw him every day, seemed to be as well. Also gone were her sense of humor, peace of mind, ability to sleep well, and most of her faith.

She wasn't a fool. She knew people could see this, her losing of self, but still she was surprised one day at work when one of the doctors approached her out of the blue.

She was just leaving the room of a patient who had been in an automobile accident and was still in a lot of pain, when Dr. Evans pulled her aside and asked her if they could speak in private.

At first Joni was worried that she had made some error and was about to be reprimanded, but it was unlikely. She always made it a point, even in her present state of mind, to be exceptionally careful; and Dr. Evans, who insisted on being called by her first name, Tobie, wasn't really the type to get someone alone and then yell at them.

Tobie asked Joni to sit in one of the squashy guest chairs in her office while, instead of sitting behind her desk, she took the other one next to Joni. Tobie handed Joni the cup of tea that she had already made for her.

Tobie's brown eyes were filled with compassion. "How are you doing, Joni, really?"

Joni sighed. She hated this question. It was good to know that people truly cared, but it forced her to put the pain into words.

"I'm surviving. Sometimes I have to remind myself to breathe and sometimes I wake up screaming...I don't know, Tobie. To be honest, I'm not doing that great."

"I'm sure. No one could expect you to be." Tobie tucked a strand of chestnut hair behind her ear. She seemed to be choosing her words carefully. "In times like these, people feel really helpless. Someone we care about is suffering and everyone wants to feel like we should *do* something to help make it better." She paused, still thinking. "The problem is there's nothing anyone can do to really fix it, so everyone just tries to do what he or she can and hope that it brings just a little bit of comfort."

Joni nodded and tried to give her an understanding smile, "My church friends have said the same thing."

"I'm glad," Tobie smiled. "Well, there may be something I can do, too. I know it isn't much, and I hope you aren't offended, but I'd like to prescribe you some antidepressants."

Joni was a little surprised by this statement. She hadn't known what she was expecting, but it wasn't this.

"Now let me make it clear that it has nothing to do with your job performance. I've spoken with Kenya and, although she's concerned about you as well, she has told me that your work is exemplary as always."

The Valley Without Her

Kenya Priest was Joni's director of nursing and a wonderful woman to work for. Kenya was always professional and fair. She was tall and beautiful with close cropped hair and skin the color of cocoa. Joni had always thought of Kenya as regal, like an African queen. She carried herself with poise, but not arrogance, and Joni had a great deal of respect for her. She felt a twinge of dismay that they had been discussing her, but it was to be expected. She believed Tobie when she said that it was out of concern for her well-being. Tobie and Kenya had not been gossiping about her.

"Joni," she said firmly, "we don't have perfect bodies and we don't have perfect minds. If you were a diabetic, you would need insulin and if you were nearsighted, you would wear glasses or contact lenses. I'm going to write you a script," she picked up the little pad from her desk and scribbled as she spoke, "just a month's worth. Take them as needed. If, in a month, if you decide you need more, then we can talk about getting you on an automatic refill." She tore off the little piece of paper and tucked it into Joni's hand. "Let me do this for you. It'll make me feel a little better to think that maybe I've helped in some way."

Joni thanked her and left. She tucked the little piece of paper into the pocket of her scrubs and even made a mental note to stop by the pharmacy before she went home, but she doubted that she would use the pills. She truly appreciated the gesture, but didn't have any hope that this would change anything. Emma was gone and no little pill was going to bring her back.

Chapter 15

Joni sat in an uncomfortable chair in a depressing room that was trying valiantly to be cheerful. She supposed that was part of its problem. If this were a cheerful place that her father lived in, then it wouldn't have to try so hard to *appear* cheerful, it just would be.

The people here used to be confident, capable adults. They used to have jobs and families who depended on them. They made important decisions and people respected them. Now they were like children again. They made very few decisions for themselves and had forfeited a great deal of their dignity to old age and their disease. Joni's father, Hal, smiled at her vaguely. She missed her dad. *Just one more person to slip away from me,* she thought. She watched him as he played with bits of yarn, pretending to tie them into knots. He had been in the Navy and, even if he did remember the knots, his hands didn't have the dexterity to tie them properly. It was just something the staff let him do to pass the time.

"How are you doing today, Dad?" she asked him. Joni didn't try for long to have a conversation with him. He simply wasn't there with her.

"We found out about the clock today." He nodded importantly. "That boy with the hat. He found one, too."

The Valley Without Her

Joni never knew if her father was speaking out of some deeply buried memory, if he was actually talking about something going on in the present, but couldn't call forth the proper words, or if it was all simply gibberish from beginning to end. She sat with him for a little longer, remembering him as he was. Joni tried to come and see him at least twice a month. It was difficult to see him this way. She rose to her feet and kissed him on the head. "Bye, Dad. See you soon, okay?" Hal didn't respond to his daughter. He mumbled contentedly to himself and rearranged his bits of yarn.

* * *

The school year was coming to a close and it seemed that the staff was trying to find ways to fill up the final days of school. All minds were thinking ahead to summer vacation and no one wanted to be in school anymore. The students sat in the auditorium and waited for yet another assembly to begin. Some of the kids knew what was coming. Claire and her friends had been told that all the schools were going to be having an interactive lecture about self-defense. The Hillside youth group knew that it was because of Emma. None of them knew what anyone had meant by "interactive."

They sat together in the auditorium and even some of the boys were there in the row with Claire, Melody, and the others. James was among them, which was probably part of the reason Lindsay Glass chose a seat not far from them. She hadn't spoken to them as much after they had invited her to youth group, but one day she had cornered Claire in a restroom (Claire had been terrified for a moment that the old Lindsay was back) to ask her a question.

* * *

"So does James go to your youth group?" Lindsay wanted to know.

Claire raised one eyebrow. *You're just figuring this out now?* She reminded herself about what Pastor Josh had said about being nice. "Well, yeah, he's my brother."

"Yeah...right." Lindsay was no longer looking at her, but staring into space thinking. Claire could practically hear the wheels turning in Lindsay's pretty blonde head.

"Okay, bye." She had muttered and darted away before Lindsay could ask her any more questions.

* * *

Claire risked a peek at Lindsay, sitting not far from them. She was just sitting quietly, waiting for the assembly to begin. Claire hadn't told anyone about Lindsay's question, but she knew it wasn't the end of it. Lindsay wasn't done with them yet.

She was saved from imagining a slide show of frightening "Lindsay's motive" scenarios by the drama teacher, Mr. Casey, getting up on the stage to introduce the speakers. Claire didn't know Mr. Casey well, being too shy to be in any of the school programs, but he was always nice to her and her friends when he had lunch duty, and her theater friends liked him a lot.

"We have some special guests with us today," Mr. Casey announced. He gestured to the backstage area and a man walked out, followed by a little girl about ten or eleven years old. Several people were intrigued by the sight of a grade school kid on the high school stage. "This is Chris Hayes," Mr. Casey indicated the man who waved politely, "and this is his daughter, Megan." The girl gave the crowd a small smile and turned her attention back to the men standing next to her on stage.

"I know you'll give them your best attention as they give you their demonstration today." This was his teacher-y way of telling them to shut up and listen. "I'm sure you'll enjoy what they have to show you, so welcome them to our school." Mr. Casey hopped off the front of the stage as the students politely applauded the guests.

Chris nodded at the kids and began his presentation. He began by telling the students a little about himself and his family. He was a music teacher and his wife homeschooled their five kids. Megan was fourth in line. The Hayes family was also involved in a program that taught people of all different ages how to defend themselves against various attacks. He explained how his wife had been mugged while shopping alone one day and, while she thankfully wasn't hurt and the man didn't get away with anything important, she had been very shaken up and frightened. She was having anxiety attacks and bad dreams until a friend suggested that they look into this self-defense program. The whole family went and to make a long story short, he told them, they were now all instructors—even Megan and her younger brother, Max.

When he told them this, there was a murmur of amused disbelief. The little girl on stage hadn't so much as wiggled since walking out there. The thought of her fighting anyone was laughable.

"Well, let's stop talking about it and start showing you what we mean," Chris suggested. "Mr. Casey has chosen one of his theater students to come up and do some demonstrations with us." He motioned to someone and everyone looked as Travis Hardy, a senior, hopped up on the stage and waved charismatically at his peers. He was obviously comfortable up there. Claire would have died of embarrassment if all those people were looking at *her* like that.

Chris shook Travis's hand and then so did Megan, or, more accurately, Megan let Travis take her hand and wiggle her arm back and forth. She gave him the same benign smile she had given the crowd.

"Now Mr. Casey tells us that you've taken stage combat classes and know how to, "fight" safely and properly?"

Travis nodded confidently.

"And," Chris looked at the students, "we haven't practiced this. This is the first that Travis has met us, right?" He looked at Travis.

"Improv!" Travis said loudly putting his fists in the air.

Everyone laughed.

Megan nodded and smiled her smile.

"All right, then. Let's begin."

Travis took a step toward Chris, but Chris held up his hand. "No, not me. You're going to try and abduct my daughter."

Travis was obviously stunned. He glanced at the little girl and gave the older man a "you've-got-to-be-joking" look.

"It's okay," Chris nodded. "You don't have to have a stage fight with her, just try and grab her."

Travis still looked skeptical. He looked back and forth between the two of them. Megan continued to stand there, quiet and serene.

"Go on." Chris prodded. "Grab her."

Travis took a breath and shrugged his shoulders. He leaned closer to the girl and reached feebly for her arm. The reaction was dramatic and instantaneous.

"NO!" Megan screamed. Claire felt her bottom leave her seat as everyone in the auditorium, except Chris and Megan but including Travis, jumped out of their skins.

Megan repositioned herself so she was actually facing Travis, who had to be at least double her size. "NO!" she screamed again. Everything about her had changed. Her stance was combative. Gone was the little girl with the bland expression; in its place was a blazing, seething spitfire about to claw, kick, and bite anyone and anything that came near her. She backed up several steps, creating more distance between the two of them, but still keeping her eyes on him.

Travis actually cowered slightly as she screamed again, "NO!" And again, "NO! HELP! 911, 911!"

And just as abruptly as she had turned into a Tasmanian devil, she returned to her original meek, little girl self. She smiled again mildly at the stunned teens.

There was a heartbeat of silence and then Travis closed the distance between them, reached out to her and this time actually took her wrist; but instead of "grabbing" her, he swooped her hand up over her head and shook it like a winning prizefighter.

The applause was deafening.

Travis was excused back to his seat and Chris addressed the students again. He explained how the element of surprise can be an ally. Chris and Megan demonstrated a few more techniques, showing how to physically escape someone. It was informative and Claire would have thought it entertaining if the reason they were having this assembly weren't because someone had taken Emma.

She felt her heart clench like a vise in her chest. *Would it have made a difference if Emma had known these things?*

Claire was mortified to realize that she was crying. She hopped up out of her seat and climbed over her friends to make it to the aisle. She dashed out of the auditorium to find a rest room where she could get her emotions under control in peace.

* * *

Kate was in a hurry. She still had to go to the bank, the post office, and the grocery store before running home to make dinner for her family. She had left her list at her shop, so she was mentally repeating the items to herself to keep from forgetting them. Thankfully, it was a short list. She was about to enter the bank, her hand pressed against the door, when she stopped dead in her tracks.

Her heart leaped into her throat. Kate blinked a few times and looked more closely at a young girl that was walking down the sidewalk on the other side of the street. The young girl had auburn hair. She was at least twenty years old. Kate's heart crashed to her feet. The girl was not Emma. Didn't even look much like her really. There was no stopping the tears that stung her eyes. She pulled herself together so the nice ladies who worked there wouldn't think she was a basket case and pushed open the door to the bank.

* * *

The end of the school year came and Pastor Ward could see the shift in his people. Attendance would decline as families went on summer vacations. Many of the kids would be attending camp. Pastor Josh would normally be holding his annual "Timmy Awards," but had decided to skip it this year. Some things were the same, of course. Pastor Ward had received his annual greeting card from Ray Crawford, the man responsible for ending Mollie Brown's life. Ray always sent him a card and a note on Arbor Day. He kept Pastor Ward updated on his prison ministry and told him he was praying for him. Though Ray never said so, Ward knew that he chose this holiday because of its obscurity. Pastor Ward assumed he chose a holiday in order to help remind himself to do it, but he didn't want to darken an important holiday like Easter or Christmas by reminding Ward of Mollie's death. At the same time, he also wanted Ward to know that he was still thinking of him. He was still sorry. Pastor Ward was glad that Ray kept in touch as he did. He was grateful though, that it was only once a year and that Ray had had the tact not to choose a significant day.

Pastor Ward noticed a few new people had attended church today. Now that the service was over, he would be able to greet them. He always tried to introduce himself to the newcomers. There was a new girl who had been sitting near the back. She was a pretty blonde girl who looked to be about the same age as Claire Thomas and the other youth group girls. She also looked quite uncomfortable, as if she thought someone were going to suddenly do something bizarre. He was shaking hands with Frank Lopez when it suddenly dawned on him who the girl must be.

"Frank?" Pastor Ward frowned.

"Yeah?"

"Who is that girl standing there all by herself?"

Frank followed Pastor Ward's gaze, and his face darkened. That told the pastor what he needed to know.

"That's Lindsay Glass," Frank said. "She's the one who's been mean to the girls all these years."

"Yes, but I hear that she's turned over a new leaf," Pastor Ward reminded him gently.

"Something like that," Frank said.

Pastor Ward could tell that Frank was torn between a father's protective nature and a Christian's duty to forgive. And here he had thought that today's *other* visitor was going to be the one to cause a stir. He glanced over to where Scott Fischer stood and shook his head. Yes, this was definitely going to get people talking. Pastor Ward looked at the lovely dark-haired young woman smiling next to Scott and couldn't help but wonder what was going on. Scott had made no commitments when it came to Brandy, but still Pastor Ward couldn't help but feel a little disappointed. Scott must have decided that Brandy's life was too complicated for him and moved on. Pastor Ward deliberated only for a moment and then quickly decided to greet the blonde, younger girl first. No one was talking to her.

* * *

Pastor Josh couldn't help but notice the lovely dark haired young woman smiling next to Scott, and couldn't help but wonder what was going on. First of all, he had been under the impression that Scott was interested in Brayle's mom, Brandy, and secondly, he felt very *very* guilty for finding Scott's companion more than a little attractive. Watching her, he felt like one of the teens. His hands were sweaty and his heart bounded in his chest. She smiled at someone. His heart did gymnastics. He allowed himself five seconds of staring at the lovely creature and then ducked out of a conveniently nearby side door. He wouldn't even introduce himself to her. He wouldn't even introduce himself to that blonde kid who had shown up today, though he should. She was obviously youth age, but he felt it was more important to get himself out of there *now*. Josh wasn't sure if he had ever had such a reaction to a stranger before. The blonde teen would have to wait. The brunette angel would have to be forgotten, or, in the event that she married Scott Fischer (Josh felt a strange and guilty stab of jealousy at the thought), Josh might have to look for a different job.

* * *

Brandy Robinson was almost *almost* thinking of maybe warming up to the idea that Scott Fischer wasn't such a bad guy. Until today. He had been making a point to speak with her after services and Bible studies and other sundry church events. He didn't ask her out or take large amounts of her time, but still he gave her an attention that seemed unique. People had starting asking Brandy what she thought of him and she always kept her answers polite, but vague. She had wanted to be very sure that he was "safe" before letting him get close.

Wouldn't you know it, she thought, *the day I decide to actually give him some encouragement and he brings a woman to church. He's already on to someone else and he* must *have been seeing her already if they're coming here together.* Brandy hated how hurt she was. She was angry and surprised by her keen disappointment. She hadn't realized that she was looking forward to seeing Scott today. She hadn't realized that she was starting to really like him. She *did* realize that her eyes were starting to sting and at that moment, Scott looked at her. She clenched her jaw. It was probably just her imagination, but his expression seemed to tell her that he wanted to talk to her. *No way, pal. I'm not interested in meeting your new little girlfriend.* She turned and dashed out of the same door that Pastor Josh had just exited, though she didn't see him. She'd wait for the kids out here, they'd find her. As for Scott she was done with him. At least it had ended before it began this time. Yes, it was better this way. Simpler.

She hung her head, hating herself for the tears she couldn't stop. Joni was wrong. God just didn't care about her like He cared about other people.

"I knew it was too good to be true," she said aloud to no one.

Chapter 16

The summer swept by quickly, as is summer's habit, and the people of Gardenville tried to keep up. Pastor Josh was even more driven than usual. He felt a little guilty for avoiding Pastor Ward, but he did *not* want to talk to him about the girl who was sitting next to Scott Fischer every Sunday at church. Instead of their usual meetings, Josh always found an excuse to talk with him over the phone instead. After Sunday morning services, Josh simply dashed away as soon as he could, without neglecting his teens. *Let Pastor Ward deal with the adults.* For instance, Julie Burish, who was still a regular attendee along with her family, had been keeping to herself and bolting for the door after services much in the same way that he had. But Julie wasn't his problem.

Pastor Josh was a little concerned about Brayle, although she seemed better cared for than she had a year ago. He knew that Brayle's mother had stopped attending church. Brayle didn't talk about it much, but he could tell she was disappointed. Her mother wouldn't tell her why she didn't want to come anymore.

Of course, there was always the Emma issue there in the middle of everything. His kids were wounded by it, and Pastor Josh prayed constantly that he would have the wisdom to help them deal with it. Emma's birthday was coming up. It seemed there was always something going on that emphasized the acute sense of loss. This was why he decided to skip the Timmy Awards this year. Every year around graduation, Pastor Josh held the annual award ceremony based on 1 Timothy 4:12: "Don't let anyone think less of you because you are young. Be an example to all believers in what you say, in the way you live, in your love, your faith, and your purity." This year it somehow seemed inappropriate, and the kids didn't question it.

And then there was the new girl in his youth group. The blonde who had shown up the same day as the pretty brunette (Josh had gone out of his way to not even know her name), and although she didn't attend faithfully, she brought an uneasiness to his group. He understood the situation, and while he was very proud of his kids for the efforts they were making to include Lindsay, she herself was obviously not at ease and it made everyone feel awkward. Josh suspected that Lindsay's attendance had a lot to do with James Thomas, and she put up with the meetings in order to be near him. This, of course, was not ideal, but it was a start.

Camp was a convenient distraction and so were the many summer activities in which his teens were involved. He just needed time. He'd get over it. He hoped. School would be starting soon, and then just around the corner would be the apple festival. That alone was plenty to worry about, without taking time to think about the lovely girl that always seemed to be hovering somewhere in his mind.

* * *

Emma's birthday loomed in the near future and Joni was dreading the day. She could not believe that one of the happiest days of her life was now such an overwhelming source of grief. Some mornings Joni had to force herself to get out of bed. Usually this happened on mornings after she dreamed about Emma. It didn't happen all the time, but when it did, it was excruciating.

One night Joni dreamed that she and Emma were sitting on a blanket on a grassy hillside enjoying an outdoor concert. In the dream, Emma leaned back against her mother and Joni wrapped her arms around her daughter. Emma's head fit perfectly in the crook of her neck, and Joni wondered why holding her daughter in this moment in time was so exquisitely wonderful. In the dream, Emma had never disappeared, instead this was just a snapshot of everyday life. Emma had turned to Joni and spoken. "You know, Mom, I've been wanting to tell you—" and then she was awake.

Reality slashed at her and she was suffocated by disappointment. It seemed so cruel. *Why do I have to dream like that? If only I could have at least heard what Emma was going to say.* Joni moaned against the ache like a knife in her heart. Greg was used to his wife waking up calling for Emma, but this time it didn't matter. Her cries didn't wake him because he had fallen asleep on the living room floor.

Joni felt her life get smaller every day. Brandy no longer met with her and Joni now realized how right Pastor Ward had been. Meeting with Brandy had been a bigger refuge than she had known. Joni couldn't remember the last time she laughed. Every time she began a conversation on the phone with the detective, she felt a traitorous well of hope spring up in her heart only to maliciously evaporate as Palmer told her, again, that they were still working, but had found nothing. Each time this happened, Joni went to bed and stayed there until she absolutely *had* to get up. Sometimes her husband was there and sometimes he was doing something illogical, like searching the basement or the crawlspace. As for Greg, they hardly spoke. Sometimes they were like strangers. They weren't angry with one another, they simply couldn't think of things to say. Joni had always heard that couples often split up after the loss of a child, one of the reasons being that they grieve differently. That didn't seem to be the case with the two of them. Each of them was slowly being eaten alive by the loss of their daughter. Neither of them had the strength to try to talk to the other.

* * *

One Sunday morning after church, it happened. Drew, Nate, and James had pulled Pastor Josh aside to talk to him, and they unknowingly kept him much longer than he had intended to stay. Up until today he had managed to avoid this moment, but the second the boys left him, Pastor Ward waved Pastor Josh over to where he was standing, talking with Scott Fischer and his brown-haired beauty. Josh wanted to escape, but it was no good. There was no way to avoid this introduction without being rude. He gulped and closed the distance between them.

"Pastor Josh, I don't believe the two of you have met," Pastor Ward extended his hand toward the beautiful girl and smiled warmly. Or at least, that's what the old man thought he was doing. Josh felt as if his mentor were inviting him to have his heart ripped out.

"Hello, Pastor Josh," said the angel melodically. She held out her hand to him and smiled in a way that made his knees weak. "I'm Macy Fischer."

Josh took her hand and tried to ignore the tingly electric feeling it gave him to touch her. His mind snagged on the name Fischer, the same last name as Scott's. Was she Scott's...

"Wife?" Josh said out loud. He sounded as if he were choking.

The Valley Without Her

Macy laughed; still holding his hand, her eyes sparkled. "Well, I'm flattered," she teased, "but we've only just met."

Josh didn't know what she meant. She was even prettier up close and his brain was fuzzy. He realized he had better let go of Scott's wife's (*wife's!*) hand before he got punched in the face. He looked at Scott to see if he'd noticed Josh's reaction, but Scott only looked slightly confused. Josh looked at Pastor Ward whose lips were twitching.

Josh shook his head like a dog shaking away a bath. "Huh?" he said intelligently.

Pastor Ward made a noise like a laugh that he tried to disguise as a cough, and came out like a snort. He cleared his throat and seemed to be trying to keep a straight face. "Could you excuse us for one moment please?" He pulled Josh away and into the church's nearby office. It was mercifully vacant.

"What's the matter with you?" Pastor Ward demanded. "I obviously am not going to offer you a stiff drink, so shall I slap you instead?"

"What?" Josh felt like he had already been slapped. *What in the world was going on? Why was he acting like this was funny?*

"Pull yourself together, young man!" Pastor Ward commanded. "I can see that you're taken with Scott's sister, but that's no reason to behave like an imbecile."

Josh flushed. "Well, how would you feel if you were attracted to someone's—did you say *sister?*"

Now Pastor Ward *did* laugh. "Oh, you thought they were a couple? Oh, dear" He sighed. "Well, that explains it." Pastor Ward stopped smiling. "That explains a lot, actually."

Josh wasn't listening. He felt relief start and the soles of his feet and rush up over him to burst out the top of his head like a volcano. He enjoyed a moment of happiness, but then remembered how he had just acted a moment ago.

"So," Josh began, trying to keep his voice even, "That girl is Macy and she's Scott's *sister,* and I just acted like a complete moron?"

"Well," Pastor Ward, seemed to be trying to find something encouraging to say, "she didn't seem to mind."

Josh groaned.

"They're probably wondering what's become of us. Let's go back and speak with them."

Josh followed Pastor Ward meekly. He was determined to redeem himself. Now that he knew that this girl (*Macy*) was Scott's sister and not his better half, he didn't want her thinking he was a compete dolt.

He could tell that the senior pastor was trying to help. When they rejoined Scott and Macy, Pastor Ward looked at Josh and said with relief in his voice, "Well, I'm glad we got *that* taken care of." He said this as if he and Josh were superheroes back from making the world safe for democracy. Obviously Pastor Ward didn't want them to know that he'd had to take Josh into another room and threaten to slap him.

By this time most of the people had left, and it was just the four of them standing in the foyer.

"Do the two of you have any plans for lunch?" Pastor Ward asked Scott and Macy.

They didn't

The Valley Without Her

"Well, why don't the four of us go out together for lunch?" he suggested lightly.

Josh found it very ironic that the idea of sharing a meal with Macy (even though the pastor and Scott would be there too), was so exciting that his stomach was doing cartwheels and he probably wouldn't be able to eat anything. He was pleased but nervous when they agreed.

"Well, the best place in town in Kate Thomas' shop, but it's closed on Sundays so why don't we meet at Mandy's Cafe? They have good pie."

Everyone agreed with Pastor Ward's suggestion that they would meet shortly at Mandy's.

* * *

If Josh had been taken with Macy after only seeing her, having a conversation with her put him over the moon. Macy was witty and fun to be around. She spoke openly and happily about her faith. They had the same taste in music and she was obviously intelligent. And, of course, he thought she was *very* pretty. He found out that Macy was a physical therapist and had started a job not far from here. Scott had told her how much he liked Hillside Church so she decided to give it a try and found that she liked it, too.

It would have felt like a date if the pastor and her brother hadn't been along. It felt like a date for Quakers. All too soon it was time to go, but Pastor Ward wasn't through with his scheming.

"Josh, would you mind taking Macy back to her car? Scott and I have a little something we need to do, and they rode here together from the church."

Now Josh understood why the older man had asked him if he could ride along with him in his car. He had been planning this little switcheroo game of musical cars all along. Josh even suspected that Pastor Ward had something up his sleeve for Scott as well. He didn't mind. This meant a little more time with Macy. He hoped she didn't mind either.

"Sure, that'd be fine," he said, he hoped casually, as his heart sang. He looked at Macy and smiled. "You ready to go?"

"All set," she smiled back.

The drive back to the church seemed far shorter than it had been on the way there, and soon they arrived. He hoped he wasn't being too forward, and was terrified that she'd say no, but he couldn't let the opportunity pass.

His heart was in his mouth, but he managed to speak as they stood by her car. "You know, Pastor Ward wasn't kidding; Kate's place really is the best in town. Have you been there?"

Macy wrinkled her brow. He couldn't help but notice how cute she was when she did that. "Um, no. I don't think so. Isn't it called Clothespin Laundry or something like that?"

"'Line Dried Laundry," he told her. "Would you like to go sometime? I mean, would you like to go there," he cleared his throat, "with me?"

He thought that maybe her cheeks pinked just a little, and she smiled.

"Sure." She said softly. "I think I'd like that."

Josh thought he might actually be able to do a backflip, but kept both feet on the blacktop and gave her what he hoped was a charming and confident grin. "Great," he said. "Why don't I call you later when we both have our calendars in front of us?" He was stupefied by his own cunning. Not only had he made what he hoped was a date with her, but he was about to get her phone number too.

She gave him her number, smiled her good-bye and left.

He stood there for several moments after she was gone, thinking he must be dreaming. He came to himself and climbed into his car and headed for home. As he drove he prayed, thanking God for this new exciting development in his life, and that whatever happened would be His will. Josh laughed out loud. This was the best day he'd had in nearly a year.

* * *

"You think that's why she stopped coming?"

Scott and Pastor Ward were still sitting in Scott's truck, parked outside the parsonage.

"Well, I can't be sure, but she did stop coming right around the time that Macy began attending church with you. If she did think that Macy was your girlfriend and not your sister, she wouldn't be the only one. I think a lot of people did. I, myself, wondered until you introduced me to her."

"Oh, I didn't think of that." Scott sat quietly for a moment.

"Now, don't think too much of her reaction, even if it is true. You were showing interest in her and then, she thought, you moved on to someone else. It doesn't have to mean that she had any deep feelings for you, but you could see how she would feel at least insulted. Do you see? You needn't feel too pleased with yourself that you had such an importance to her."

"Yeah, I see what you mean." Scott answered humbly. He stared at his work-calloused hands. "I did like Brandy. I mean I *do*. But when she stopped coming and I didn't know why... And

I didn't think I knew her well enough to call her and ask, you know? I didn't think we were, well, *there* yet."

"I understand. But at least now, we have a way to try and fix it."

Scott looked skeptical, "I don't know. I don't think she'll talk to me if I call her."

"No, I think it would be best if someone went to speak with her in person. Maybe I'll go myself. I think Joni is having a rough time right now and I don't think we should be putting any more weight on her shoulders."

Scott smiled. "Thanks, Pastor. I hope I haven't ruined it with Brandy."

Pastor Ward rubbed his chin. "I hope to help in any way I can."

Scott knew the older man wasn't only talking about him.

Chapter 17

Kate was worried about her friend. More worried than she had been before. Emma's fifteenth birthday had come and gone and the day had been very hard on everyone. Joni was thinner and her hair had lost its shine. Kate could hardly remember what her laugh had sounded like, but she *did* remember that it was lovely. They sat together at Line Dried Laundry. Kate took time to spend with Joni while Marty took care of the store. The place wasn't busy anyway. It was early, and she had just opened. The only other person there was a young woman. She was sitting a few tables away.

Kate tried to think of safe, happy topics as she chatted with Joni. This wasn't easy. Nearly everything reminded Joni of Emma. Their lives were wrapped up in their children and now Joni's was falling apart because her child was gone. Kate secretly wondered if Joni had given up hope that she would ever see Emma again, but didn't spend a lot of time analyzing the theory. The possibility was too hideous to think about. Kate didn't even consider telling Joni about how she had recently mistaken a young woman for Emma. It would do nothing but cause Joni pain. Instead, Kate talked about some plans she had for the store. She was thinking of having a sunflower theme this coming fall.

Joni and Kate had not noticed the young girl's phone ringing, but they couldn't help overhearing her side of the conversation. She was obviously talking to her sweetheart who was obviously far away. They didn't mean to eavesdrop on her, but Kate watched Joni turn pale when the words the young woman spoke became eerily fitting.

"I miss you so much." The girl said, her face betraying the fear she was trying to keep out of her voice. "You're just so far away, and I don't know what's happening to you or if you're safe. I'm thinking of you all the time."

Her sweetheart, who Joni and Kate inferred was overseas, must have been speaking while the girl listened.

"I know," she continued, as she traced the rim of her teacup with her finger, "me too. The other day I was walking to class and this was guy getting into his truck and I thought it was you. I mean I know that's not possible, but it was just for a second. It made me miss you so much."

Now Kate was doubly glad that she hadn't told Joni about the girl she had seen. But the young girl, who had no idea that she was causing Joni pain, continued.

"It's like that old lullaby, you know, it talks about having a dream that you're together, but you wake up and it's not true so it's even worse than before. You know what I mean?"

Joni began to gasp for air. Kate knew exactly which song the girl meant and that Joni did to. Mentioning the song had made it ten times worse. Joni and Kate had both sung the song to their children when they were babies.

"I have to get out of here." Joni choked. She stood and stumbled blindly out the door without looking back. Kate tried to stop her, but she shook her off and ran for her car. The young woman was smiling now as her sweetheart's comforting voice reassured her.

* * *

The Valley Without Her

Joni got in her car and jammed the keys into the ignition. She screeched out of her parking space and drove. It didn't matter where she was going, she just had to get away. For a second, she considered visiting her father, but she was too upset and it would only agitate him so she just continued to drive aimlessly until she ran a red light and almost got hit by a car coming from the other direction.

She needed to calm down so that she or someone else didn't get hurt. Joni pulled into a nearby parking lot and slowed her breathing while she tried to get her hands to stop shaking. *Why did she have to hear those things? Why did she have to have these cruel dreams about Emma that gave her hope, only to have her hope snatched away?*

Joni knew she should pray. She didn't feel like praying, but maybe she should try. She concentrated again on breathing. Slowly her heart rate returned to normal and she could begin to think clearly again.

Joni began to form a prayer, but then she looked up and realized where she was. The sign on a building she had never entered, greeted her with sickening cheeriness.

"The Mollick Center."

Joni felt like someone had kicked her in the stomach.

"NNNOOOOOO!" She wailed. Any composure she had gained in the past few seconds was blown to bits and Joni put her car in drive and sped out of the parking lot, even more reckless than she had been before. She knew she was behaving dangerously, but she didn't care.

* * *

Pastor Ward looked up when Kate walked into his office. She didn't have an appointment and it wasn't like Kate to barge in unannounced, so he knew it must be something important. She didn't even knock, she just walked in and sat in one of his guest chairs.

"I'm really worried about Joni," she said without preamble.

"What is it? What's happened now?" he asked.

"Well, nothing new, really; she just seems to be, I don't know, *crumbling*."

Pastor Ward set aside this week's sermon notes. "Tell me what's going on," he said.

* * *

Joni needed to get her mind off of what had happened today. First there was the young woman talking about dreams, and then she stumbled upon that wretched Mollick place. She came home and set up her canning things. Irene Holland had given her lots of fresh produce from her garden, and Joni thought that maybe if she got busy putting it up, it would serve as a distraction.

* * *

Kate told the pastor about what had happened earlier that morning, how she and Joni had heard a young woman and the things she had said, mentioning the lullaby that Joni had always sung to Emma. She told him about how the words had upset Joni with their painful significance. Kate wanted to go and talk with her friend, but she wanted to talk with the pastor first. She had waited until a time when things weren't busy, and left the shop to her assistant and came to see him. She was hoping he would have some words of wisdom for her.

* * *

The Valley Without Her

Joni had always found the sound of cans sealing to be extremely rewarding. The soft little popping noise meant that the canning process had been a success, and that in the months to come she and her family would be enjoying the fruits of her labor. She sat in the quiet kitchen listening to the sound. It reminded her of something. From somewhere deep inside her came the memory. The sound she was hearing now was similar to the sound made when she used to kiss baby Emma. She would hold her baby girl close to her face, and Emma would grace her with one of her slobbery, sweet, open-mouthed, baby kisses. The tiny echo of Joni's kiss against Emma's mouth sounded just like the soft clicking noise the jars of peaches and green beans were making now.

Joni felt despair like poison, spreading through her body. *Why does absolutely everything have to remind me of her? What did I do to be punished like this? Has God abandoned me so completely that He would allow me to suffer this slow torture every day?*

Joni picked up one of the pint-sized jars from the counter. It sealed in her hand. *Click.*

She gripped the jar as if to crush it. Just as she had done all those months ago with Tesla's tennis ball, Joni brought her hand back and threw the jar as hard as she could. It smashed against the wall and shattered, sending peaches and broken glass flying. A small part of her mind was thankful that she had put Tesla in the backyard before she began her project. He wouldn't be cutting himself on the shards while trying to lick up the peaches.

Joni crumpled to the floor and pulled on her hair. She just lay there in a ball, and she cried out as if she were in physical pain. She hadn't heard herself make a sound like that since...since Emma was born. *Why?* She thought. *Why, why, WHY? Does everything come back to her? If only there were some escape... escape...escape.*

* * *

"I don't know, Pastor Ward, for some reason it was just... different this time. I can't explain it."

Pastor Ward could tell that Kate was frustrated. She felt as if she should be with her friend right now, but had wanted to seek some guidance first.

"Joni's in a lot of pain," Pastor Ward told her. "You know that. Pain makes people do things they wouldn't normally do." He turned his chair to face his bookshelf. "Now where is that C.S. Lewis book? Well, it's several books in one, actually. Have you ever read *The Problem of Pain?*" He asked her. "Now what did I do with it?" He rubbed his chin, thinking. "Oh, yes! I lent it to Scott Fischer some months ago. I'll have to find my old one."

* * *

Joni pushed and pulled herself up off of the floor. She stumbled and half-crawled her way to the bathroom. She closed the door and sat on the floor, leaning against the bathtub.

* * *

Julie Burish had something to say to Joni. She had put it off for a long time and today was the day. She sat parked outside of Joni's house, taking deep breaths. She set her chin, got out of her car, made her way to Joni's door, and knocked. There was no answer so she went around to the side door, and then the kitchen. Julie could see through the glass door that Joni had been canning. Something was wrong. Julie opened the door and went inside. "Joni?"

The Valley Without Her

Julie felt something crunch and squish under her sneakers. There was a broken jar of peaches all over the floor and against the wall. Now she was concerned. She made her way down the hall. "Joni?" she called again. "It's Julie! Are you okay?" She didn't even know if Joni could hear her.

* * *

Joni could hear Julie Burish, of all people, calling to her from somewhere in the house. She was coming closer and calling her name. Joni didn't feel like talking to anyone. Julie was asking her if she was okay. *Of course I'm not okay. How could I be okay?* "Leave me alone!" Joni shouted. "Go away! I don't want to see anyone!"

* * *

Joni could hear Julie outside the bathroom door. For a moment, she thought Julie was going to force her way in and start giving orders, but then Joni heard Julie's footsteps grow quieter as she walked away.

* * *

Pastor Ward had used his compilation copy of the C.S. Lewis classics so often that it was falling apart. The last time he had used this particular copy was when he was away at a conference. While he was there, he came across a new copy and bought it. He didn't get rid of his old beat-up book; instead he put it on his bookshelf and forgot about it until today.

"I lent my newer copy of this book to young Fischer months ago, and he still hasn't returned it." Pastor Ward held up the old book for Kate to see. "I'll have to speak to him about it." He began to thumb through the book as he spoke. "The part I wanted to read to you—" A page of the tattered book fluttered out and landed in his lap. "Whoops!" He picked up the page. "This is why I bought a new copy. This one is, it's..." Ward stared at the paper in his hand. It was not a page out of a book.

* * *

Joni stared at the pills in her hand. She hadn't taken any of the antidepressants that Dr. Tobie Evans had prescribed to her all those months ago. There were thirty or so pills in the little amber-colored bottle. Tobie had told her to take the pills as needed. Maybe she needed them now.

* * *

Ward felt his hands begin to shake as he stared at the little piece of paper. Slowly he began to understand what he was seeing. The last time he had used this book, he had been away from home at a conference. While he was there, he had purchased a new copy of the book before he had even opened his old copy. The piece of paper that had fallen out of the book was not a part of the book at all, but a note from Mollie Brown. She had left it in his old book, thinking he would surely find it, but he had never opened it again. Until now. Pastor Ward covered his mouth with his hand and read the words she had written for him.

"*My beloved, I know we have to be apart for this short while, but you'll see me again soon, and I'll be waiting here with a kiss for you when you come home. All my love, Mollie.*"

* * *

What did it matter? Joni thought. *There's nothing left for me. I've lost Emma and because I've lost Emma, I've lost Greg, too.*

The Valley Without Her

I suppose people would be upset for a while, but they'd move on...I just don't think I can do this anymore.

* * *

Kate watched as her pastor's face turned ashen. He was staring at the piece of paper that had fallen out of the book he was holding and now his eyes were full of tears and the expression on his face was peculiar. He was beginning to frighten her.

"Pastor Ward? Are you feeling all right?"

* * *

Ward knew that Kate was talking to him, but he couldn't focus on what she was saying. He was holding in his hands his last love note from his Mollie Brown, and while she had written it years ago, it had meaning for him today. It was an echo of her last words for him. *"Tell Glenward I'll see him at home."* He would see Mollie again someday. She was waiting for him in paradise.

Out of habit, or perhaps because he was hungry for more of her, Ward turned the note over to see if Mollie had written anything on the other side. There was something there, but it was not one of Mollie's love notes to him. It was something she had most likely written as a reminder to herself.

"Oh, no!"

* * *

"Pastor Ward!" Kate was getting more and more concerned as the seconds ticked by. He still wasn't answering her. "Glenward!"

* * *

Amie M. Johnson

Call Joni. Just two words. That was all that Mollie Brown had written on the other side of her note to him. He was startled when he heard Kate shout his full name. He was fairly certain she had never addressed him thus, and it had finally gotten his attention. He looked at her. "We have to call Joni. Now."

Chapter 18

Kate was confused. Although he was finally, *finally* answering her, he was still behaving oddly so her apprehension decreased very little. She watched him pick up the phone and dial Joni's number. As he did, he tried to explain what had just happened. Kate's jaw dropped; and as the understanding of Mollie Brown's note dawned on her, so did an icy cold dread. They waited for Joni to pick up the phone.

* * *

Joni still sat on the floor with the pills in her hand, but by this time she had also taken the cup that always sat on the bathroom sink and filled it with water. *It would be so easy,* said the voice in her head. *In no time at all, all the pain could just vanish.*

She held the hand with the pills up to her mouth when the phone rang. It sounded loud, nearby. That's right; she had put it in her pocket before she started canning in case someone called her while she was working. Now she wished she had taken it out of her pocket before she came in here. Of course, she hadn't known that she'd end up on the bathroom floor, contemplating ending her own life. Suddenly she was stricken by the thought of what she had been about to do. She took the phone in her hand.

* * *

"Joni!" Pastor Ward shouted with relief. Joni must have answered. Kate felt like a spring that had been wound too tightly. She listened to Pastor Ward's side of the conversation as he spoke for a few moments with Joni. His tone and his words told Kate what was happening on the other end of the line, and suddenly the sickening fear she had been feeling was replaced with white-hot anger. She almost felt fevered.

"Stay on the line with her until I get there." And Kate was gone.

* * *

Pastor Ward sounded shaken. That was to be expected, she supposed, of a pastor calling one of his trusted church members to find her pondering suicide. He had seemed flustered right away though, before she had confessed what she had been up to. She didn't have the strength to try to figure it out. She merely listened as he alternately quoted encouraging Scriptures and prayed for her.

She listened meekly without interruption until-

BOOM!

Joni jumped a foot in the air, dropping the bottle of pills she had returned to the bottle and spilling the cup of water when Kate kicked in her bathroom door.

"Pastor, I should go. Kate's here." Joni spoke as if they had been chatting about the weather, but she now needed to end their conversation for a little girl in a uniform who had shown up to sell cookies.

Kate was so angry she could hardly form the words. "How... *dare*...you!" she seethed.

Joni sighed. "Kate..."

The Valley Without Her

"Don't you "*Kate*" me!"

Kate grabbed the bottle from the floor, opened it, dumped its contents in the toilet, and pushed the handle.

"You're not supposed to flush them like that." Joni said flatly.

Kate looked like she might breathe fire. "You're not supposed to swallow the whole bottle at once, either! What on earth are you thinking? How could you be so selfish? How could you be so *stupid?*"

Now Joni was angry as well. "Do you have any idea the kind of day I've had?" Her voice rose in volume as she spoke.

"Some." Kate shot back. "I was there this morning remember?" She didn't sound very sympathetic.

Joni sat up straighter. "Well, after I left you I went for a drive. I didn't know where I was going; I was just wandering around trying to calm down and, oh yeah, I was almost in an accident because I ran a red light, and then when I pulled over to get a hold of myself do you know where I realized I was?"

"No." Kate said coldly. "Where?"

"The Mollick Center." Joni spat the name as if it tasted bitter in her mouth.

Kate gasped. Her rigid body went slack. "You're lying," she whispered.

Joni was aghast. "When in this miserable lifetime have I ever lied to you?"

Kate was silent for a moment. Of course it was true. Joni had never lied to Kate. And the old Joni never would have called life "miserable."

"I'm sorry," Kate said softly. "That must've been awful for you."

"You think?" Joni said sarcastically. "You don't know what I'm going through. You don't know what it feels like to be me every day."

Kate began to get angry again. "Now wait a minute. Are you telling me that if it had been...if it had been my daughter instead of yours that this would be a cakewalk for you?"

It had not gotten by Joni that Kate couldn't bring herself to actually say Claire's name in the context of this "what if." She let it slide. "No, but it's not the same…"

"Of course it's not the same. But I love her too; *we all* love her too, and we want Emma to come home. And she still could, you know. What if Emma came home and you weren't here because you gave up on her?" Kate paused. She spoke more softly now. "I know that I don't know what it's like, Joni. But I *almost* do."

She crouched down and looked Joni in the face, holding Joni's hands between her own. "Don't you love my daughter as if she were your own?"

Joni could only nod.

"Then you should be able to put yourself in my shoes. In everyone's shoes. You aren't the only one who misses Emma," She waved her hand at Joni to preempt the interruption she knew was coming, "and of course you miss her more, we all know that...but you don't have the right to make us miss *you,* too." She looked at her friend. "What about Greg? If something happened to you it would kill him."

The Valley Without Her

Kate suspected that Joni doubted this, but she knew it was true. Greg was not doing well since Emma's disappearance, but if something happened to Joni, it would finish him off.

"Won't he be home soon?" Kate asked "Let's go make Greg some dinner. If you want, I'll call Alan and the kids and they can bring something over and we can all eat together."

"That sounds nice," Joni said. She was surprised how appealing the idea of company was. Not long ago she had ordered Julie Burish out of her house because she had wanted to be left alone. Joni gasped and put her hand to her mouth. *I was so rude to her,* she thought. As if she needed another thing to be ashamed about.

"What? What's the matter?" Kate asked.

Joni told Kate about her meltdown in the kitchen, how she had thrown a jar up against the wall, and how Julie had come over (Joni still didn't know why), but that she had yelled at her to leave.

"It'll be all right," Kate told her as they got off the bathroom floor. Kate gave Joni a long hug before they started down the hall. "We'll clean it up and tomorrow you can give Julie a call, I'm sure she'll—"

Kate stopped in the doorway of the kitchen. She turned to look at Joni.

"I thought you said you broke a jar," she said, confused.

"I did," Joni told her. She stepped around Kate to show her the mess. "It's right th—"

The smashed mess of glass and peaches was gone. Julie must have cleaned it up.

* * *

"I feel really dumb." Brandy told them. Kate gave Joni a look that only Joni noticed. They sat in the kitchen at Kate's house while the little kids played in the backyard and the older ones watched a movie.

"Believe me, you don't win first prize in the Stupid-Things-People-Have-Done-Lately contest." She ignored Joni's narrowed eyes. Although she was for the most part truly compassionate about the whole thing, Kate still got angry when she thought about what Joni had been about to do. "Besides," she continued, "you're not the only one who thought that Scott and Macy were a couple instead of brother and sister."

Brandy looked slightly comforted by this news. "Really?"

Joni and Kate exchanged a smile. "Pastor Josh thought so, too." Joni told her. "Apparently he was quite taken with Scott's little sister and when he found out that she *was* his sister and not his girlfriend, he asked Macy out."

"Yep," Kate confirmed. "They were at the shop having dessert the other day. That boy is over the moon for Miss Macy," she laughed.

Brandy smiled, but then sighed. She traced a pattern with her finger on the tabletop, avoiding their eyes. "It's not like I thought we were together, or he had any obligation to me or anything. It's just that I thought that he liked me and I thought maybe it would be different this time and then...well, you know."

"I can see how you felt that way, but that's what happens when you shut everyone out. That's what a church family is for, to get you through tough times and to help you sort things out when you're confused." Kate told her.

"Yeah, that's what Pastor Ward said when he showed up on my doorstep. He figured it out and came to set me straight."

"And, for the record, I *do* think that Scott likes you. A lot of other people think so, too." Joni added.

"I don't know. I think I may have messed this up, too."

Kate and Joni let it go. They knew it was going to take some time for Brandy to really start believing in herself. She had already made miles of progress; she no longer depended so heavily on Brayle and was doing much better at controlling her temper, but she still struggled with past wounds. Her new friends knew that only God would be able to give Brandy the peace she longed for.

* * *

A few weeks later, Joni got a phone call from Brandy. Scott Fischer had called her up to ask her if she would go out to lunch with him.

"I said, yes." Brandy's voice sounded nervous. "Is that okay?"

"Well, of course it is, why wouldn't it be?" Joni asked her.

"Well...I don't know...I always picked the wrong men before so I doubt my decisions."

Joni could tell that Brandy was not proud of her past, and that she was afraid that Joni was going to judge her.

"We all make mistakes. And, you know, maybe Scott isn't the person God has in mind for you, but it's okay to just take it slow and get to know him. Going out to lunch with him isn't a lifetime commitment. Wait and see how it goes, and if you two decide to keep seeing each other, just make sure you make wise decisions along the way."

* * *

Brandy and Scott *did* keep seeing each other, and while they behaved only as two good friends would, it was obvious to them and to everyone around them that they liked each other. A lot.

When Brandy talked with Kate and Joni about her budding relationship with Scott, she joked that he sometimes ignored her for her younger kids. Brayle knew that her mother and Scott had feelings for each other and Brayce may have had some idea, but the twins thought that their mother had simply picked out a really fun guy for the two of them to hang around with. Brandy loved it that her kids liked Scott, and didn't really mind at all when they got the lion's share of his attention.

One night Scott took Brandy and her kids to Kate's for dessert. Claire was there, too, and while the girls chatted at their own little table and Brayce finished everyone's cheesecake, Brandy watched as Scott talked to the twins about their artwork. Alan and James had decided to stay home for some quality "guy time"—which meant there was a game on TV that they wanted to watch. Scott and the twins shared a little artistic common ground, him being something of a photographer, and the kids loved it when he gave them advice. "See, the blue should touch the green," he told them. "Look out the window." They did. "See how the sky looks like it comes all the way down to the ground?"

The two looked from the window to their drawings. It clicked. In typical little-kid fashion, they had been leaving a big white space in the middle of their drawings because, of course, the ground was below them and the sky was above them. Now that Scott pointed it out, they happily set about coloring in their horizons. Scott agreed with everyone else that the twins were very talented.

The Valley Without Her

"You know, you two should help me take pictures sometime. The apple festival is coming up and I was there last year and... and I..."

At the mention of the apple festival, Brandy, Brayle, and Claire all froze. Claire stared down at her hands and bit her lip. Brayle and her mother avoided one another's eyes. Neither had forgotten the awful events of that day, including Brandy yelling at her daughter.

But Scott wasn't looking at them. He smacked himself on the forehead. "I've got to go!" he said loudly. Everyone had been lost in their own thoughts, but suddenly all eyes were on Scott.

He jumped up out of his chair, knocking it over. He picked it up, knocked it over a second time and picked it up again.

"What's wrong?" Brandy wanted to know.

"I have to go," he said again as he dug some money out of his wallet and threw it at the table. He made brief, but sincere, eye contact with Brandy. "I'll call you," he said, and he dashed out the door.

Chapter 19

It was a dreary fall day. It wasn't exactly raining, but it wasn't *not* raining either. It was almost like the sky was spritzing Gardenville with one of those little spray bottles used for watering ferns. Joni did not enjoy being spritzed like a fern, but Tesla didn't mind one bit and came to Joni with pitiful puppy dog eyes and his leash in his mouth. Joni didn't like to think about it, but she suspected that Tesla insisted on these walks, at least in part, because he thought they were looking for Emma. She sighed and grabbed her raincoat. When she hooked his leash to his collar, his attitude changed immediately to wiggly-dog glee. He wagged his Tesla coil happily.

Twenty minutes later Joni and Tesla returned their soggy selves home where, upon entering, Tesla, predictably, shook fern spritz all over the kitchen floor. Joni scolded him and was about to find an old towel to clean up the wet when the phone rang.

"Hello?" She hoped she didn't sound as impatient as she felt.

"Mrs. Leonard?" A man's voice asked kindly.

"Yes?"

"This is Walter Horn...I'm sorry to have to tell you..."

Joni didn't need to hear any more. Walter Horn was the director of the facility where her father lived. Mr. Horn had never called her at home before. Even though she had known it was coming, had known for months and months, she still couldn't believe her father was gone.

* * *

Detective Doug Palmer was afraid to hope that he had been handed some good news. Out of the blue, he had received a phone call from a man named Scott Fischer. Fischer apologetically explained that he had attended the infamous apple festival a year ago and had taken pictures of the event. The man was clearly ashamed that it had taken him this long to draw the conclusion that his pictures may be of use. As soon as he had remembered the pictures, he called his pastor who gave him Palmer's phone number. Palmer gave Fischer his email and waited.

* * *

Less than an hour later, Palmer felt like a kid on Christmas morning. He carefully studied Fischer's photos one by one. Palmer was a little miffed at the guy for waiting so long to realize he had something useful to the case, but mostly he was grateful for the possible lead. He was determined not to turn away from them empty-handed. So far, though, he had found nothing of use. They were very good, as photos go, but of no purpose to his case. There was one in particular of the sun setting behind a gorgeous apple tree that Palmer would have liked to hang on his wall, if he were the type of man who hung things on walls. He wasn't though. He was the type of man who found missing people. Undaunted by the first fifteen unusable images he kept going, spending at least two minutes on each one. He brought up the sixteenth picture and began his examination. This one was a busy street scene. Lots of people, lots of action. Something in the background caught his eye. He zoomed in on it. Paydirt.

* * *

"Hello?"

"I'm sending you an email and I need you to look at it. Right now."

Josh found the voice vaguely familiar, but couldn't place it.

"Who is this?" he asked, bewildered.

"Detective Palmer. Are you checking your email?"

Josh blinked. *The detective was calling him. That must mean he's found something!* "Um, no. I mean, I will. I'm on my way home." Josh had taken Macy out for dinner. He had had a terrific time, and would usually have spent the drive home reliving the evening, but the call from the detective pushed everything from his mind except Emma. It was no small thing that could get Josh to stop thinking of Macy, and he hoped that whatever it was that Palmer had for him would point them to where she was. He was glad that he had given his email address and cell number to the man all those months ago. Josh's throat closed when he realized it was very near a year that Emma had been gone. These thoughts zipped through his mind in a matter of seconds, and he listened to Detective Palmer's instructions.

"I just want you to look at the picture and tell me what you see. Tell me if anything jumps out at you. I don't want to influence you, so I'm not going to tell you what to look for, only that you need to look closely, understand?"

"Got it," Josh answered. "I'll be home in five minutes."

"I'll be waiting," Detective Palmer said and he hung up.

When Josh got home three minutes later, he bolted through the door and flung himself into his computer chair without taking off his coat.

The Valley Without Her

He pulled up his email, located the one from Palmer and downloaded the image. It was just a picture of the apple festival. Main Street. Lots of people milled around. He recognized the mayor who seemed to be buying a candy apple for his granddaughter.

Surely that couldn't be what Palmer wanted him to find. He kept looking.

There. In the background of the picture, down one of the side streets, was a woman with unnaturally blonde hair throwing an old quilt into the trunk of a car. He recognized the quilt and he recognized the woman.

Josh's hands shook as he pulled up the email again and found the phone number that Palmer had included. The older man picked up on the first ring.

"Well?" Palmer demanded without saying hello.

"That's the woman," Josh panted. "That's the woman who yelled at Emma at the fundraiser."

* * *

Joni and Jennifer sat at Joni's kitchen table. It had been over two years since Joni had seen her sister and now that the funeral and all its related activities were over with, the two had time to talk.

Jennifer hadn't changed much. She still had ridiculously long, thick hair. It was much less red than Joni's, but there was a whisper of auburn in the blonde. Joni had always thought that Jennifer was the beauty of the family with her long lashes and cute little nose, but Jen had always insisted the same thing about her.

"I'm so ashamed, Joni." Jennifer confided. "I should have come home months ago."

"Well, that wouldn't have changed anything," Joni soothed, "Dad would still be gone. I don't think he really knew the difference anyway. When I saw him last week, he didn't know who I was. He hadn't for a really long time."

"Well," Jennifer gulped. "It's not just that. I should have come when you told me..."

Joni felt her world go dark. They hadn't talked about Emma yet. She knew it was unavoidable, but she also knew that it was going to burn like fire when the subject finally came up.

"I think about her all the time. I pray every day." She looked away. Jen had always hated to cry in front of people. Even Joni.

"I'm such a coward. I just didn't think I could stand it, you know? Being here and not seeing my little peanut Emma-nem." This had always been Jennifer's nickname for her favorite, and only, niece. "I mean, being in London...I don't know...the distance made it easier to deal with. Less real." She hung her head. "You must think I'm a terrible person," she whispered.

"No," Joni told her. "We all deal with it differently. It would have been nice to have you here, but I understand."

"What about Greg?" Jennifer asked. "He seems so, I don't know, *removed* that I don't think he even knows I'm here."

"I'm not sure he knows *I'm* here," Joni said flatly.

Jennifer looked at her for a moment. "How are you doing? Really."

Joni sighed. The time had come. She was going to have to tell her sister what she had been about to do and why. She got the worst of it out first, starting in the middle of the story with Kate kicking in her bathroom door like a swat team. Jennifer was, of course, hurt and enraged and needed a few minutes to calm down after giving Joni a piece of her mind.

Joni waited patiently and meekly without interruption until Jennifer was ready, and then began to fill in the holes of what had happened that day. Jen held her hand while Joni began by telling her about hearing the young woman mention Emma's lullaby, and how she had left in a panic.

Memories came flooding back as she told her sister that she had stumbled upon the Mollick Center. As Kate had, Jennifer knew exactly what contempt Joni held for that place. Although it had been over a decade ago Joni remembered it like it was yesterday.

* * *

Greg and Joni had been trying for years to have a child. When, at last, they discovered that Joni was pregnant they were beside themselves with excitement. Joni pored over baby name books and Greg researched home safety and child-proofing. They started eating healthier, taking walks in the evenings and went faithfully to each check-up. The Leonards looked forward to the day when they had their first ultrasound appointment, and they would hopefully get to hear their baby's heartbeat.

The day came and Joni gasped when, for the first time, they heard the amplified flutter of their baby's miraculous little heart. It was impossibly fast and the most beautiful sound she had ever heard.

The technician smiled politely and told them they would have the results soon. Joni was only half listening. She wanted to go on hearing the heartbeat forever. It was after the second ultrasound that it happened.

They knew something was wrong when, the next week after their appointment, Joni's doctor called and asked them to come in to meet with him in his office. Dr. Ash showed them prints of their baby's ultrasound, which they couldn't tell from an inkblot, and gravely explained that in all likelihood, their baby would be physically or mentally handicapped. Possibly both. He waited for them to compose themselves after this difficult news and then with the perfect balance of professional authority and cool empathy, handed them a business card. Joni took it from him mutely.

"This is for the Mollick Center. It's nearby and they can handle things for you. If you'd like I can have my staff call them. I can make you a referral."

Joni felt like her bones had turned to steel. She clenched her teeth until her jaw hurt. Joni nodded at the man sitting across from her keeping her voice even. "Yes. I think you'd better."

Out of the corner of her eye, she saw Greg swivel his head to look at her. He was thunderstruck that she had agreed to this man's offer for a referral to this place.

"Very well," Dr. Ash continued, "We'll have them make you an appointment and then…"

"No." Joni's voice was dangerously soft. "I meant you can make me a referral to a different doctor." She got to her feet and beside her, Greg did the same. She was aware of his relief, but right now she was too angry to appreciate it.

"On second thought," Joni looked down her nose at the doctor, his jaw hanging open, "I don't think I really trust your judgment. I'll just find another doctor on my own." She threw the business card down on the desk and stalked out of the room, still reeling from the double punch she had just taken. Greg gave the man behind the desk a look of contempt and followed his wife out of the building.

Later that year Emma Katherine Leonard was born to her parents, healthy and beautiful. There was a slight problem with Emma's left hip and she would always walk with a faint limp. Other than that she was exquisitely perfect: all dimples and sweetness and cuddly soft, with hair as downy and touchable as a baby chick. There had been complications with the pregnancy, though. After a difficult labor and an emergency C-section, Joni was told that she would not be able to have any more children. They were lucky to have Emma. After that, Joni always said that Emma was a miracle.

Every once in a while Joni would run into Mr. Ash (after that day she never again gave him the honor of the title of "doctor," even in her mind). She went out of her way to show him her beautiful, and obviously intelligent, baby. Joni always introduced Emma to him, enumerating her many charms and accomplishments. Ash would smile politely and walk away meekly after Joni was through talking with him. On one occasion the man had the grace to turn red-faced when the adorable baby Emma blew him a kiss. Joni assured friends and family that she had forgiven the man, but she still refused to respect him and hoped that seeing Emma would cause him to think twice before jumping to conclusions concerning other babies.

* * *

Jennifer already knew all of this when Joni told her that she had unintentionally visited Mollick's parking lot. She understood why just seeing the place would be painful for her sister.

"It's almost like someone has always wanted to take Emma from me." Joni whispered. "Before she was even born, there was that imbecile Ash and now...and now..." Joni couldn't finish. She shuddered a sigh. "Oh, Jen, I miss my baby girl."

Jennifer didn't know what to say. She wrapped her arms around Joni. She wrapped her prayers around her, too.

Chapter 20

Joni and Julie had not been avoiding each other. On the contrary, they had each wanted to speak with the other, but it simply hadn't happened. Julie had attended Joni's father's funeral with her family, but knew that it wasn't the time or the place to say what she wanted to say. Joni had tried calling Julie, but could never get a hold of her.

Finally one Sunday night after church, Joni decided enough was enough and walked up to Julie after the meeting was concluded.

Joni took Julie's elbow gently. "Julie, could I talk with you for a minute?"

Julie nodded. "I have something I'd like to say to you, too," She said quietly.

As one, they turned and entered one of the vacant Sunday school rooms. Joni went first.

"I just wanted to tell you how sorry I am for how I spoke to you that day you came to my house." She looked at her hands. "I was having a very," she took a deep breath, "very difficult day, and I snapped at you. I shouldn't have done that."

"I can understand that," Julie said gently. "I imagine you have a lot of difficult days."

"And then you cleaned up that mess in my kitchen." Joni looked at her. "You didn't have to do that."

"Yes, I did," Julie said humbly. "Could you hold on a moment, please?"

Julie got up and left the room. Joni was very confused. She almost wondered if the conversation was over, but Julie had indicated that she was coming back. Sure enough, here she was. However, this time she wasn't alone. She had brought Kate, Sherry, and Ruth along with her, all looking as confused as Joni felt.

"I owe all of you an apology," Julie said, looking to her own feet. "I have been rude and prideful." She looked at Ruth. "What you said all those months ago upset me," she held up her hand and raised her voice to keep Ruth from interrupting with an apology of her own, "because it was true." She looked at her shoes again. "I deserved it. When we got to the car, I started to complain and even snapped at my husband. He waited until we got home, told the kids to go to their rooms, and he told me that he agreed with what Ruth said." Julie's voice was trembling. "At first I was furious with him, but I knew he was right. I've been unkind to you and other people at Hillside, and I've been disrespectful to him. I still mess up, I mean, it's taken me *this long* to apologize, but I'm trying to do better and I'd like it if you all would forgive me." She took a deep breath and kept going. "I guess I owe Brandy an apology, too, but she didn't hear the awful things I said, and I don't want her to know, so I'll say I'm sorry to you instead."

For a moment no one moved, and then as one, all four women moved and put their arms around Julie. No more needed to be said.

***

Palmer couldn't believe his luck. He supposed that kid preacher would tell him it wasn't luck at all. Before they had hung up Pastor Josh had given God the credit for this new lead. He hadn't known what to say, but he sure was thankful that the picture Fischer took of the bleached blonde woman included her car *and* license plate. The detective wasted no time using this new information to find out who this woman was and where she lived. He began to make the preparations to pay her a visit.

* * *

Melody had had a rough day at school. Dena Roberts had again acted as if she wanted to talk to her, and again evaporated when Lindsay appeared. Melody wasn't exactly happy to see Lindsay, but at least she had some idea what to expect from her. She was afraid that Dena wanted to pick up where Lindsay left off and begin torturing her and her friends.

Melody was very glad when the final bell rang and it was time to go home. She came in to find Charlotte waiting for her at the kitchen table. While this wasn't unusual, nearly everything else about her little sister was. Melody stopped in the doorway, her backpack halfway to the floor when the look on her sister's face made Melody freeze midstep. Charlotte's eyes were wide and her face was pale under her blonde curls. She was sitting still with her hands in her lap. Charlotte wasn't doing any homework or reading *A Little Princess* for the forty-fifth time.

"What's the matter? What's wrong?" Melody demanded.

"Something happened at school today," Charlotte said, her voice soft and unsure.

Melody cautiously took the seat across from her sister. "Are you okay?"

"Uh-huh," Charlotte nodded. "It wasn't me."

"What wasn't you?" Melody asked.

It had been a long time since Melody had suffered a nightmare. Sometimes she had foggy, vague bad dreams, but nothing like the ones she used to have. Charlotte was sleeping in her own room again; and while she had liked her sister's company, she hoped that whatever had happened today, it wasn't going to trigger more insomnia for either one of them.

"Well...remember last year when that girl and her dad came to school to tell us about what to do if... if someone tried to, you know, take you?"

It was hard for Lottie to talk about what happened to Emma.

"I remember," Melody told her. Everyone knew that Emma was the reason for the school-wide assemblies and, although she thought it was a great idea to present them, it made Melody's heart ache when she thought about that day in the auditorium.

Charlotte took a deep breath and swallowed hard. "It happened today at recess. I was playing on the monkey bars with Chloe. Natalie usually plays with us, too, but she was absent today. I think she's sick. Well, then a car pulled up and stopped close to the playground where everyone was playing. There was a man."

Melody shivered.

"Davy Ballard—remember him? He's the one who accidentally put taco sauce on his hamburger instead of ketchup at lunch that time."

"Okay..." Melody prompted. This was the way Lottie told stories and Melody was trying to be patient. Sometimes, like now, it was hard to do.

"Well anyway, Davy was playing over there by himself and a car drove up and a man rolled down his window and started talking to him. Well, Davy just stood there and even went a little closer to the guy and the guy looked like he might get out of the car. He was trying to get Davy to go with him."

Melody gasped. "What happened?" Melody realized that her whole body was tense. She pressed her hands against her cheeks, bracing herself for what was coming.

"Landon saw what was going on. Remember Landon Nichols? He was the one who won the spelling bee last year. Well, he saw Davy talking to that creepy guy and ran over and grabbed him—Davy, I mean. The creepy guy was still in his car. Then Landon started screaming like that girl did when she came to school to show us what to do. You know, like, 'No! Call 911!' and stuff like that.

"Then the teachers saw, 'cause they heard Landon yelling, and they started yelling, too. One of them called the police, I think, and the guy drove off real fast anyway, 'cause Landon yelling made him leave. He knew he was going to get in trouble, I think."

"So he saved that other boy?" Melody asked through her fingers.

"Yeah. The principal—remember Mr. Barnes? Well, he came in and told Landon in front of the whole class that he was a hero. Landon got all embarrassed, but I think Mr. Barnes was right."

"Me, too," Melody agreed. She wiped her eyes. She wondered if, in some weird way, Emma's disappearance had kept another child from being taken. Melody shivered again.

"Hey, Lottie Lou, do you want to have a sleepover in my room tonight?" she asked her little sister. *Might as well be proactive*. Melody had a feeling that when they turned out their lights, they would both have trouble sleeping.

***

Detective Doug Palmer checked the address one last time to make sure. This was the place. The blonde woman, whose name he now knew was Tonya Hamilton, was the one who had cussed and yelled at Emma at the apple festival over the price of a quilt. He knocked on her door and waited. He heard the sound of a television being turned off and the door opened a crack. The woman from Fischer's photo peered at him with suspicious eyes through the tiny crack in the door.

Palmer showed the woman his badge and asked her if he could come in. This was just out of politeness. He had a warrant and told her so, but he wanted her to be cooperative.

Hamilton opened the door to let him in and immediately began babbling about her ex-boyfriend, Jimmy, and his many flaws and escapades. "He was into all kinds of stuff, that's why I kicked him out," she declared, puffing nervously on a cigarette. "I told him to shape up, 'cause I was tired of all the trouble, you know?"

As she complained, Hamilton edged her body inch by inch along one wall until she came to a stop in front of a closed door. She leaned against the door frame diagonally with her shoulder resting against the trim on one side, and her feet crossed at the ankles on the other. She was trying and failing to look casual. She looked very uncomfortable in that position. Hamilton continued her attempt to shift attention off of herself and on to her notorious ex while Palmer studied the room in a way that she wouldn't know he was doing it. So far there was nothing here

The Valley Without Her

that pointed toward Emma. When Hamilton took a breath, he took his chance.

"I'm going to need to see what's behind that door." He said, his voice calm.

As he suspected, she became more agitated. "Oh, that's just a bunch of junk; you don't want to see in there." She held her cigarette up to her mouth for a fortifying drag with one hand, while grasping the doorknob with the other.

"Ma'am," Palmer said firmly, "you're going to have to let me see what's in there."

She moved away from the door slowly, but still yammered. "Well, okay, but my boyfriend, I mean my *ex*-boyfriend, kept his stuff in there so—"

Palmer swung the door open and found a small bathroom. He saw what she hadn't wanted him to see. He hadn't wanted to see it either. It wasn't Emma. This woman had been growing, and most likely selling, marijuana. He turned to face her.

"It isn't mine," she declared, shaking her head.

Palmer sighed. Someone had obviously been taking care of these plants. There was no way her boyfriend could have had them without her knowing about it. They were even under a lamp. Besides, this was the only bathroom in the tiny apartment.

He hadn't been prepared for how disappointed he would be if this lead turned out to be a dead end. Somehow, Palmer knew instinctively that there was no point, but he took out of his pocket the flier with Emma's picture and information on it, and showed it to the frightened woman.

"Do you remember this girl? Have you seen her?"

Hamilton studied the flier for a moment and then blurted, "No, the redhead that buys from me is way older than that."

Palmer sighed again, and then he arrested her.

* * *

Miles and miles away from where Palmer stood, someone else held the very same flier. She had been putting groceries away when she noticed the piece of paper stuck in with the dry goods. Her hands shook as she studied the photo and the information, trying to decide what to do about it. There was no denying that Mother would recognize the girl in the picture, as she had, but there was no predicting what Mother would do. Sometimes everything was fine and then all of the sudden, out of nowhere, Mother would have one of her rages. She set the paper down on the tiny kitchen counter and stared at it. The face in the photo smiled up at her, and seemed to be demanding *"Do something! Help me!"* She had never felt more powerless.

* * *

"Lydia?" Mary Louise frowned when she watched Lydia jump as if she had been scalded. "Sorry, I didn't mean to startle you," she said quietly.

"Um, that's okay, Mother. What, um, what did you want?" Lydia's voice sounded funny. She didn't just sound startled; she sounded afraid. It annoyed her when her daughter acted like this, but it also made her feel guilty which annoyed her even more. She tried to get a handle on her emotions before they cycled themselves into a problem. Mary Louise took a calming breath and tried to cast off the irritation that had flared at the sight of Lydia's skittishness. "I just wanted to tell you to set the table after you put everything away."

Lydia nodded wordlessly, still looking unsettled. Again, Mary Louise pushed aside her vexation and turned to leave the room. Mary Louise could understand why Lydia could sometimes be jumpy, and she *did* feel bad about it, but couldn't her daughter see that she was trying? She didn't like to think about the times when she let her emotions get the better of her and she had one of her headaches and then one of her blackouts. When that happened, Mary Louise would lose time and suddenly it would be four hours later, and she would find Lydia, puffy-eyed and scared with an angry, red handprint on her cheek. Unlike years ago, when Lydia had been a little girl, that hardly ever happened anymore. When Lydia was little, it had happened all the time, but now Mary Louise really was trying.

Back in the kitchen with Mother gone again, she stared sadly at the flier. "I'm so sorry," she whispered.

* * *

Joni was glad when the apple festival was over. She, and a lot of other Hillsiders, had avoided it altogether. Palmer had arranged for there to be at least a dozen undercover agents attending the festival, in hopes that whoever had taken Emma would return and somehow catch their notice.

There was one man who had been behaving oddly, but when apprehended by a blonde female agent who looked like a college student, he was found to be guilty of nothing more than shoplifting. The agent alerted the local police and turned him over to them so she could continue her work on Emma's case. There was nothing to be found by her or anyone else. Even though Joni and Greg hadn't been expecting anything to come of it, they still couldn't help but be disappointed.

The two of them had mixed emotions when they heard about the little boy who had saved another child from being taken by a stranger. Of course, they were glad and relieved to hear that the man had been caught. While they shared everyone's opinion that Landon Nichols was a hero (Joni had even told Kate that she thought that Gardenville should throw the boy a parade), it reminded them that no one had been there for Emma. It reminded them that *they* hadn't been there when she needed them most.

Chapter 21

Christmas this year at least was a shade better than last year. Joni had been dreading the holiday. Emma's absence made everything ugly and off-balance and Christmas was especially painful. Joni didn't want to ignore the holiday completely, but she didn't have the heart to do all of the wonderful things she had always done with, and for, Emma. She pondered this problem one dreary evening as she drove home from work. *Should she try? Maybe just put up the tree? Forget the whole thing?* Her musings were crumbling into apathy as she opened the front door and was greeted by Tesla who, for a moment kept her attention away from the changes in her home. Her Christmas tree was up and decorated, complete with presents. She absently patted Tesla's head and looked around the room. Someone had strung garland around the doorways and even put the Christmas tablecloth and centerpiece on the table. As she stood drinking in the comforting surroundings, Joni wondered who had done all of this.

Kate. She suspected Sherry and probably Julie, too. As she stood there in thought she didn't notice Greg come in behind her.

"Well," he said softly, "that looks nice."

Joni jumped. "Oh!" She shook her head. "It wasn't me."

He frowned. "What wasn't you?"

"I didn't do all this," she swept her arm at the room, "I just got home and it was like this."

"Hmm. Well, that was nice of someone to come do this for you."

Joni could tell he was trying to say something nice to her. He didn't know what to do for her so he made these small attempts. She hugged him. "I'm glad they did it. I wasn't sure what to do about..." she sighed, "about the holiday."

Greg returned her hug. He said nothing else, but she understood.

***

Claire, Brayle, Melody and the others had gotten used to Lindsay's presence at youth group. Sort of. Things were still uncomfortable and awkward, but at least now they knew what to expect from her. Lindsay hadn't once made fun of, or insulted, any of them while attending youth meetings. In fact it had been several months since she had been overtly mean to any of them. She did, however, say unkind things about other people they all knew and tried to get the girls to go along with her. On one such occasion, Lindsay was making fun of a quiet sophomore named April. Lindsay was going on and on about April's clothes and hairstyle, and wondering sarcastically if April's family owned a television, so great was her lack of fashion sense. Lindsay had been happily bashing this girl whom she barely knew for several moments before she realized that no one was laughing at her jokes.

The other girls sat in stony silence. Claire was torn. They had all agreed that they had been wrong to shun Lindsay's overtures of friendship, but the way Lindsay was talking about April was wrong, too. *Should she say something? What would she do if one of her "real" friends was talking about April this way?* None of them would do that and Claire sat there feeling miserable.

Brayle, on the other hand, didn't have as much trouble deciding what to do. "April's nice." She declared bluntly. "I've never really paid attention to what she wears, but I think she's pretty." She sat up straight as she looked Lindsay in the eye. Everything from her tone of voice to her body language told Lindsay that she and her friends weren't going to be playing Lindsay's little gossip game. Brayle's boldness immediately gave the other girls more confidence.

Ashley tilted her head. "Yeah," she added, "she's really smart, too. She was in one of my classes once, and everyone always wanted to be her partner when we worked on stuff together."

"We all really like her," Mia concluded, her voice full of meaning. Each girl had been careful to keep her tone polite, but made sure she got her point across. Lindsay got their message.

Claire sighed with relief. She was glad her friends were brave and could think on their feet. She could just nod in agreement, and not have to confront Lindsay herself.

"Oh." Lindsay tossed her head "I didn't mean anything bad about her, I was just, you know, talking..." She was obviously not used to being challenged when stirring up trouble. The Hillside youth girls were turning out to be disappointing as lackeys. A few of them were wondering if Lindsay missed Dena and her gratuitous laugh, which was like the insincere canned laughter on a lowbrow sitcom.

On the other hand, they didn't want her to feel left out or unwelcome. Mia changed the subject. "Are you going coming to the Christmas program?" she asked her politely.

Lindsay was saved from having to answer when Pastor Josh called for their attention to start the lesson. The girls rose from their seats on the couches and armchairs and made their way over to the folding chairs, facing the small platform where Pastor Josh spoke. Lindsay chose a seat next to James who acknowledged her briefly with a cordial smile.

It had not escaped Claire's notice that Lindsay frequently sat next to James. She was often trying to get his attention and engage him in conversations. Lindsay laughed loudly at the smallest and, in Claire's opinion, stupidest of his jokes. Claire was used to girls being interested in her good-looking brother, but it had never really bothered her before. James usually didn't realize when a girl was trying to flirt with him. Even Lindsay's overacting seemed to be beyond his notice. Lindsay wasn't really used to being not noticed nor denied something she wanted, so in her bull-headed way, she redoubled her efforts, partly out of sheer stubbornness. James began to pay her small bits of attention.

* * *

While Claire was dismayed by Lindsay's chasing after James, she was positively ecstatic about Pastor Josh's relationship with Macy. Her friends were in agreement with her on both counts. The Hillside girls tolerated Lindsay and strove to find reasons to like her, but they all but fought over Macy Fischer.

Macy attended the meetings now as one of the youth sponsors. She was pretty and funny and kind. She had an uncanny gift for giving advice and encouraging teenaged girls. Macy added a big sister element to the youth group and most of the girls had gone to Macy for advice or encouragement at some point. She was patient and approachable and easier to talk to about some things than Pastor Josh was. What was more, Pastor Josh had obviously fallen hard for her, and it was endless fun to see him so lovesick. They were all thankful that Macy had come along and were hoping to see a ring on her finger very soon.

* * *

Excepting Lindsay, who didn't care, there was a friendly jealousy of Brayle amongst the Hillside teens. Everyone had worked out that if Pastor Josh married Macy and if Scott married Brandy, then Macy would be Brayle's aunt. While Brayle was excited to see Pastor Josh with Macy, seeing her mother with Scott was a different story. It wasn't that she didn't like Scott, she did, but with her mother and Scott there was more at stake. If Macy and Pastor Josh didn't end up together, everyone would be disappointed, to be sure, but if Scott and Brayle's mother broke up, it would crush her mother and her siblings. Even Brayce had hinted once or twice that maybe it would be nice if Scott could be his dad. Brayle had seen her mother hurt before and it was tough on all of them. This time, though, would be even worse because Scott was such a good guy and all of them, including Brayle, liked him so much. She waited and prayed and told no one about her fears—not her mother, not Macy, not Claire. In the past she might have considered telling Joni or maybe Kate about what she was feeling, but things were different now. She couldn't go to Joni because she knew that it would somehow, in some way hurt, and she didn't want to cause Joni any more sadness. If she went to Kate, Kate would have to know that she couldn't tell Joni and it would circle around to the same problem as before. It wasn't fair. Whoever had taken Emma had also taken away life as they knew it.

* * *

The months slipped by and Emma Leonard's family and friends continued to cope with her absence. While everyone that knew and cared about her had adapted to life without her, it was easy for no one. A Hillside member had been heard to describe it as learning to function after an amputation or living with a broken limb that had healed improperly. Many of them felt as if they were living in a strange and frightening alternate reality. Even the happiest of moments were dimmed by Emma's absence, but still, life continued.

* * *

Brayle felt more and more secure with the idea of Scott Fischer and her mother. Scott and Brandy saw each other nearly every day and had fallen into a predictable and comfortable routine. After work, Scott would take a quick detour to his apartment to wash the sawdust out of his hair before heading over to the Robinson's house for dinner. He helped with groceries since he ate with them so frequently and after dessert, Scott would help the kids with their homework while Brandy cleared everything away. They would all settle in the living room together for TV or maybe board games. Sometimes everyone just read quietly while the twins drew pictures. It was like a family, and Brandy wasn't the only one who felt Scott's absence when he went home every evening.

* * *

Scott's sister, Macy, still wasn't wearing a diamond and everyone was wondering why it hadn't happened yet. She and Josh were obviously in love with each other, but when anyone with enough boldness asked Josh what he was waiting for, he would tell them he was waiting for the right moment. The end of the school year was approaching and many people thought that maybe Pastor Josh was waiting for the busyness of graduation and the Timmy Awards to subside. Macy didn't seem to mind; it was everyone else who was getting impatient.

One budding romance that was not as well received, though everyone tried not to let it show, was between James and Lindsay. It was especially difficult for Claire when her brother realized that Lindsay existed, that she was pretty, and that she liked him. He wasn't exactly crazy about her, but he paid her enough exclusive attention that Lindsay claimed the right to call him her boyfriend. Claire didn't tell her brother what she thought of Lindsay for fear that it would sound catty, and worse, earn her brother's resentment. They may not have been the best of friends, but Claire didn't think she could handle his disapproval, especially not over Lindsay Glass. Claire just hoped that he would see Lindsay as she truly was before she caused him too much grief. It was still very new and the two of them really didn't know each other all that well. Claire admitted it to no one, but part of the reason she didn't like James and Lindsay being together was that she knew it would hurt Emma. The fact that Emma was gone somehow made it worse, and Claire's heart ached even more than before.

* * *

Pastor Ward tried to lead his people and encourage them as he knew that they were still suffering. He himself still struggled. He knew that people were giving up hope of ever finding Emma and, though he didn't blame them, it broke his heart to see the sad resignation on the faces of these people he loved so much. He took courage in the fact that Joni still held out hope. Sometimes it was only a glimmer, but Pastor Ward knew that she hadn't given up yet. The day that he had found Mollie Brown's note, Joni had been wounded in this battle, but she was still fighting to believe that she would see her precious daughter again. He prayed that they would win the war. Greg was much harder for Pastor Ward to assess. He still attended Hillside with Joni, but this was more for Joni's sake than his own. He rarely spoke to anyone and seemed more locked inside himself than he did a year ago. When people tried to talk to him or encourage him, Greg would be polite but he never let anyone get close. Pastor Ward prayed for him and Joni every day. He also prayed for Detective Palmer. Pastor Ward knew that the poor man was trying everything he could, and coming up with nothing. He prayed for Emma. God knew where she was and Pastor Ward prayed that He would bring her home, whether it was the detective who found her or not. He, too, tried to keep up hope. Some days were harder than others.

* * *

Melody seldom had nightmares anymore. When she did have them she would talk to Macy about it and Macy always found ways to encourage her. Melody suspected that Macy was part of the reason she was doing a little better. Just knowing that she was there for her, gave Melody courage. Macy had told her that she was sorry she hadn't met Emma, but that she hoped she would get to someday soon.

* * *

Kate and Alan were concerned about their two children. Claire was more withdrawn than ever. She, who was already thin, had begun to lose weight. Before, while she would be subdued and shy in public, she was bouncy, animated and engaging around her family and close friends. Now she kept to herself even at home. She shut herself inside her room and inside herself. Claire talked to her family if they spoke to her. She was respectful, but removed. It was nearly impossible to draw her out of herself or get her to laugh and smile. Alan and Kate knew that the major part of the reason for Claire's suffering was Emma, but there was more to it than that, and they didn't know what it was or what to do about it.

They were concerned about James as well. He had never had a girlfriend before and they didn't know Lindsay well, only what Claire had told them back in the days of bullying, and they were not impressed. The two of them were aware that Lindsay was now attending youth group and had not picked on Claire or the other girls in a long time, but it wasn't enough to set them at ease. They wanted to get to know Lindsay and they told James so.

There wasn't much that really upset James and this was no different. When Alan told him that he and Kate wanted Lindsay to come to their house for dinner so they could get better acquainted with her, James showed no more emotion than moderate surprise and agreed to tell Lindsay that his parents wanted her to visit with the family. Alan suspected that James wasn't taking his relationship with this girl all that seriously at the moment, and wondered what was the big deal.

One person who did have strong emotions about the arrangement was Claire. Having Lindsay in youth group was one thing, but the idea of having her in her home was another. It felt like a violation. She considered asking her parents if she could go to Brayle's that night and thereby escape the whole evening, but she knew it was futile. Not only would she most likely be denied, her parents would want to know why and Claire didn't want them to know how upset she was about the whole James and Lindsay issue in the first place. The truth was Claire felt betrayed. Lindsay Glass had made her life miserable and now her own brother had stamped her with his approval. It was as if all the cruelties just didn't matter, as if he thought it was okay that Lindsay had tormented his sister. Claire knew that James really didn't know everything that Lindsay had done to her, and the other girls, and that helped. But not much.

    She anticipated with dread the day her former enemy would come to her house. Fortunately it seemed that it would be a few weeks away. Mom was getting ready for spring at Line Dried Laundry and this was a busy season for Dad at work, too. She and James were working hard to finish end-of-the-year projects for school, and Claire supposed that Lindsay had her own fair share of homework to do. What was more, Pastor Josh's annual Timmy Awards ceremony was approaching, and everyone was helping with preparations for them. The teens were all looking forward to it, especially since it had been canceled the year before.

    Claire felt guilty at her relief that their parents had told James that he could only "see" Lindsay at church and school until they met with her. He, in his James way, took it in stride and let Lindsay know. She was much less understanding of the arrangement than James, but chose to hide her outrage from him. Claire, however, could sense Lindsay's contempt, and it was the reason she felt guilty. Claire was ashamed that she couldn't help but feel some satisfaction at Lindsay's disappointment.

Chapter 22

The night Claire had been dreading was finally here. Up until now, James and Lindsay had only seen each other at school and at church (Wednesday and Sunday nights; Lindsay didn't attend Sunday morning services), but now everything would change. At least Claire suspected that Lindsay expected them to change. She had overheard Lindsay telling someone that she was glad that they were getting this evening "over with" so she and James could go on "real dates." Claire told no one anything about it, not even Brayle.

It was almost funny. It would seem that James should be the one to be nervous about his girlfriend coming over to meet his parents, but Mom had had to remind him at least twice that today was the day. Claire, on the other hand, felt sick to her stomach. Mom was making cheeseburger soup and homemade rolls, which was a family favorite, but the idea of eating anything made Claire queasy. She didn't know if she could make it through the whole meal without having a panic attack.

***

Lindsay arrived right on time at six o'clock. Claire would have thought Lindsay looked gorgeous if she didn't know her, and if a little more of her skin was covered. Even in her anxiety, she had to shake her head. *Who wears a skirt that short to meet her boyfriend's parents?* She felt another stab of guilt at the hope that Lindsay would lose points with her mom and dad because of her outfit.

Claire was spared having to have much to do with Lindsay because, after a moment of something like surprise at seeing her (Claire suspected that Lindsay had forgotten she would be there), Lindsay largely ignored her. All of her attention was for James. In fact, for some unfathomable reason, Lindsay was bolder now with him than she ever had been. *Maybe*, Claire mused from her chair in a corner where she hoped no one would bother her, *Lindsay thinks that meeting our parents makes the relationship "serious."* Claire quietly looked on the bookshelf behind her chair for something to read, but nearly fell on the floor in a dead faint when she heard Lindsay ask James if they could go up to his room until it was time to eat.

Fortunately for Lindsay, neither of the parents heard her brazen request. Of course, the meaning was lost on James who blandly told her that it was almost time to eat and he'd bring his guitar downstairs to show it to her after supper.

Claire rolled her eyes. *Doofus. He thinks she's interested in his music. Like anyone wants to hear his unrecognizable version of his favorite country song.*

Claire surprised herself by nearly shouting James some sisterly wisdom (such as, *It's a wonder you can even dress yourself, you stooge!)* when her thoughts were derailed by her mother telling them it was time to eat.

* * *

The meal was uncomfortable for Claire. She kept her eyes on her bowl, playing with her soup. If she sensed anyone looking her way, she tried to take a bite. As always, her mom's soup was delicious, but having a bully at her table made it all but impossible for Claire to eat. James was, not surprisingly, unaware of the tension in the atmosphere. He scarfed down his meal in single-minded determination. As soon as he had begun to eat, he had forgotten about Lindsay and everyone else.

Lindsay, now faced with her boyfriend's parents, wore her "good-girl" mask. She was obviously uncomfortable, but tried to answer Alan and Kate's questions sweetly, and give the replies that she thought they wanted to hear.

"So how long have you been going to youth group with Claire and James?" Kate asked her politely.

"Oh, um, a long time." Lindsay beamed. "I was just so glad when Claire invited me." She took a tiny bite of her roll.

Claire looked up. Although she had been there when it happened, she hadn't been the one to do the actual inviting of Lindsay to youth group. What was more, to say that her reaction to the invitation had been "gladness" simply wasn't true. When Mia had asked Lindsay to come to church, Lindsay had made some excuse and scampered away. Claire sneaked a peek at her mom to see if she had caught this truth stretching. If she did, she didn't let on.

Lindsay didn't seem worried about being caught in a lie; on the contrary, she seemed almost bold.

"I'm really glad we finally got to do this," she said with exaggerated relief. "Now that you know me, James and I can start actually spending time alone together."

You could hear a pin drop. Even James stopped cramming his third roll into his mouth to turn and look at Lindsay as if she had just dropped out of the ceiling. Whether he was surprised that she expected him to spend more time with her, or that she had just told his parents how it was going to be, Claire didn't know, but she was sure which one it was for her mom and dad.

Dad looked concerned. Mom's brow wrinkled and she cleared her throat. "What do you mean?" She asked evenly.

Lindsay seemed to realize she had overstepped. "Oh, you know, I mean not just church stuff."

Claire was angry. She knew Lindsay had evaded the question, that she had big plans for James.

"Well," Mom began, "Alan and I would prefer it if, for now, whenever one of our children is thinking of spending time with someone that they do it here with the family. They really are both too young to be thinking of seriously dating anyone."

Now James looked uncomfortable. He obviously hadn't taken any of this as seriously as anyone else in the room. Claire could tell that he was sorry he had asked Lindsay to come over, even though it had been their mother's idea. Mom and Dad both seemed to have their guard up now, altered by what Lindsay had said.

Lindsay's face was a collage of confusion, dismay, annoyance and disappointment. Claire hid her first smile of the day behind her napkin. *It's not funny! I am a horrible worm of a human being!* She thought to herself.

"What," Lindsay cleared her throat, "what do you mean here with the family? Like tonight, having dinner together?" She was obviously trying to make her voice light and casual, but Claire could hear an undertone of *you've got to be kidding me.*

Dad spoke up, "Well, yes," he assured her kindly, but firmly, "Kate will make us all dinner and then after we get the dishes cleared away, we can all play games or watch a movie together.

The Valley Without Her

Maybe the five of us can even go mini-golfing sometime. Won't that be fun?" His eyes twinkled.

Claire almost laughed. Not only were things not going at all the way Lindsay wanted them to, but Dad had just told Lindsay that Claire would be present for her "dates" with James. Again Claire felt a little guilty about finding humor in watching Lindsay squirm.

James stared at his food. He seemed to have lost his appetite. This was unprecedented.

"Well..." Lindsay was obviously trying to pull herself together. "Well then, when is he *allowed*," she nearly choked on the word, "to go on real dates with me?"

Mom answered this time. "We'll just have to wait and see. When James is a little older, and if, after Alan and I get to know you better, James wants to date you more seriously, we can talk about it then."

Claire could tell that Lindsay was surprised that there would be a question in anyone's mind that James would want to date her. Claire shook her head and peeked at her brother. She wondered what he thought about all this. He looked as if he had been thrust onstage during a play that he had not rehearsed, and had no way of knowing any of his lines. Claire almost felt sorry for him, but was still angry with him for paying Lindsay any attention in the first place.

Slowly, painfully and eventually, the evening came to a close and Lindsay left. They did not play games after dinner; Lindsay merely said she had things to do and bolted for the door. Alan had to remind James to walk her out and say good-bye to her. Claire was glad she didn't have to be a part of that awkward farewell.

* * *

Later that night after everything had been cleared away and everyone was winding down for the evening, Claire found her mother reading in bed. Dad was watching the news and James was in his room, butchering an old John Denver song. Claire wore her favorite pajamas and a pair of fuzzy slippers. Her hair was still wet from her bath and she smelled like soap. She felt miserable.

"Mom?"

Kate set her book aside. She could immediately sense the pain in her daughter's eyes. "What, honey, what's the matter?"

Claire shrugged. Kate opened her arms and Claire climbed up next to her on the bed. She rested her head against Kate's shoulder and Kate combed Claire's damp hair with her fingers.

Claire took a deep breath, "I feel bad." she said softly.

"About what?" Kate asked. "Is it something about Emma?"

"No," Claire said sadly. "Not really, anyway." There was a long pause before she continued. "It's about Lindsay."

"What about her?" Kate's tone had changed a shade. It was hard for Claire to define the mood behind it.

"I feel bad because," she swallowed, "because I don't like her."

Kate could hardly hear her daughter's voice. Claire was whispering, but her tone was fierce. "Lindsay has always been so mean to me and my friends. I know she's different now, but I still don't trust her. And then James goes and acts like everything's okay. Like it's okay that she, she always called Melody a fat cow and pretended that the ground was shaking when Melody walked. Or that Lindsay said that Brayle's dad left their family because he couldn't stand to look at her. Or that she kept telling people that Mia sleeps with everybody (and that's not true *at all*). One time she stuck a pad to the back of Ashley's shirt and Ashley didn't know why everyone was laughing at her until Mrs. Frank saw it and took it off of her. She always tried to embarrass people in front of everyone. There was that time that she said that I'm—I'm so ugly that people look at my yearbook picture when they want to throw up...She used to call Emma the most...the most *awful* names."

By now Claire's voice was creaky with misery and Kate held her close and rocked her.

"What kind of a person *does* that, Mom? The only reason I don't hate her is because the Bible says to love your enemies. It's already *so* hard, and then James acts like she's the best thing since French fries." Claire's voice had an uncharacteristic edge of bitterness. Kate held her closer.

"Well, first of all, I think that you've overestimated your brother's opinion of Lindsay." Kate soothed.

"What do you mean?" Claire sniffed.

"From what I could tell, James treated Lindsay almost like one of the guys, except if Nate or Ben had been here tonight, James would have talked to them a lot more. He hardly spoke to Lindsay at all."

Claire said nothing, but Kate knew she was thinking about what she had just said. Kate wanted to alleviate her daughter's suffering, but she knew it wouldn't be appropriate to tell her everything she was thinking. She had to choose her words carefully. Kate silently prayed for wisdom to say the right things and for peace to calm her spirit from the fury that had risen in her mother's heart when reminded of the cruelties inflicted on her dear ones by this dubiously reformed bully.

She breathed before she spoke. Kate wanted her voice to sound calm so Claire wouldn't perceive the rage that had bubbled up inside her. "I have a feeling that Lindsay is taking this 'relationship,'" Kate made little quotation marks with her fingers, "far more seriously than your brother is. He may even think of her as one of the guys...just prettier. Daddy and I have talked about it, and we don't really think it will last long when Lindsay finds out that James isn't going to give her the kind of attention she sees guys giving girls in the movies."

"But James—"

"Don't be so hard on him. Does he even know about all those things that Lindsay did?"

Kate felt Claire's tense body soften a degree and go from granite to fiberglass. Kate rubbed Claire's back.

"I don't know. I don't think so." Claire said in a low voice. "I didn't tell him. I can't say anything now though, it's too late."

"No, you probably shouldn't go and try to get involved. Things have a way of working themselves out, and Daddy and I are not taking it lightly. Try not to worry too much about it, okay? I really do think that you are taking Lindsay far more seriously than your brother is, and I *know* that he didn't mean to hurt you."

Kate felt the rest of the tension lift as the little body next to her melted from fiberglass into Claire. Kate prayed with her daughter and told her she'd have Alan come and kiss her goodnight before she went to sleep. She could tell that when Claire left her room that she was feeling better. Kate breathed a prayer of thanks and asked again for wisdom. She and Alan had been dismayed when James had mentioned casually that Lindsay was interested in him. They could have sat him down immediately and forbade him to see her, but they thought better of it. Kate and Alan were afraid that if they took the authoritative approach, it would only make Lindsay more appealing. Instead they decided to mark out some boundaries, knowing that Lindsay would be indignant and James would most likely be indifferent.

Kate and Alan were very grateful that James had made a commitment to himself and to God, to save himself for marriage. They both got the sad impression that Lindsay was "that kind of girl." Because of these differences, they were confident that James would see Lindsay's true nature and lose interest in her. Kate and Alan didn't want to make these decisions for him, but hoped that he would learn from this experience with Lindsay and, in the future, make wiser choices.

Kate could not tell Claire that she and Alan were working to sabotage James' relationship, but she had been tempted. Again she prayed for her children and hoped that soon this would be behind them. She even prayed for Lindsay. Kate knew that happy, well-adjusted, and secure people did not behave as Lindsay had. It was true that Lindsay hadn't bullied Claire or any of her friends for quite a long time, but Claire still came home from school with stories about Lindsay's mistreatment of other people. Kate prayed that Lindsay would surrender her wounds to Jesus and become a new person for her own sake and the sake of others. However, until and unless Lindsay did make a decision to start treating others with kindness, Kate didn't trust her with either of her children.

Chapter 23

Alan decided to take James on one of their father/son outings. Alan knew he didn't do it often enough, and after talking with Kate last night, he decided that the time was right.

They drove to their favorite steakhouse. It was several miles away and the long drive gave them time to talk. James was used to these heart-to-hearts with his dad and was not surprised when Alan asked him about Lindsay.

"So, what do you think of this Lindsay girl?" Alan asked casually. "She the one?" he joked.

"Dad, I'm still in high school. I don't even know her that well." James gave his dad the "parents-are-so-clueless" look.

"Well, if you're too young to be serious, and if you don't know her that well, then why is she your girlfriend?"

James fidgeted a little in his seat and began searching through the radio stations. "I don't know. I'm not sure I'd call her my *girlfriend*."

Alan raised his eyebrows. "Really? 'Cause you'd better believe she calls herself that."

James stopped fiddling with the radio and stared at his dad. "How do you know?"

Now it was James' turn to get the patronizing glare. "It doesn't take a relationship expert to see that she thinks of the two of you as a serious couple."

Now James looked alarmed. "Serious?" His voice squeaked. "She said that?"

"Not out loud." Alan shook his head. "It's the way she acted."

James frowned. "I don't know. I mean, I just kind of thought of her as a friend who's a girl. She's cute and everything, but..."

Alan laughed in spite of himself.

James looked at him alarmed. "What? What's so funny?"

"Oh, nothing." Alan smiled. "It's just your mother."

"Mom?" James held his head as if he thought it might explode. "What's Mom got to do with it?"

"She's just one smart cookie, that's all."

Alan let the silence stretch like the road beneath their tires before he asked his next question.

"So what's Lindsay like, though; is she a nice girl?"

James looked out of the window. He ducked his head a little. "I don't know. She's always nice to me. Like I said, I don't really know her that well."

This was the part of the conversation that Alan had been dreading. He took a deep breath and prayed a silent prayer.

"There's something you need to know, James."

James listened quietly while Alan told him some of the things that Claire had told Kate. Of course, Kate told Alan about her talk with Claire and they had decided that maybe he should tell James some of the things that had Lindsay had said and done.

When he finished he waited as James sat quietly next to him, looking sick. "Now I know people can change, and your mother and I aren't telling you that you can't see her if you want to, but you need to be careful about the kind of people you choose to get close to. Just think about it, all right?"

James nodded. Alan let James sink into his own thoughts and didn't give any more advice. He didn't want to overwhelm his son and he had already given him quite a lot to think about.

After several minutes, Alan asked James a question about his music and for the rest of the evening, they kept things light and fun. They had a delicious meal and ate way too much; they laughed together and had a great time. Although the subject of Lindsay didn't come up again, Alan could tell that James was still thinking about what he had told him.

* * *

For several days, the Thomas home was uncharacteristically silent. James was thinking hard about what Alan had told him, but nothing had really changed between Lindsay and him. She still sat by him in youth group, but always with a slightly sour expression. It was assumed that she was unhappy with the nature of her relationship with James, but was digging in her heels in the hopes of making things the way she wanted them to be.

Any encouragement that Claire had enjoyed from talking with Kate was gone, as her brother continued to pay attention, albeit in small amounts, to Lindsay Glass. It made Kate's heart ache to see Claire so discouraged, and she was thankful that Claire didn't know that Alan had enlightened James about some of the awful things that Lindsay had done. If Claire knew that James was aware of Lindsay's cruelties and still chose to "date" her, Kate could only imagine how it would crush her daughter.

The Valley Without Her

Kate suspected that James regretted allowing Lindsay to get close to him, but that he didn't know what to do about it now. Kate and Alan were concerned about their kids and prayed that they would pass through this valley soon. Even then, however, they, like everyone else, would still be in the valley of Emma being missing. And it was dark in the valley.

* * *

Claire was thinking how glad she was that the school year was almost over. She gathered her books to go home for the day and tried not to think about how everything was going wrong. Things were so different from the way they used to be, and she simply couldn't adjust. She could not shake the sadness that had been draped across her shoulders ever since the night Emma didn't come home. It was her constant and unwelcome companion. She missed her friend so much. And then there was James. Claire wanted to like Lindsay. She tried to have an attitude of forgiveness and not of resentment, but she did not trust her. Claire had hoped that when the school year was over that she'd see less of her former bully, but Mom and Dad had stated that any "dating" would be done in her very own living room. There was no escaping the situation, and there was no escaping the discouragement it caused her.

Claire closed her locker and shouldered her backpack. "Good job with the positive thinking, Claire." she mumbled to herself sarcastically. Claire started down the hall to find James. Dad was picking them up from school today, and tonight they were having the Timmy Awards. At least that was something to look forward to. Claire turned the corner and found not only James, but Lindsay. James' back was to her, so Claire couldn't see his face, but Lindsay was smiling up at him and laughing at something he had just said.

Claire couldn't stand it. She knew that her dad would be there any minute and that James would come looking for her, probably with Lindsay trailing after him like a bodyguard, but she didn't care. She couldn't stand to look at the two of them right now. Claire dashed back around the corner and almost ran smack into Dena Roberts.

Claire threw her hands up. "Sure! Why not!" She shouted, surprising both Dena and herself.

After a moment of staring at each other, Dena recovered. "Are you all right?" she asked, and looked closely at Claire with an expression that Claire had never seen on Dena's face before. It took Claire a moment to realize that it was compassion.

She didn't know what made her do it, but Claire shook her head. "No," she whispered. "I'm not all right." And then she began to tell Dena about James and Lindsay. She didn't know why she was doing it, it went against all logic, but for some reason telling Dena seemed like the right thing to do. Dena didn't interrupt, even when Claire described some of the moments that Lindsay had tortured her where Dena herself had not only been present, but a participant. When she was through talking, she wiped her eyes and glanced at Dena.

"I'm sorry." Dena whispered.

Claire shrugged. "It wasn't you as much as her." She said softly. "I always kind of thought you just went along with it because you wanted her to like you."

"Well...that's kind of true, I guess." Dena said slowly. "I'm sorry about that, too, but that's not what I was talking about." She sighed and looked at her shoes. "There's something I should have told you a long time ago."

* * *

The Valley Without Her

A few moments ago Claire wanted nothing more than to get as far away as possible from Lindsay Glass, and now she was tracking her like a bloodhound. James and Lindsay were not standing in the same spot they had been when she saw them last, so Claire sought them out by Lindsay's locker. She knew where that was because she made it a point to know where Lindsay was likely to be at all times so she could avoid those places. This was different. For the first time in her life, Claire intentionally went looking for Lindsay.

She had been right. There she was, still smiling her Hollywood smile at James who was clueless as usual. Claire would deal with him later. Right now, she only had eyes for Lindsay. As Claire approached she saw that Lindsay was giggling and telling James a story about some reality show she liked while she opened the door to her locker. Lindsay didn't see her coming. Claire stomped herself in between the two of them and slapped her palm against the cool metal of the locker door.

BANG! Lindsay and James both jumped, startled by Claire slamming Lindsay's locker shut.

For a second the old Lindsay was back and she appeared to be outraged that someone as insignificant as Claire would dare to cross her. Dena, who had followed Claire, prepared herself for one of Lindsay's tirades. But then Lindsay got a good look at Claire's blazing eyes, and took a step backward. She actually looked intimidated.

"YOU!" Claire nearly screamed at her. "This is ALL your fault!"

"What's going on here?" Lindsay's locker was near the main entrance of the school and Alan, who had come inside to find them, had suddenly shown up and was wondering who was this crazy person who looked just like his daughter.

It was a testament to how angry Claire was that the sight of her father didn't calm her down. James just stood looking bewildered and scared while Dena seemed contrite. Lindsay, however, looked afraid and defiant. The perfect picture of someone caught in wrongdoing.

Claire pointed at Lindsay. "Tell them what you did!" she commanded.

Lindsay said nothing. She lifted her chin and avoided everyone's eyes.

"It all makes so much *sense* now." Claire shouted. "I can't believe I was so *stupid*. I mean we just couldn't figure out *why* in the world someone who went out of their way to treat us like dirt would all the sudden want to be best friends! You felt *guilty* and you were trying to cover it up! Trying not to look suspicious!"

"Claire..." Alan began.

"Daddy," Claire sobbed. "She knew and she didn't say anything. If she had just let her be..."

"I didn't *do* anything!" Lindsay spoke for the first time, her voice belligerent.

"What's going on here?" Alan asked again.

Dena spoke up. "We were there that day," she began, "the day that Emma disappeared at the festival."

"Shut up, Dena, you obviously don't know what you're talking about." Lindsay spat.

"You obviously don't remember that I don't take orders from you anymore," Dena glared.

Lindsay reached for James' arm, "Let's go, James," she sniffed, "you don't want to hear them tell *lies* about me."

James pulled his arm out of her reach. He looked at her as if he'd never seen her before. Lindsay crossed her arms over her chest and set her jaw as Dena continued. Claire was breathing hard, as if she'd just sprinted a mile. Her eyes were still shining with anger.

Claire looked at Dena. "Tell them."

"Well," Dena said softly, "Lindsay and I saw Emma walking by herself. She was coming from Claire's mom's store, you know?"

Alan gasped and Claire shook her head as tears slid down her face. She watched her brother, studying his reaction as Dena spoke.

"Lindsay said something like, "Look there's that freak," and went to stand in Emma's way. I followed her. Emma was all by herself, you know, and Lindsay started...saying things to her. Mean things. She called her names and said that her parents should have gotten rid of her before she was born or drowned her at birth or something because she was a defective cripple and worthless and, and, things like that." It was obvious that Dena didn't want to repeat everything that Lindsay had said. They all got the point. It had been really bad.

"Well, then," Dena sighed, "Emma ran off. She had been walking down the street toward that big tent where her friends were selling stuff, but instead she ran off by herself. She went a different way. We didn't know anything until the next day. The next day people were saying that Emma was missing. That she never went back to her friends." Dena broke down. "I'm so sorry," she whispered. "I think we might have been the last ones to see her."

Chapter 24

Kate sat with Alan as they watched quietly from a corner while Pastor Josh welcomed everyone to the Fifth Annual Timmy Awards. She was glad that they had decided to wait to tell Josh and Macy about what Dena had told them today. Alan and Kate agreed that it would be best to let them know after the big event was all over. If Pastor Josh wondered why Lindsay wasn't there or why Claire had brought a girl named Dena he had heard about but never met, he didn't act surprised. He had prepared for visitors and had a few little newcomer awards for them in the form of candy bars.

As for Lindsay, Kate doubted that she would be returning to Hillside any time soon. While Kate felt bad about this for Lindsay's sake, she was relieved that she would no longer be stirring up trouble for her kids. When her family came home, Alan had pulled her into their bedroom to relate the afternoon's revelations to her. Apparently after Dena told them what had happened Lindsay had tried to deny any responsibility for what had happened that day, and even went so far as to suggest that Emma had simply run away. According to Alan, Claire had nearly exploded with fury at the slight on her friend. After that, Lindsay tried to downplay the whole situation and proceeded to try to sweet talk James. She batted her eyes and asked him to call her later and even hinted that he might skip the awards to spend time with her instead. James was clearly uncomfortable, and he did his best not to be rude, but he let Lindsay know that he didn't want to miss the awards, and he didn't think it was such a good idea for them to be spending time together anymore.

Lindsay had tried to leave with her dignity. Alan told Kate that he thought she may have showered her peers with spiteful and venomous words if he had not been standing there. She merely gave Claire, Dena, and James each a look of pure contempt and stomped away. All three of the kids seemed to wilt with relief to see her go. It was then that Claire asked Dena if she wanted to come to the Timmy Awards with her and her friends. While Alan was telling Kate what had happened, Claire called Brayle and the others to tell them what she had learned. All of the Hillside girls were ready to welcome Dena into the group. Kate was glad she had come. At first she had seemed shy and afraid that the girls would, at the very least, ignore her, but it was clear that Dena was having a good time. She smiled and laughed with her brand-new friends and even sat up a little straighter. Kate had known Dena before, back during her days of being Lindsay's sidekick, and this new role of just being herself suited her much better. Kate thought that maybe Dena was even a little slimmer than before. These past several months must have been so hard on her. Kate shook her head but then smiled as she watched the girls laugh at something Dena had said. Yes. The new Dena was going to be just fine.

*　*　*

Pastor Josh was obviously excited about having the Timmy Awards again. The purpose of the event was to recognize the teens' accomplishments and inspire them to be effective for Christ. Pastor Josh gave the kids awards based on all sorts of things, some silly and fun, others serious and meaningful. Pastor

Josh believed that was how God worked. God invented fun and had a wonderful sense of humor, so those things were to be celebrated in His children. God also had an awesome sense of purpose. It was okay to be silly, but not to be foolish. It was good to be childlike, but not so good to be child*ish*.

Pastor Josh had a way of being a clown one minute, having everyone laughing and cheering, and the in the next minute you could hear a pin drop as he spoke about spiritual truth and awarded one of the teens for honesty, courage, or generosity. Kate was proud to see her two amazing children receive their awards. She applauded when Brayle received her award for having a servant's heart and laughed when Nate got the Timmy for "best impression of Pastor Josh." That one had been Macy's idea. All in all, it was a great evening, but Kate dreaded what needed to be done after the event was over. Josh and Macy weren't the only ones Alan and Kate had waited to tell about what had happened earlier that afternoon. Joni and Greg needed to know, too. Still, Kate enjoyed the program with the rest of the parents until the final award of the evening. Kate's heart sank when she knew that the time had come to pay her visit to Greg and Joni. She and Alan had decided that he would tell Pastor Ward, Pastor Josh and Macy while she went and spoke to the Leonards. Alan stayed behind while Kate, James, and Claire started the walk home. The days were long this time of year and the sun would not set for at least another hour. Kate told them she, and Dad, too, would be home soon and to lock the doors when they got inside. She walked alone to Greg and Joni's house.

* * *

Joni answered the door and didn't seem surprised to see Kate, but she didn't look like she had actually been expecting her either. Kate was simply here now and Joni let her in. Kate missed the days when Joni would answer the door with a perfect hug and her smile that always looked like she had some wonderful secret. Kate missed a lot about the way things were before.

"Can I come in?" she asked "I have something to tell you."

Joni led Kate into the living room and they sat down. Greg was there, too, but it was quiet. The TV was off and Greg's and Joni's hands were free of newspapers or novels. It was as if they had been just sitting there, enduring the silence. Kate took a breath before she began to recall the events of the afternoon. She tried to relay the information while sparing them as much as she thought she could. For example, she didn't give them any details about what Dena had told them that Lindsay had said to Emma that day. Kate knew that hearing that someone had told her daughter that she ought never had been born would have been excruciating for her. Kate breathed a silent prayer of thanks that they did not ask for those specifics.

After she was through, the two of them sat quietly for a moment. Kate could tell they were absorbing the information. After a while Greg spoke.

"It doesn't make any difference," he sighed. "Even if we'd had this information then, it wouldn't have helped us find her. We looked everywhere. We tried everything to find Emma."

He put his head in his hands and Joni got up to pace, but Tesla, who had been lying at the foot of Greg's chair all this time, began to go berserk. He kept dancing toward the door and barking so hard that his front feet left the floor. His Tesla coil was a blur.

Joni was the first to catch on. "He heard us talking about Emma and he thinks we're going to get her." She explained, her voice stretched thin by misery. "He heard us say the words "find Emma" and he doesn't understand."

Joni was right, for when she said the words again, Tesla threw back his head and howled. He ran to the door and scratched at it. Joni sighed. "He hasn't been out in a while. Maybe he'll run around the yard a while and forget what he was so excited about." She opened the door and Tesla was out in a flash of fur.

Kate stayed a while and accepted the cup of tea that Joni offered. She didn't really want anything, but it gave Joni something to do, and it gave her a reason to stay a little longer and talk with her friend.

Kate told Joni about how Claire had struggled with James' semi-relationship with Lindsay, and how Alan had told her about Claire finally standing up to her. She asked Joni what she thought about James paying attention to Lindsay in the first place, and if she thought they should be concerned about his choices in girls, or even friends.

Joni gave the answer Kate thought she would, that this was a good experience for Claire, learning to trust God and helping her to have more confidence. Joni thought that James would learn from this too, and would probably be more careful next time.

While Kate did value Joni's opinion, really she was just hoping to keep her mind occupied for a while. She knew that the days stretched long for Joni and Greg and they had many discouragements. Again and again they talked to Detective Palmer and while he always tried to sound positive when he updated them, he had very little information for them that gave them any hope.

After about an hour, Kate hugged Joni and said she needed to go home. Kate said good-bye to Greg, and Joni walked her to the door. When Kate stepped outside, it was then that the two of them realized that Tesla had not yet come back inside. Usually he would come to the door and bark when he was through sniffing all the trees and barking at the squirrels, but they hadn't heard even a yip out of him since Joni opened the door to put him out.

Greg joined them and the three of them spent a quarter of an hour looking nearby and shouting for Tesla. Greg decided to get in his truck and drive around the block and look for him. After another fifteen minutes, Greg returned, but without the little beagle.

Kate knew it wasn't just because of Tesla that Greg looked like he was going to break into pieces when he told Joni he couldn't find him. She turned away so they wouldn't see her heart break for them. *What else, God?* She cried in her spirit. *How much more can they take?*

* * *

In the middle of the night, Greg would wake up as if someone had suddenly shouted in his ear. He wondered briefly what it was that woke him before the events of the day came rolling back over him. What would haunt him would not be Tesla's running away, or even finding out that that horrible girl had caused Emma to go off her planned path. No. It would be the half-truth that he had spoken that night. *He hadn't done everything he could do. Everyone one else had, but not him. He just didn't see what good it would do. He would think about it. He didn't want to do it, didn't want to trust a God who would take his girl away. But maybe he should. Maybe he should pray for Emma to come home.*

* * *

Amie M. Johnson

Kate slowly walked home feeling weary and lonely. When she walked in the door, she found her family all curled up on the couch. She was forcibly reminded of the night Emma disappeared when she found them here on the sofa bed in their pajamas. She squeezed herself in between the guys and took Alan's hand, lacing her fingers through his. She hated to tell them about Tesla running away, but she knew that it had to be done. When she told them, all three of them seemed to sink under the weight of the news.

Then suddenly Kate remembered. With all that had happened today, she had completely forgotten to tell even Alan. She was glad to have some good news to give them and it was just the thing they needed right now. "Hey, I forgot to tell you; I got a phone call today," she told them. "Aunt Bertie called and invited us to use her lake house up north. Maybe, after school's out, it would do us all some good to take a little vacation."

Chapter 25

Present day

She was dreaming. She had to be dreaming. It couldn't be possible that she was actually seeing Emma, talking to her, touching her hair. But it was real. *It's real and we need to get her out of this truck. Now.*

Kate tried to keep her voice calm. Emma was obviously distraught, and Kate didn't want to upset her any more than she already was. However, it was imperative that they get her to safety.

"Come on, honey," she crooned softly, still stroking Emma's hair. "Come on out and get into the car with James and Claire, okay?"

Emma lifted her head. "James?" She sniff-hiccuped, "Claire?" Her young face, full of joyful hope at hearing the names of her friends, was the most beautiful thing Kate had ever seen. But then Emma's expression crumpled.

"No," she gasped. She shook her head, her eyes wide. "I'll get in trouble!"

Alan stepped in. "We're not going to let anything happen to you, Emma." His voice was strong and confident, and Kate had never loved him more than she did in this moment. "It's all over and we're going to take you home. Now come on out of there and get into the car with Claire."

Emma was trembling, but she nodded. Alan opened her door and was taking her hand to help her down. It was then that Kate saw what Emma was wearing. She had on a dress that was most likely secondhand and looked like it belonged to someone's grandmother. Before Kate had time to make sense of this, she noticed Emma freeze. The look on the girl's face was a mask of terror.

Kate's heart slammed into her throat and in the split second before she turned around, her imagination presented her with a hundred different horrible possibilities of what she was about to face. Who would be the monster that had taken Emma?

Kate and Alan turned, but there was no one standing there but a pale, middle-aged woman with long silvery hair. She was staring at them.

"Lydia?" she frowned. "What's going on?" Her voice was sharp and snapped like a whip.

Alan and Kate stepped closer together, hiding Emma behind them with their bodies. Kate bent her arm behind her back in order to hold Emma's hand. She could feel her trembling. Emma's fear brought out the mother bear in Kate and, in a flash, all of her own fear was burned to ashes by anger.

"Who are *you*?" Kate demanded.

The woman ignored her. "Lydia! I asked you a question!" She chastened harshly.

"Her name is not Lydia," Alan said firmly.

Again the woman pretended not to hear them. "Come on, Lydia; we're leaving."

Kate was surprised to feel Emma tug her hand away from her own as if to obey this stranger. Kate clamped her hand tighter around Emma's.

"She's not going anywhere with you. We're taking her home." Kate was shaking as she stared this madwoman down.

"You can't leave," Alan informed, as if to reason with this person, "you have a flat tire." There was nothing in his voice that gave away the fact that he himself was the one who had vandalized the vehicle. Emma, however, was clearly terrified, as if *she* had been the one to stab the tire and was about to be punished for it.

Enough was enough.

Kate turned her back on the woman. She put her hands on the trembling shoulders and looked into the sweet brown eyes. "Emma," she commanded, "go get in the car with James and Claire. You're safe now. You're not going anywhere with her; we are taking you home."

Emma seemed to lighten with relief and was about to obey Kate's instructions, when several police cars and emergency vehicles arrived on the scene. They had come in response to the call that James had made moments earlier. Kate continued to hold Emma to her side while Alan kept an eye on the strange woman who kept referring to Emma as Lydia.

Two men in uniform approached the little group of people, and Kate glanced at her own children to see if they were all right. James and Claire had exited the car, but were standing huddled together in the shelter of the open door. Kate wanted to open her arms to them and have them close to her and Alan and Emma, but she thought it would be best if they stayed where they were for now. She attempted a brave smile and gave them an encouraging nod. Their eyes blinked at her out of their pale, scared faces.

"What seems to be the trouble here?" asked the older of the two policemen who approached them. Kate nearly laughed.

Trouble? We have Emma back; the only trouble is that we're still standing here and not driving home to Joni and Greg. The thought of Joni nearly brought Kate to her knees, so she was grateful when Alan began to calmly explain the situation to the policemen. It was bizarre. How in the world had they ended up in the same place at the same time as Emma? They were standing smack in the middle of a miracle.

The woman, who they learned was named Mary Louise Crable, declared that she came out the door to find these people trying to take her daughter. It was just a little confusing for the officer because at one point in all the chaos, he did hear the girl call the older woman "Mother."

Things kept escalating until, at last, the officer raised his hands and called for peace. "Just everyone simmer down," he told them. He leaned down and made the girl look him in the eye. He could tell she was afraid and he spoke gently to her. "Now, honey, I want you to forget that there's anyone else here. It's just you and me talking, all right?"

She nodded.

"Why don't you go ahead and tell me your name, darlin'?" He was almost one hundred percent sure he knew the answer. They had checked it out on the way to the scene and she fit the description. He wanted to hear her say it.

She looked at him. Her voice was confident when she whispered, "Emma Katherine Leonard." And she hid her face in her hands.

The woman named Mary Louise was about to protest, but the officer held his hand up to her. He was about to say something, but was interrupted by the voice of a young girl. Everyone was

The Valley Without Her

surprised to see that Claire had joined the group. James was standing behind her.

She was clearly terrified. "I'm sorry, Dad, I know you said to stay, but I had to bring this. It was in the glove compartment." She handed the policeman a piece of paper. It was Emma's missing poster.

He looked from the poster to Emma and back again, reinforcing what he already knew.

"Here." The girl he knew was Emma Leonard spoke, reaching into her pocket. "I have one too."

Mary Louise Crable's jaw dropped. "Where did you get that?" she spat.

"It was in with the groceries." Emma told her. Her voice gained confidence, "I found it one day after you came home—I mean back from town and I kept it with me ever since." She looked at Kate. "I knew you were all looking for me, but I didn't know what to do." Her chin trembled. "I'm sorry."

Kate pulled Emma into a hug and then threw out an arm to scoop Claire close as well. They held each other and then no one was sure if they were laughing or crying.

* * *

After about forty-five minutes of red tape, Mary Louise Crable being stuffed into a police car in handcuffs, and making sure Emma was okay, the Thomases were permitted to take her home. Alan had talked the officials into allowing him to drive her home in their car. They were still five hours away and heading home anyway. They had also asked that they be allowed to call home to tell everyone that they had found Emma. They didn't want to call now and then have them wait for a long time.

They had waited long enough and Alan had a plan. They were granted permission, and an officer would follow them home. After Emma changed into some of Claire's clothes, at Claire's insistence, they were given the green light. It was time.

The drive home was surreal for everyone. Emma sat in the back huddled between James, who stared at her, and Claire, who wouldn't let go of her hand. Kate turned in her seat so she could watch Emma, and Alan glanced frequently into the rearview mirror as if to reassure himself that she was really there. Everyone cried at least once during the long drive home as they swapped information. They told Emma about the months without her. It was heartbreaking for Emma to hear about her grandfather passing, and she sobbed in Claire's arms when they told her that Tesla had run away.

Emma told them the story of what had happened.

* * *

"Well," Emma stared at her hand holding Claire's, "you told me that you already know about what happened with Lindsay." She huffed. "So stupid. What she said was really mean, but I shouldn't have let her upset me. I should have just come back to you guys and none of this would've ever happened."

"If Lindsay had just left you alone none of this would have happened." Claire grumbled through clenched teeth.

Emma shook her head. "She's not in charge of what I think about myself. I should have been stronger. I know that now."

Claire was obviously still angry, but let it go. She wanted to hear what Emma was going to say, even though Emma had told the police, and she was promised, there would be more interviews when she arrived home. Claire and her family had not heard the whole story.

Emma took a breath. "Well, after Lindsay said that stuff to me I ran off to be by myself for a little while before I came back to the fundraiser. I went down that side street that the Fredricksons live on. You know, the one with all the trees? Well, there was no one out there but this woman. She was lugging a big bag of clothes into the trunk of her car. She saw me and...I don't know... she had this weird look on her face like she recognized me or something." Emma fidgeted. "She didn't *seem* scary, you know? Just a little strange, so I wasn't scared or anything when she asked me to help her with her bag.

In the front seat, Kate closed her eyes and hung her head.

"She pushed me," Emma whispered. "She pushed me really hard. I was surprised how strong she was and the next thing I knew, it was dark because I was locked in a trunk and we were moving. She was driving away. I was so afraid."

Emma paused to compose herself. There was nothing but the sound of the road beneath the tires. "We drove for a long time before she stopped. She opened the trunk, but only long enough to throw in a bottle half-full of water and then she slammed the door again. I was thirsty so I drank the water.

"She started driving again and I got the idea to try to do something to the car. I pulled back some of the carpet and I found some wires and I pulled them out."

Alan made eye contact with Emma in the mirror. "That was a good idea," he told her softly.

"Yeah, I think it almost worked, too." Emma's voice sank under the regret she felt. "She got pulled over, but we were on a road with lots of traffic. I yelled and kicked and banged on the trunk, but he didn't hear me. Then I was just so tired. There was something in the water that made me sleep. I found out later that Moth...Mary Louise took medicine. Lithium, I think it was called. She must have used it to drug me.

"I think I slept for a really long time and when I woke up she told me we were home and started calling me Lydia. She acted like I should know things about her and her house and her life, and she'd get really mad when I didn't act like she thought I should. Sometimes, at first, she would talk about how I should be grateful to her and how she rescued me. I didn't know what she meant, but that just made her mad, too."

Kate tried to keep her face from betraying the rage she felt as Emma told her story. She could tell by Alan's knuckles, white from gripping the wheel, that he felt the same way.

"She didn't have a phone. We lived really far away from everything and she never let me leave. She would go to get supplies sometimes, but we ate food from her garden and things she had canned. I never want to see beets again for as long as I live.

"It wasn't like she told me why she was doing what she was doing, or why she thought my name was Lydia and made me call her Mother. I had to figure it out myself. She didn't leave very often, but when she did, I would snoop around to try to figure out where I was and what was going on in her crazy world. After a lot of little clues I figured out that she had a daughter named Lydia who died. She drowned, I think. After that, Moth...I mean Mary Louise kind of lost her mind. She had to take medication, but she still was...I don't know...not right.

I know she was confused because I wasn't like Lydia. I didn't even look like her, I know because I found a picture. Sometimes she would get madder and madder and madder and then...she'd hit me. She would kind of wake up and not know what she'd done. She didn't really say she was sorry, but I could tell she felt bad, so she would just get quiet for a while and try to be nicer. It always came back, though. She always got mad again. I just tried to play the game with her. I tried to act like Lydia so she wouldn't get angry, but it was hard. It was like the rules changed every day. I didn't go to school because Lydia was homeschooled so I tried to use some of her books, but I know I'm behind now. I think there were people who were asking her questions. She must have been acting suspicious, you know? One day she came home and told me we were moving. I think she moved around a lot. That's what we were doing today. That's why we were in a truck. She was taking me somewhere else.

"Anyway, one day a long time ago, she brought home some supplies and told me to put them away. I found my picture, my own missing person poster, in the bag. It was so awful. I was afraid that if I showed it to her, you know, to tell her that I wasn't Lydia, that she'd get mad and hit me or worse. I didn't know what to do. There was no one I could talk to. I just prayed. I prayed that someone would find me and take me home."

* * *

Pastor Ward sat in his office. He was expecting a phone call from his grandson, Micah, who wanted to tell him about his first time at camp, so Ward was unsurprised when his phone rang.

"Hello?" He smiled into the phone.

"Pastor Ward?" It wasn't Micah. It was Alan Thomas, and his voice sounded strange.

"Alan?"

"Pastor Ward, are you sitting down?"

Chapter 26

Pastor Ward looked around him. His beloved people never ceased to amaze him. After Alan's phone call, and figuratively picking himself up off of the floor, he had driven the short distance to Joni and Greg's house. He had been weak with relief to see that they were both home.

"I need to come in," he had told them, rubbing his chin nervously. "I have something to tell you." Pastor Ward could tell by their bland expressions that they had no idea what he was about to say to them.

He had asked for a cup of water, but didn't drink it. He sat it on the coffee table, thinking one of them might need it in a moment. He asked them to please sit down and then began by telling them that just a few moments ago he had received a phone call from Alan. Pastor Ward took a deep breath and grinned as tears of joy sprang into his eyes. He began to give them the information, piece by piece, that Alan had given him.

As he had expected, their reactions were dramatic. Joni nearly fainted and Pastor Ward held her shoulder to keep her from falling on the floor as Greg went to his knees and sobbed.

They had so many questions. *Were they sure? Why didn't they call us? Who had taken her? Was she okay? Were they sure? Did someone hurt her?*

Pastor Ward had patiently answered every question, even the ones they asked more than once.

Now he looked around at all the people that had gathered in the Hillside parking lot to welcome Emma home. It was a glorious day and they had set up for the greatest homecoming any of them had ever seen. He had called a few people and word of Emma's rescue had spread like wildfire. He was astonished at what they had put together in such a short period of time. Ruth, Irene, and Sherry had organized an impromptu potluck/cookout so there would be food for everyone. Someone had made a giant banner that read, "We Love You, Emma." Pastor Josh and Macy were there, leading the youth and some others in singing praises to God for bringing Emma home. Julie Burish was buzzing around giving people tasks and assignments. A few actually listened to her. Thankfully for now, the news people hadn't heard about what was happening, so there were no cameras or microphones intruding on the joy.

People kept asking Pastor Ward if Greg and Joni had talked to Emma on the phone, but he told them no, that they had wanted to see her in person. Like Thomas, they wanted to see their beloved in the flesh before they believed. He knew that what Alan had told him was the truth and that they would all be seeing Emma before the sun went down that day, but he didn't blame them. He knew loss, and the cruel games it played.

Joni and Greg stood a little apart from everyone else. Rather everyone stood apart from them. It was as if they were circled by these people who loved them, bodily and prayerfully protected by them. And then, after nearly two years, Kate and Alan pulled into the church parking lot in their SUV. Everyone made way for them and stood back, forming a path between the car and Joni and Greg. The door slid open.

* * *

Joni was trembling all over. She thought she would probably fall over if not for Greg's arm around her, though he was trembling too. It seemed an eternity from the time that they caught sight of the Thomas' car, to when the door slid open and finally, *finally*, after a lifetime's worth of heartache, there she was.

It was her. It was Emma, running to them with open arms, inexplicably wearing the same t-shirt she had been the last time they saw her, for they did not know that Claire, not making the connection, had loaned Emma her own *Brushfire* shirt—identical to the one Emma had been wearing when she was abducted.

Joni and Greg fell to their knees and nearly crushed their daughter between them in their embrace. Greg thought he had never in his life seen anyone so beautiful as his daughter as she ran to them from the SUV. He cried like a child— they all did, as he and Joni kissed her and touched her face and told her they loved her.

After several moments of happy reunion, Emma spoke. "I remembered what you said, Mama." She whispered to Joni.

"What's that, baby?" Joni laughed through her tears.

"The last thing you said to me and my friends. You said to remember who I am and whose I am. I thought about it every day. Because even though she called me a different name, even though she said I was *her* daughter, I remembered. I remembered that I was Emma, and that I was God's and Daddy's and yours."

* * *

People nearby, though respectfully maintaining their distance, could overhear what was being said by the little family and everyone broke out in song, laughter, or tears. They clung to one another and rejoiced.

One such spectator was Scott Fischer who, moved beyond words by what was happening in front of him, was trying valiantly to keep it together. He stood there, chest heaving and sniffling. He was actually rather proud of himself, because what he felt like doing was throwing his head back and yowling like a newborn. Pastor Josh, for example, was unabashedly sobbing and laughing at the same time, but Scott was uncomfortable showing that level of emotion. He had his arm around Brandy with her kids gathered around them and he wanted to be strong for them. At least, that was what he was telling himself.

* * *

Pastor Ward couldn't help but think of Mollie Brown. He missed her terribly and, though he knew it was selfish to want her to leave paradise, he wished she were with him right now. He smiled a sad smile at the irony. This moment, a joyful reunion, was just a taste of what heaven would be like; just a shadow of the joy that was yet to come. Ward raised his hands in worship.

* * *

After a moment, in a small degree of quiet, Emma asked her parents about Tesla. The Thomases had told her that he had run away, but she wanted to know what had happened.

Greg hung his head. "I'm so sorry, honey," he whispered, "we looked and looked for Tesla, but we just couldn't find him. We think he wanted to go looking for you and—"

"RROOOWRL!"

It was the unmistakable sound of a beagle barking. There was a heartbeat's measure of silence and then...

"NO! WAY!" Greg shouted as Tesla, covered in mud, burrs, and probably ticks, came bounding out of some nearby bushes and into the middle of the celebration.

"Tesla!" Emma shrieked.

"Rrooowrl!" Tesla answered. He threw himself into Emma's arms and covered her in slobbery beagle kisses.

Once again the crowd roared with joy. The sight of the little dog being reunited with his favorite girl nearly knocked them off their feet. Scott bit the inside of his cheek to keep from crying out loud.

* * *

Greg couldn't believe his eyes. He could never have imagined anything making this moment better and now *this*. He was overwhelmed. Greg knew what he had to do. He raised his hands and called for silence. If it had been anyone else the revelers may have ignored him, but Greg Leonard drawing all their attention to himself was unprecedented. With the exception of a few sniffles, giggles, and the sound of Anna Lopez humming softly, silence fell like snow over the people of Hillside.

"I have something to say," Greg began. He looked at Emma and Joni and seemed to draw strength from the sight of them. "I blamed God for taking my girl away from me and from Joni. I thought you all were fools to pray to Him to bring her back when He was the one who let it happen in the first place. Well, the other day I told Joni and Kate that we'd done everything we could to find Emma, but then I realized that wasn't true. You all were praying for my little girl to come home...but I wasn't. Not once. I was angry at God for taking her and I didn't want to give Him the satisfaction of praying to Him when He did something I hated. But then I got to thinking about it. If I had thought that

Emma would come home if I would put my shoes on the wrong feet and walked around backwards all day, quacking like a duck, I would have done it. I would have done anything. And I realized that if I was willing to do something foolish, then why not let go of my pride and pray for my girl? It took me a while to decide to do it. I was still mad at God... But I did it. I decided to pray for my baby to come home." Greg hung his head. His voice broke. "I prayed this morning. I was praying when Pastor Ward knocked on our door." He looked up. "And if you wouldn't mind, pastor, I'd like you to pray with me right now. God brought Emma home to me and I want to spend my whole life thanking Him."

* * *

The crowd cheered, and Scott Fischer hung his head and sobbed.

* * *

The young officer who had followed the Thomases home stood back and watched this amazing thing happen in front of him. He was aware that he ought to be doing something, but he was glued to the spot, witnessing this outpouring of love and welcome. Something was happening here that he had never experienced before and he wanted in on it. Maybe he would talk to that preacher, too. Maybe he would have some answers for him.

* * *

A few hours later, after more instructions and questions from the officer (who for some reason was grinning like a maniac), a small group was gathered in a half-lit Line Dried Laundry. The sign on the door said "Closed." Kate was glad to share some chocolate chip cookies she had baked from the dough she kept in the freezer and she was grateful that Greg and Joni had chosen to spend some time with them when they had every right to take Emma home and hog her all to themselves.

Along with their two families were also Scott, Brandy, Brayle and the kids. Scott was happy to meet Emma for the first time and Emma was happy to see the change in Brayle's family's life.

There were so many questions; so much time to make up for.

"So," Claire asked slowly, "She acted like you were supposed to be *grateful* that she took you away?"

Emma nodded, a frown of confusion wrinkling her forehead. "Yes. At first, anyway, before she started calling me Lydia. I don't know, it's almost like she thought she *knew* me or something. She said things like, 'After what I did for you, you'd think you would show some respect.'" Emma fidgeted. "It's so weird. I had to be Lydia for so long, and now I get to be Emma again, but I'm not sure if I remember how. I keep thinking I'll wake up and this will all be a dream."

Emma was sitting between her parents, so Kate leaned across Joni to put her hand over Emma's. "You're safe now, honey. We all feel like it's too good to be true too, but it's real. You're home now and you're safe."

Everyone was curious about Mary Louise Crable, this person who had altered their lives by taking Emma. Scott got out his laptop and pulled up a picture of her from the address that Detective Palmer had given them. He had been informed right away when Emma had been found, and was now involved in the follow-up on Crable.

The group, excepting Emma, scrunched together around the little screen in order to get a better look at the woman who had called Emma "Lydia."

They studied her photo for a few quiet moments before Brayle gasped.

"I...I recognize that woman. I've seen her before," she whispered.

Everyone swiveled their heads to stare at her.

"You have?" half of them asked.

Brayle nodded, looking miserable. "I saw her that day." She avoided her mother's eyes. It was obvious that she didn't want to tell them what she knew and that she was choosing her words carefully.

"I saw her the day Emma disappeared," Brayle gulped. "She was there watching when...when Mom got mad at me. She was staring and shaking her head like she felt sorry for me."

For a short while, everyone pondered the mystery before them. Suddenly, Brandy clapped her hands over her mouth as the gravity of the implication hit home.

"It's my fault," she choked, "That—that *person* thought Emma was Bray and that she was saving her from me," Brandy gasped. "*I* did this!"

The faces around her showed her varying degrees of skepticism and confusion.

"No, just think about it," Brandy cried, "I was yelling at Brayle and that woman saw it." She pointed at the picture on the screen. "That's why she expected Emma to be thankful." By now Brandy was nearly hysterical. She shook off Scott's hands as he tried to calm and comfort her. "They both have red hair and they were wearing the same tee shirt, and she thought she was *rescuing* her from *me!* This is all my fault! It's all my fault; oh, you all must hate me! *I* hate me." She turned agonized eyes on

Emma, Joni, and Greg. "I'm so *so* sorry for what my stupidity caused." Brandy grabbed Brayle by the arms and looked in her face. "Bray. I should never have talked to you that way. I was just so tired and angry at everything, but none of it was your fault." She looked at her other children who were watching wide-eyed. "None of you, it wasn't your fault. *All* of this was because of me." Brandy let go of Brayle, slumped in her chair and covered her face with her hands. There were a few moments of silence as everyone absorbed what had just happened.

Greg cleared his throat. He patted Brandy's shoulder awkwardly. "You can't do that," he said softly. "Sure, you shouldn't have been yelling at your daughter like that, no question, but it doesn't make what happened your fault. The same with that Glass girl who bullied Emma. She was mean and awful, but she didn't know what she was doing; she didn't know what would happen."

"I blame myself too," Claire mourned. "If I hadn't left Emma alone, if I had just gone with her—"

"If I had been there that day," Joni added

"If I had walked the girls back to the fundraiser," Kate shook her head sadly.

"If I had just been braver, both with Lindsay *and* with—with *her*." Emma said.

"If that woman had just left you alone," James whispered, looking at Emma.

Joni put her hand on Brandy's shoulder. "So many things went wrong that day. I'm sure there are other people who feel responsible," Joni said gently. "Detective Palmer told me on the phone today that he thought he should have caught it, but I don't see how he could have. Please don't take this on your shoulders, Brandy. It's not yours to carry."

* * *

Kate watched as Joni wrapped Brandy in a hug and then as the three girls joined the embrace. She, too, participated and curled herself around her daughter. Alan and Scott slapped Greg on the back. The three younger children huddled together with their sweet faces smudged with chocolate chips while James watched everyone like one waking from a dream. Kate knew that all of them had a long road of healing ahead of them. They had survived the dark valley and would all be stronger now for having passed through it.

Chapter 27

Later

It was the perfect day for a wedding. Warm, but not uncomfortable; breezy, but not windy. The sky was ocean blue and scattered with clouds that looked like they had been placed as decorations in honor of the day. Music played softly and the air smelled like daises. The people of Hillside Church gathered together to honor this new union with a jubilation that was no longer smudged with the soot of sadness. It made the day all the sweeter that they could celebrate knowing that their long and painful trial was over. Emma Leonard was home to witness Scott Fischer and Brandy Robinson become man and wife. It made the day all the more joyous.

* * *

Kate sat at one of the little round tables at the reception and drummed her fingers on the pretty white lace tablecloth. She looked around her and reflected on all that had happened in the past few months. Not long after the day that Emma returned home, Scott had asked Brandy to marry him. She was still dealing with a lot of guilt, but with the help of Scott, Joni, and Pastor Ward, she was healing. Brayle and her siblings were all delighted to add Scott to their family. The twins had already asked him if it would be all right if they called him Daddy, and

The Valley Without Her

Scott told them that it would make him as happy as it did when their mom agreed to marry him. Kate smiled at the thought. She knew that Scott liked to put on a tough-guy appearance, but those twins could melt him into a puddle of goo.

Kate's eyes fell on her son. She could not believe how grown-up and handsome James looked in his suit. No wonder girls were chasing after him. Once again Kate felt a flutter of relief that Lindsay was no longer a part of his life, and, once again, Kate breathed a prayer for that mixed-up girl. Then she smiled as she noticed James' gaze was resting shyly on Emma. It wasn't the stare of curious disbelief that he had worn on the day that God had dropped Emma into their laps. James' face was the pure, sweet, and timeless picture of innocent puppy love. Kate hid her grin behind her hand and turned to look at her daughter. Claire, whispering and giggling now with Emma, took her breath away. Her rich brown hair fell around her shoulders and her dress of palest blue made her skin glow. Gone was the look of lonesome despair in her daughter's eyes. Now Claire sparkled. Joni wasn't the only one who had gotten her daughter back that day. Claire had returned to them too, just as beautiful, but stronger and braver than before.

Kate was sure that Emma would have been blushing if she had noticed James staring, but she was unaware of his attention. Emma looked lovely. Her yellow dress brought out her creamy complexion, and her coppery hair shimmered like a new penny in the sunlight. It had not been an easy few months. Joni told Kate that there were times when Emma hardly seemed herself. One night while Emma was setting the table, she dropped a glass, shattering it. Joni jumped and was startled by the noise, and Emma was nearly beside herself in a panic of apologizing and an effort to clean up the broken pieces. In her haste, she had cut herself. Joni was heartbroken to see her daughter so anxious and afraid. Emma was getting counseling, and friends and family were helping remind her that she was safe and loved. Joni's sister, Emma's Aunt Jennifer, flew home from London to stay with them for two weeks. Joni told Kate it was good medicine for all of them. Kate praised God again for His miracle in bringing Emma home.

The ceremony had been beautiful. Brandy looked like an angel in her silvery-white dress, but it was her expression when she looked at Scott that made all the difference. Brandy was shining with hope and it lit her up inside. Scott looked like he was ready to burst with happiness.

There was a shift in the mood at the reception as it was time to honor the traditions. It was time to cut the cake and Kate grinned to herself at what was coming. Joni was all smiles, too, as she settled into the vacant chair next to Kate. Their husbands were hovering somewhere near the large bowls of mints and nuts, waiting patiently for cake.

"So," Joni whispered conspiratorially, "it's almost time!"

Kate laughed. Not only was she as excited as Joni about what was going to happen, but she was so glad to hear the smile in Joni's voice again now that her heart bubbled over with happiness. Joni was becoming her old self again and Kate had missed her so much it hurt.

"I know! I think it's perfect. Did you know it was all Brandy's idea?"

"Yes! I love it." They giggled like their daughters and turned to watch Brandy and Scott cut the cake and feed it to one another. The photographer snapped several shots of the happy couple.

* * *

The Valley Without Her

Then it was time for the bouquet toss. There seemed to be more participators than usual. Even Widow Perkins joined the unmarried females as they took their places behind Brandy. It was all part of the plan.

The teen girls giggled and blushed as if they had a shy secret, and the people sitting on the sidelines smiled at the happy moment.

"Is everyone ready?" Brandy called teasingly over her shoulder.

The people cheered and Brandy tossed the bouquet, made for this moment, over her shoulder.

Everyone scattered.

Macy Fischer was left alone on the grass as all the women, young and old, ran off and left her. The bouquet fell at her feet. She stared at it, dumbfounded.

"Here let me get that for you." It was Josh. He had appeared out of nowhere. He knelt down and picked up the bouquet and still on one knee, he held it up to Macy. She was beginning to understand.

"I would consider myself blessed, and truly honored," Josh said softly, "if you would accept this."

Macy took the flowers from him and when she did, her fingers brushed the cool circle of an engagement ring. She gasped.

"Macy," Josh pulled the ring free from the bouquet and placed it on Macy's finger. "Will you marry me?"

"Yes," Macy whispered. Josh jumped to his feet, gathered Macy close and kissed her.

Everyone shouted and clapped.

"To new beginnings!" Brandy cheered.

"To new beginnings," Pastor Ward prayed.

"To new beginnings," Josh smiled.

Joni pulled Emma onto her lap and kissed her pretty hair.

"To new beginnings," she whispered.

About the Author

Amie Johnson graduated from Indiana Wesleyan University with a bachelor of science in Christian education and is a member of Bryant Wesleyan Church. *The Valley Without Her* is her first novel, written in small installments during nap time and after her boys went to bed. Ideas were scribbled on little scraps of paper, and her efforts were often interrupted by diapers, drinks of water, and requests for impromptu puppet shows starring plastic coin pouches. Amie lives in rural Indiana with her husband, Keith, and their two small sons, Jesse and Samuel.

More Titles by 5 Fold Media

A Heart for Grace
by Bethany Largent
$16.95
ISBN: 978-1-936578-60-3

Olivia Marston struggles against the pain she carries inside from a past abusive husband. Alone and destitute, she moves to Arkansas and accepts a job caring for the daughter of widower Jed Bailey, who she soon finds herself falling for. Vivian Wrathers also has her sights set on Jed and will stop at nothing until she gets him. When Vivian disappears, Jed is the prime suspect. Suddenly Oliva's past comes colliding into her future and she struggles to find the grace to forgive and the courage to face her destiny.

The Miracle at Hope's End
by Kathy Dolman
$18.95
ISBN: 978-1-936578-41-2

A grieving young mother, a young man betrayed by his own father, an emotionally scarred woman, and a man mentally tortured by his past are all about to come face-to-face with greatest their need and desire... their very own miracle at Hope's End.

This sequel to The Light at Hope's End takes the townfolk to the next level of the journey of God's love and power to transform lives.

"To Establish and Reveal"
For more information visit:
www.5foldmedia.com

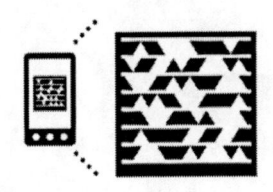

Use your mobile device to scan the tag above and visit our website.
Get the free app:
http://gettag.mobi

Like 5 Fold Media on Facebook, follow us on Twitter!